Tsunami

Book 4 of The Witch, the Dragon and the Angel "Trilogy"

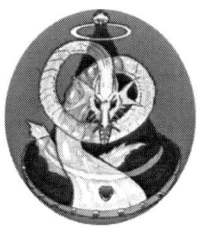

*Titles available in The Witch, the Dragon and the Angel Trilogy
(in reading order):*

Witch Way Home?
Witch Armageddon?
Witch Schism and Chaos?
plus two more (it's a magical trilogy!)
Tsunami
Change

*Related books
(in the same Multiverse)
The Witches' Brew Trilogy:*
Hubble Bubble
Toil
Trouble

And on a similar theme:
Oberon's Bane

Tsunami

Book 4 of The Witch, the Dragon and the Angel "Trilogy"

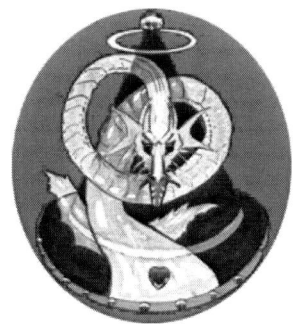

Paul R. Goddard

© Paul Goddard 2014, 2015

The right of Paul R Goddard to be identified as the author of this work has been asserted by him in accordance with the Copyright, Designs and Patents Act 1988

All rights reserved. No part of this publication may be reproduced, stored in a retrieval system, or transmitted in any form or by any means, electronic, mechanical, photocopying, recording or otherwise, without prior permission of the copyright owner

All characters in this publication are fictitious and any resemblance to real persons, living or dead, is purely coincidental.

First published in the UK 2014
2nd Edition
ISBN 978-1-85457-070-3

Published by: Clinical Press Ltd., Redland Green Farm, Redland, Bristol, BS6 7HF, UK.

*Innumerable thanks are again due to Jem, Allan and Lois.
Thank you!*

*Cover photograph: St Andrew's Church, Burnham-on-Sea
Lois Goddard 2014*

Prologue

Clang!

The sound of a filing cabinet closing woke me up. Or at least I thought I was awake. It was pitch dark, very cold and there was an unusually acrid smell in the air. I lay still trying to work out where I was. I heard voices. Were they in my head?

'We must hurry,' said one voice. I pictured a middle-aged balding man with glasses.

'What about this one?' asked a timid female voice. Young, mousy hair and also bespectacled, or so I imagined.

'He's dead. Leave him.'

'But we haven't done the PM!'

'Too late now. We've got to run before the wave hits.'

The voices stopped and I relaxed. I realised that I was dreaming. It was just a nightmare. All I had to do was sleep then wake up. All would be well. It always was.

I lay there but deeper sleep would not come. I had identified the smell now. It was formaldehyde. We used it at school, sparingly.

Then there was the drip, drip, drip on my head. Just like the Chinese Water Torture but thicker and with a slightly acid-sweet odour and a metallic taste.

*

I had just sacked my psychotherapist. Ever since childhood I had suffered from recurring nightmares along the same themes and they had recently worsened. The therapist, a very pleasant lady from Australia, had taken me through various psychotherapeutic regimes including cognitive behavioural therapy and Jungian analysis. She had now suggested Freudian analysis also and I had finally lost patience. The dreams had become worse and I was convinced that there was a practical reason for them. Perhaps they were a warning, a premonition of future events? Perhaps they were punishment for sins of omission or commission? When I had suggested this to her she had immediately fallen back on the CBT response... she had taken me through the logic of my conclusion and tried to persuade me that my thinking was flawed. She had become exasperated with me and had told me that the ideas were ridiculous!

The first, and most common of my dreams, was that of a tidal wave or tsunami. I was running but my legs were like rubber and I was getting nowhere. I knew the water was coming as I had seen the sea recede far out. Only a relatively small channel of Severn River flow had remained and mud could be seen right out to the small islands in the Severn. So I had turned tail to run but could not move.

I had been told that this is common in dreams due to the immobilising effect of sleep. I was not convinced.

The second and in many ways more disturbing dream was to wake up in a coffin and know that I had been buried alive. That used to wake me screaming but now I was used to it. This dream was just a variation on the coffin theme.

So go back to sleep properly.

Chapter 1

'On this the XVII day of January 1606 it has pleased the Lord to take unto himself His servant John Appleshanks of Burnham'

I could read this on a piece of rough paper pinned above my head on the inside of the coffin. The lid was off and nobody was in the room. The sun was only just up, a weak and watery sun and if the date was right it must be about eight o'clock. I felt very cold, almost frozen.

Two or three major problems here, I thought as I sat up in the coffin and looked round the cluttered cottage room, empty of people but not of antique style worldly goods.

Firstly, I'm not John Appleshanks.

Secondly it should be 2015 not 1606.

And I'm not dead or I could not be sitting up….and, most importantly, thinking.

Cogito ergo sum, I think therefore I am. Or, as Descartes originally wrote in French in 1637, je pense, donc je suis.

In thirty one years time from now, I pondered. *That's when he will write it. Another reason why the inscription is not just wrong but also impossible.*

And does it mean Burnham in Buckinghamshire, Burnham on Sea or Burnham on Crouch?

I climbed out of the wooden casket onto the rough stone floor.

Someone had to be playing a joke. One of my drinking pals, most probably.

That was almost my only vice…..excessive drinking on a Saturday night after the inevitable rugby game. They must have slipped something into my drink and then set me up in a film studio. But why? It wasn't my stag night.

I'm not getting married quite yet and I have three girlfriends.
Peter Chambers is the name and PE is the game.

I've said that a few times before now. I'm a physical education teacher at a local school. It is called an academy but I never liked academia too much. I do, however, also teach geography and do a little dabbling in history for the year 12 pupils. I'm big, strong, broad and heavy.

I looked at my legs. Thin and spindly.

That's not right!

My legs should be powerful and muscly, with scars at the knees from repeated operations for the cartilage.

That was it! I had not been drinking...I was in hospital for another operation. This was to be keyhole surgery on my lumbar spine. They had told me that I would wake up in no pain with my back cured!

My hands now looked skinny and worn, brown age marks on the wrinkly skin.

That's not right at all. I'm just off six feet tall and only thirty-six years old. Not even near forty!

Or at least I should be but judging from the appearance of my body I'm one hundred and thirty-six and only five feet tall. Or maybe older and shorter.

So it's not a trick perpetrated by my drinking mates. It is some after-effect of the surgery and I'm hallucinating.

I walked round the room. It looked as if I had been left in state, perhaps for the wake. Maybe the date was now the 18th or 19th of January, old calendar and my body had been left out overnight? Or even the 20th?

That made sense but why was nobody in attendance?

Maybe I was very old and they were old too and had gone home to bed? After all, what harm could come to a corpse.

A corpse? How could I be a corpse? I was up and walking. A

corpse should not be up and walking.... it defied Descartes' logic.

I felt my head with my hands and then really carefully examined myself all over. Everything seemed to be working fine, albeit shakily.

I walked over to the door and opened it.

Sitting on a small wooden stool in the next room was a middle-aged woman, dressed like a milkmaid. She was fast asleep with her head in her hands, leaning on the adjacent table.

Presumably she was the person designated to keep the night vigil over the body of John Appleshanks.

'Good morning!' I said brightly. 'Does anyone know how I ended up in that coffin?'

The maid awoke, took one look at me and screamed piercingly loudly. She jumped up and ran for the backdoor and was off down the dirty cobbled road like a shot.

I followed to the door but stopped. She was already almost out of sight and I felt rather weary and strangely hungry. I certainly could not run after her. I had to sit down to rest.

*

Drip, drip, drip.

Back into the darkness with the smell of formaldehyde or something similarly acrid and a constant dripping on my head and around me.

Yes, I concluded. It is a punishment for my sins.

Drip, drip, drip.

Did I feel something touch my leg?

Drip, drip, drip.

*

I woke up in my apartment in Bristol. It was a first floor flat over a dental surgery in Clifton. The building was Victorian but had been completely modernised in the early nineties. I had redecorated since and the flat itself was a very comfortable one-bedroomed apartment with a decent kitchen off a large dining room and with a good sized bathroom. The only drawback was the noise from the dental surgery....during working hours you could sometimes just about hear the high pitched whine of the drill and I could not help but imagine the anguished groans from the patients although they did not, in reality, penetrate through to the floor above. Well, not too often....

I climbed out of bed. It was good to have woken and to have stopped the dreadful dreams. Today was Saturday and I remembered that I was putting on a small dinner party in the evening. I had to get out to the shops nice and early in order to get some provisions in.

Should I go to the small Sainsbury's on Whiteladies Road, the bigger one further down the hill, the Tesco Express or Waitrose? Perhaps the guests would appreciate some meat from the organic butchers on Lower Redland Road? It was expensive but could be very flavoursome. Perhaps not.... most of the lads were not that discerning and it was mainly a boys do tonight, guys from the rugby club. I would probably make a curry and we would have a few beers then say a semi-serious goodbye.

Monday I was going into hospital for the surgery on my back and I was feeling particularly nervous about the appointment.

*

I woke from a short nap. I had been sitting on the maid's stool and a quick glance showed me that I was alone in the small cottage, a two up, two down affair. In the room that the maid had just deserted I found the remains of the funeral wake meal. There were a few small loaves of dry bread and a piece of unattractive meat, not exactly what I would call a feast. I tried to eat the bread but it stuck in my throat. I had a little more success with the meat and swallowed a few mouthfuls of water. From the back room a timber staircase rose to the next floor. I padded up the construction into the two small rooms upstairs. One housed a large wooden double bed and a rough chest of drawers. The other room was very small and was full of junk including an ancient soldier's uniform which was laid out on a narrow wooden bed. I looked at the nightdress affair that I was wearing and decided that the uniform was better than my present garb.

I discarded the funereal gown and I started to put on the uniform. It had a distinct smell of camphor, used to discourage moths, but otherwise was in good condition. Perhaps it had been the old boy's pride and joy from the days when he was an active soldier? That would explain why it had been left out on display for the visitors to see.

Working out exactly how to wear the clothes was a problem. There was no underwear so I had to do without. Leather trousers tied with string, not buttons, a tunic with a lace front and collar, a rounded hat, a bit like a bowler, with a feathered plume. I donned all of these. They were on the big size for me but maybe I had shrunk, or at least old Appleshanks had....

I definitely know that I have decreased in size significantly if any of this is real and not just a dream!

On the floor were leather boots. I strapped these on also. Although the body and limbs were strange they obeyed my commands with no trouble and once having started on the dressing they had worked like clockwork, the hands doing what they should without much conscious intervention.

Next to the uniform were a few nicknacks, a locket and a bugle. I picked up the horn, examined it and put it down again. I looked for a weapon but could not find one. As I replaced the bugle on the bed I was alerted by a sudden noise outside so I peered through the small, mean window. In the distance I could see the familiar shape of St. Andrew's church with its leaning tower, nearly eighty feet in height and leaning to one side due to poor foundations, just like the Leaning Tower of Pisa. So I knew that the place was Burnham on Sea, Somerset. But close to the house a mob was gathering led by the milkmaid. Several were holding pitchforks and there were at least two clergymen in dark clothes.

I knew instantly that they were after me. Rising from the dead had never been a common activity and in the seventeenth century it would have been considered the work of the devil or a particularly clever witch. I knew this was bad. To be considered a demon or a witch in a time when the king, James the First, was a man who wrote an entire book about demonology and thought that witches were constantly out to get him! Very bad indeed!

As I looked I noticed some people at the back of the crowd pushing their way forward. The mob parted in front of them as they approached, which was no surprise as they were carrying flaming firebrands.

I was suddenly very scared. I was trapped in a tiny cottage, mostly made of wattle and daub, wooden floors and thatched roof. It was a tinderbox from which there was no escape.

Not only that I was also trapped in an octogenarian's body, or possibly older, and I could not wake up from the nightmare. If, by good luck, it was a nightmare and not some kind of horrendously displaced reality.

I ran to the back of the house and looked out of the other window. There was a crowd gathering there also. The place was surrounded and there was no obvious means of escape.

The men with the flaming wood came closer to the house and then beckoned to women who were moving along behind them carrying bundles of fagots for burning.

I ran through to the small front room where I had found the soldier's uniform. Some instinct, perhaps not my own, made me pick up the bugle and put it to my lips and open the window wide so that all of the world could hear.

I had blown trumpets and bugles only a few times in my life and had made a noise like a drowning walrus but today, whichever day it was and whichever century, I blew like the archangel Gabriel. I did not just blow a single note... I blew an entire tune. I initially played Reveille followed by the Last Post.

The fire makers paused in their allotted homicidal task and looked up to see me standing at the window, resplendent in my uniform and standing stiffly to attention playing the soldiers' age old songs. Then my lungs and lips took over again and I played several more bugle tunes that I could not name but was vaguely aware of from attendance at military tattoos with the Army Cadet Force.

The halt in proceedings would not last long and the arsonists would soon proceed. I knew this but could think of no way of capitalising on the time gained.

I did not need to worry.

A cry came from the back of the crowd and the mob parted once more. Four horsemen rode up to the front of the house. On the largest horse was a man in half armour who was quite clearly in charge.

'Prithee priest,' said the man to the older of the two black clad clergymen. 'What is the meaning of this rabble?'

I could hear all of the exchange through the open window of the small cottage.

'Sir George,' replied the clergymen. 'We have come to burn a demon or witch.'

'Priest, how long has it been thine custom to do this with no trial?' asked the beknighted horseman. 'Hast thou not heard the declarations that public gatherings be curtailed?'

'Sir George, this is an emergency,' countered the priest. 'Of course I hast heard of the curfew due to the plague but this is a case of demonic power.'

'Demonic power, pah!' exclaimed the Sir George. 'It is my sworn and honest duty to keep the peace. Canst thou not give me better explanation? Thou, a priest!'

'The old bugler who lived in this house has risen from the dead,' replied the black-clad clergyman.

'Hah, hah,' laughed the self-professed peacekeeper. 'Then

perhaps the poor fellow was not quite dead when you laid him out. Hast thou been drinking too much mead?'

The priest looked most offended.

'Sir George,' he replied. 'Whilst I accept thine admonishment for the gathering of this necessary exorcism, I will not be insulted. In thy position as leader of the militia remember that God is not mocked.'

'But you will be, priest, if I so wish,' laughed the horseman. 'The church does not have the power it once had in this land. But come, let us not argue. We shall capture this once-dead bugler and take him for trial. If it is deemed that the man is possessed you shall have your way and he shall be burnt at the stake.'

'Very well, Sir George,' muttered the priest. 'But I shall not forget the insult.'

'And I shall not forget this illegal mob, priest,' replied Sir George, all semblance of amusement now missing from his voice as he looked around at the gathering.

The people shrank back from the horsemen leaving just the milkmaid, the two priests and a couple of older women who could not move quickly enough to get away.

Now is the time to escape, I thought. *But where should I go? Will running make matters worse?* Whilst I was stuck in this dilemma two of the horsemen had dismounted and entered the house.

Too late for fleeing, I thought. *I shall have to reason with them.*

*

- A leading geologist is blaming a shift in the magnetic poles for the emergency but other eminent scientists dispute that this is the only cause. They agree that the poles have shifted but also suggest that there has been a change in the universal constants. This is the BBC World service.....

Chapter 2

'Come on down, John Appleshanks of Burnham!' cried one of the soldiers. 'We know thou art up there.'

'I give up,' I shouted down the stairs. 'Don't shoot.'

One of the soldiers was indeed carrying a primitive looking musket and I did not relish the thought of a hard metal ball in my leg.....or worse!

'Methinks thou speakest in a strange way, Appleshanks,' shouted the soldier. 'But mayhap I understand thee. Thou wilt surrender?'

'Yes, yes,' I replied. 'I surrender. I'm not armed.'

I climbed down the stairs and was grabbed very roughly by one of the men.

'I have 'ee,' the soldier cried exultantly.

'Well done,' came the educated voice of Sir George. 'Bring him out here.'

The man dragged me, protesting, into the daylight.

'Is that the way you treat an old soldier?' I asked as I was thrown at the feet of the local militia leader.

'As yet I have treated you well, bugler,' countered Sir George. 'I have saved you from the baying mob because of your horn blowing and will arrange for you to have a fair trial.'

'What will you put me on trial for?' I queried. 'Being alive when they thought I was dead?'

'There is that,' mused the baronet. 'It does take some explaining. But more to the point is whether you are really John Appleshanks or somebody else impersonating him.'

'What makes you think that I'm not Appleshanks?' I asked.

'I knew Appleshanks,' replied the militia leader. 'He looked much like you but was very old and ill. It could be that you are an impostor. We have had too many Catholic plots recently and this smells of the Pope.'

Gunpowder treason and plot, I thought. *Guy Folkes and the fifth of November.*

'Lost for words?' Sir George stared at me accusingly. 'Perhaps you are indeed a Frenchman or other papish knave.'

'No I'm not!' I protested. 'I'm innocent until proved guilty. I claim Habeas Corpus.'

'So you wish to be placed before a judge,' smiled the militia commander. 'All knavish plotters say the same. Well hear this. My brother is the local magistrate and he will hear your case. If you are cleared of being a Catholic schemer we will try you as a witch. I suspect that you are one or the other.'

Realising that my careful reasoning approach was getting nowhere I decided to make a run for it and I immediately unleashed a judo throw on the soldier holding me and kicked the musket-holding soldier right on the chin. I then started to run and would have got away but for the dairymaid who stuck out a foot and tripped me up. I fell forward and hit my head on a small rock.

*

Drip-splat, drip-splat, drip-splat. The sticky Chinese Torture continued and I lay in the nightmare metal drawer in the stink of formaldehyde, decay and clotting blood. To calm myself I thought about the last rugby game I had been playing during which I had hurt my back. We were playing a Welsh team and they had been playing dirty. Gamesmanship rather than sportsmanship was their style. Before I had been stretchered off with the lumbar injury I was in a scrum and somebody had bitten my ear. My pinna was lacerated near the base with my neck...it was almost as if the assailant had meant to get my neck rather than my ear it was that violent. I could not be sure who had done it but the person needling me right up until that moment had been a tall, thin, dark haired player who was reputed to be a cousin of the Queen from the wrong side of the blanket. I had presumed that he was a distant cousin but you could never be too sure.

I had been playing roughly myself and that was probably what stimulated the biting retaliation. I contemplated the thought that the guilt was mine.

Drip-splat, guilty, drip-splat, guilty, drip-splat guilty.

Was someone or something in this box with me? There was a strange crawling sensation creeping up my back

Go back to sleep.

Drip-splat, drip-splat, drip-splat.

*

I woke up in a dark cellar. The door was firmly locked and the room was unlit so I spent time exploring the scene with my hands. This was more of a glory hole rather than a cellar. It probably belonged to a large house....perhaps that of Sir George? There was only one entrance and it would not budge.

A rattling noise came at the door and a scraping sound, followed by a bright light in the middle of the wooden panel. A small square window, maybe six inches by six inches, set centrally in the portal was admitting the light. A hand poked through containing a small metal plate. More bread and meat! It was followed by a cup containing water. I had an insane desire to bite the fist holding the container. It would have done me no good at all as biting the hand that feeds you has never been a survival trait so I resisted the urge.

I ate the meat and discarded the bread. I drank enough water to flush down the meat but could stomach no more.

This was all very strange for despite my rugby playing butch image I was an avowed vegetarian. Perhaps being an ancient dead, but now resurrected, bugler turned one into a carnivore?

A rat scuttled across the floor of my prison and I shied away from the creature. With the light spilling in from the small aperture I was able to more adequately assess my cell. I discovered nothing new except that it was all definitely made of stone. I could not break out so the best thing to do was to rest.

I lay back on a cold slab but could not sleep. What was happening to me? How could my mind have been displaced into that of a Jacobean soldier.....or should he more correctly be considered as a retired Elizabethan bugler? My knowledge of the man consisted solely of his name, his recently supposed death, his uniform and his bugle.

If they questioned me closely I would have to plead amnesia. I doubted that it would go down well.

Eventually I dozed off.

*

Drip-splat-splat, drip-splat-splat.

The pool of liquid around my head was getting bigger and I could not stay asleep. But waking still put me in the nightmare of a metal entombment.

Perhaps this was not a bad dream but was my reality? Maybe I could break out?

My arms were bound to my side and I could not move them. My legs were tied together.

It must be a dream.

So back to the rugby game. I was playing well, catching and passing with excellent success, feinting past the opposition and running like the wind until the Fitzroy fiend bit my ear and neck and minutes later somebody almost broke my back. I had been playing physically hard but there was no reason to break my back. Well, that's what it felt like but the orthopaedic surgeon told me it was a simple disc prolapse. He could sort that with keyhole surgery but he preferred to do the operation under general anaesthetic.

So I came into hospital expecting to have a short operation and here I am, waking up in a metal filing cabinet, unable to move but still able to think.

It has to be a bad dream brought on by the GA.

Drip-splat-splat, drip-splat-splat. Splat!

Close your eyes Pete Chambers and go back to sleep. You'll wake up in a comfortable hospital bed with nice clean linen. Except my eyes are not really open are they? They won't open.
Go to sleep.
There is something in here with me!
Drip-splat-splat.

*

A whole day had passed so it was probably the nineteenth or twentieth of January. I woke up when light started to stream through the small window in the door. I was feeling very stiff but did a few shaky press ups and just two sit ups. This old body I appeared to be inhabiting was getting stronger by the minute... how weird was that?

A hand appeared some time later holding a cup. The receptacle contained weak ale. I normally avoid alcohol until the sun goes down but today felt different. Heck, it was different. I was either in a metal filing cabinet in a mortuary or I was inhabiting an old bugler's body in Somerset. Or perhaps still dreaming? Either way it was no ordinary day so I swallowed the ale gratefully.

Perhaps this was virtual reality? Maybe someone had plugged me into a VR suit and just left me there and I was half dreaming, half computer driven.

I could see, smell and taste the ale, swallow the ale and feel the ale in my stomach. It was real in every sense. Nobody had perfected virtual smell and taste beyond scratch and sniff, which always had a peculiar chemical quality to it.

No, I had to accept that this was, in some way, reality. But whose reality and why?

About an hour later the door swung open and the leader of the militia, Sir George, was standing there flanked by several big burly soldiers all holding sticks. Sir George climbed down the few steps into the cellar room. I did not get a chance to see into the house above before the door was swung shut. The militia leader stood looking at me thoughtfully, he was holding an oil lamp which was lighting the damp dark cellar,

'I have discussed your case with my brother, the magistrate,' stated the baronet, eventually. 'And we have decided to extend mercy to you in your capacity as an old soldier.'

'So you are letting me go?' I queried.

'Of course not, bugler,' replied the militia leader. 'That would not be acceptable. We have agreed that you should be tried by a military court. You shall be court-martialled.'

I looked at the man, amazed that he thought this was merciful.

Sir George Merriford was looking back at me and I found that I could read his thoughts.

What am I to do with the fellow? Merriford was thinking this.

I knew somehow that he was a pragmatic man who did not believe in devils. Or gods for that matter although he tried to keep these views to himself.

All this I could pick from his mind. Could this new found ability of mind reading help me to get out of the place? Or did it simply tell me that none of this was real?

These are dangerous times to be a disbeliever, Merriford was pondering this. *You could so easily be mistaken as a Catholic.*

It was such a short time since Guy Fawkes, or Guido to his friends, had been caught perpetrating the gunpowder treason and plot. The agents of King James were still roving around looking for Catholic plotters.

Perhaps the old man really is an impostor?

I caught that thought very clearly.

Merriford remembered meeting John Appleshanks on a couple of occasions and although this man looked very much like Appleshanks he also seemed considerably younger and had a strange accent....and there was that peculiar look in his eyes that the clergymen had found so disturbing. There were also, of course, the accounts from numerous sources that the man had been dead for a couple of days. He was not too worried about that. John Appleshanks had apparently died from old age. No more specific diagnosis had been made and no doctor had certified his death and in Merriford's opinion even the doctors were particularly useless at pronouncing on death correctly. Only last year his own uncle on his mother's side had been announced as dead by the physician, had awoken and had sat up from his sleep with a start as the priest was giving the last rites. The uncle in question had chased both the doctor and priest out of his house denouncing them as charlatans.

In the navy he knew that the surgeon sewed the dead sailors into their hammocks. Before burying them at sea the doctor would put a stitch through the nasal septum to check that they were dead. If the sailor was still alive tears would appear in their eyes.

Clearly the doctors would not do that if it was easy to tell that someone was dead by other means.

But the superstitious peasants were always stirred up so easily by the clergy. It was in the interest of the Church to keep the populous in ignorant fear with devils and witches an ever present threat in their easily led minds..

If he left the old bugler to the mercy of the laymen it was highly likely that they would obey the mean-minded priest, the Reverend Theodore Dean. The man was only 39 years of age but his thin, sallow face and his Cassius-like character made him seem a lot older. His side kick was his curate, the Reverend Johnson, the leader of the militia did not know his Christian name.

The clergy are bad enemies to have.

Despite his laughing dismissal of the priest Sir George knew that the clergy were bad people to have as adversaries, particularly for someone like himself who was not religious.

For appearances sake Merriford attended church every Sunday and sat in his own wooden pew with the family. In fact people who did not attend church were likely to be fined for their disobedience. It was even rumoured that William Shakespeare, the great playwright, had been fined in that way or if not the playsmith himself maybe his father.

Sir George pondered this half remembered fact and I could hear his pondering as clearly as if he was speaking out loud .

Probably the father, he mused. *William tries very hard to keep in the good favour of the authorities.*

Sir George was a great follower of the theatre whenever he got a chance. In Bristol, the second most important city in England and less than half a days ride away, he had seen many of the travelling theatre troupes. He had been a great fan of Marlowe, particularly the plays Doctor Faustus and The Jew of Malta. But poor Christopher had died in an inn brawl more than ten years previously. Stabbed to death. A sad ending to such a fine writer's life. Sir George reflected on this as he thought about the bugler. He would rather be watching a play about an imaginary pact with the devil than pronouncing as to whether or not this old soldier had made such a pact. If he really had done so why had he allowed himself to be caught? In fact the man seemed quite clueless and confused by his condition.

Eventually the baronet stopped staring at me and the connection was broken. I stopped reading his mind.

Sir George turned and made his way up the steps and banged on the door. His men let him out and shut the door firmly behind him.

*

Drip-splat-splat, drip-splat-splat. Splat! Drip-splat-splat, drip-splat-splat. Splat!

The sticky dripping substance was now all around me. I had become convinced that it was blood. Moreover the filing cabinet did not feel as cold as it had done previously. Where was I? Was I in a mortuary drawer and if so where were all the people... the technicians and pathology staff?

The operation....that was it. I had gone home with a painful back. It clearly was not broken as I could walk but the pain had not gone away with ice and pain killers. I had seen the surgeon in his private clinic. The surgeon had told me that I would have to wait for two years on the NHS so he had arranged for me to go into the private hospital immediately. I was going to have emergency surgery on a prolapsed disc and it would all be done under local anaesthetic.

But that wasn't what happened was it Pete Chambers? Go on, remember what happened.

No....It's no good. It's all muzzy.

'You have not lived your life as blamelessly as you think Chambers. You will now suffer the consequences.'

Did I think that or did someone whisper it in my ear?

Drip-splat-splat, drip-splat-splat. Splat! Drip-splat-splat, drip-splat-splat. Splat!

*

The door closed with an ominous bang. Somehow I felt at home in the pitch blackness. it was soothing. Mysteriously I was beginning to be able to see in the dark. Not just in the gloom but in the absolute darkness. How I was doing that I had no idea. In addition I was feeling fitter and younger. The pains in my joints were receding and I was definitely filling out my uniform. This was all inexplicable.

In addition I had a strange urge to try new foods, particularly raw meat.

I had to stop myself from eating a live rat when it tried to nibble my leg.

*

Drip-splat-splat, drip-splat-splat. Was the drip slowing down?

'Just a small scratch and you won't feel a thing.'

The anaesthetist had definitely decided that it would be better if it was done under full general anaesthetic. I had hoped that the surgeon would opt for the local anaesthetic alternative but it was not to be. So I had been prepared for GA, something I dreaded the thought of but somehow felt I could not refuse. Anyway, the back pain was so bad that I wanted to have the operation straight away. I let him insert a cannula.

'One, two, three, four, four, four……..'

Drip-splat, drip-splat, drip-splat.

*

- *"This is a recorded message from the British Government. All travel has been suspended and the State of Emergency has been extended. There is a curfew at twenty hundred hours and no travel is permitted beyond a two mile radius from your home at any time unless on official business."*

Chapter 3

'The nineteenth of January in the year of our Lord, Anno Domini, sixteen hundred and six. We shall let the proceedings begin. Heretofore we have heard how the aforesaid John Appleshanks of Burnham was a bugler in the Queen's army. Long since retired he is reputed to have recently died in his own bed from old age.'

The clerk was reading out the charges and background to my case and I was listening very carefully. We were all sat in a small hall adjacent to the village church.

I had been taken out of the cellar blindfold and led the short distance through the hamlet to this hall where they had removed the impediment to my vision. I looked round at the assembled company.

'On the eighteenth day of the month of January of the year of our Lord, sixteen hundred and six .... that's yesterday,' the clerk looked up from his notes and peered around the court as if to see if anyone disagreed with him before continuing to read. 'The aforementioned bugler is reported to have woken up from his state of mortal death and arisen from his coffin, thus scaring the maid who was carrying out a silent vigil. He also subsequently resisted arrest by the King's militia.'

Silent vigil? I thought. *Some vigil that, she was fast asleep!*

'The charges placed against him by the leader of the militia, Sir George Merriford, are that John Appleshanks is an impostor. Charges brought by the Reverend Theodore Dean are that the bugler is either a witch or is possessed by the devil. Sir George wishes us to proceed with the charge of impersonating Appleshanks first since it will be the easiest to prove or disprove.'

The clerk sat down and Sir George stood up and spoke.

'I have asked the maid and two of Appleshanks' relatives, a nephew and a cousin, whether or not the bugler had any distinguishing marks. They all three agreed that he had been wounded in 1688 at the time of our great victory over the Spanish. The real Appleshanks has a long jagged scar on his back.'

Two of the burliest soldiers walked over to me and roughly pulled up my tunic at the back. There was a gasp from the small crowd.

'So he is the real Appleshanks,' concluded Sir George.

I presumed that my naked back did sport a large jagged scar as predicted.

'Or he is the spawn of the devil and has been made as a perfect copy,' stated the elder of the two clergymen who had tried to burn me alive in the cottage.

'Would Reverend Theodore Dean please refrain from speaking until he has his turn,' said the clerk, solemnly. 'Sir George, do you have anything to add?'

'Just that it was clear from the horn playing that Appledore was a bugler. That concludes my evidence.'

So far so good, I thought, but my attention strayed again to my half-existence in a metal drawer and my replayed memories.

*

Drip-splat, drip-splat, drip-splat

I can't move!

I seem to remember waking up during the operation. I couldn't move then either and I could not breathe.

I opened my eyes. That I did manage to do. Could I remember this or was I imagining it? I was on my side facing the hapless anaesthetist and he should have been looking at me but he wasn't. He was doing a crossword, or a codeword. Something that involved filling in letters on a piece of paper.

'Is he ready?' asked the surgeon.

'Yes, he's under,' replied the anaesthetist.

No I'm not, I wanted to shout this out but all I could do was think it. *I'm wide awake.*

Urrgh, urrgh.

I thought that the surgeon had cut into my skin but all it had been was the cleansing fluid. I could feel it dribbling down my back. Cold liquid which smelt of alcohol. Then again the shock of the cold fluid followed by green towels thrown across my back and down to my front. I knew they were green as I could see the one over my chest and part of my head.

'What's the funny mark on his ear and neck?' asked the anaesthetist.

He's looking at me now, I thought. He's bound to notice that I'm staring at him.

'He was bitten during his last rugby game,' replied the surgeon. 'Told me that it was a member of the royal family that did it.'

'Confabulator,' said the gas man, clearly disbelieving me.

'Probably,' replied the surgeon. 'Have I told you the one about the patient who told his GP he was a pair of curtains?'

'Yes, you have,' replied the gas man in a bored voice. 'The doctor said he should pull himself together.'

'No,' replied the surgeon in a slightly hurt voice.... he clearly considered that it was the duty of the gas man to laugh at his jokes. 'This GP told the patient to stand over by the window to cut out the draft.'

'Same joke,' replied the anaesthetist. 'Five down. Mad jumper out of rehab?'

'How many letters?'

'Only four.'

'Hare,' replied the surgeon.

'Where?'

'No, hare the animal. Like a rabbit.'

'Oh yes,' replied the gasman in a grouchy voice. Damn, you're right. Eight across Beast of burden backwards in a mall.'

'Llama.'

'Damn it.'

I was panicking. I still could not take a breath in and the anaesthetist was more concerned about his crossword than he was about me.

Drip-splat, drip-splat, drip-splat

*

'I am the Reverend Theodore Dean, vicar of the parish Church of Saint Andrew's, Burnham,' stated the clergyman. 'And I present the evidence for the prosecution of John Appleshanks for consorting with the devil, malicious witchcraft and conspiring against the king.'

All of which carry a sentence of death, I pondered. *Perhaps this priest had something against Appleshanks when he was properly alive?*

'Firstly I present the recent parish record of attendance,' stated the clergyman. 'You will all note that John Appleshanks was conspicuous for his absence throughout most of that time.'

'For pity's sake remember that he was ill for the last nine months,' cried the cousin, a buxom lady who looked to be in her late fifties.

'Which simply leads me to the next point,' smiled the sinister priest. 'How could such a sick man, a man who was so ill that he was pronounced dead, recover and step out of his coffin? There is no way without the assistance of the devil himself.'

The hastily gathered military court turned to look at me.

'Now is your chance to answer,' stated the clerk.

'Certainly' I replied. 'That is difficult to answer. I do appear to have come back to life but we can cite at least one recent example in which the person came back to life without the interaction of the devil. Sir George's uncle was pronounced as dead by the doctors but turned out to be alive and kicking.'

'He may have been in league with the devil also,' sneered the black-clad priest, to the clear discomfort of the baronet.

'There is the famous case in the scriptures,' I added. 'And that was definitely not the devil's work.'

'Thou blasphemes,' cried the clergyman pointing his accusing finger at me. 'Thou art trying to use the example of our Lord Himself who came down from glory that we might live!'

The clergyman then turned to the rest of the people in the room and continued his tirade.

'To suggest that this mere bugler, this horn playing ex-soldier, this Appleshanks is equivalent to our Lord is nothing less than the very worst blasphemy and thou, Sir George, should agree with me that he be taken away for burning. Suffer ye not that witches be allowed to live!'

All the people in the room looked for a moment towards Sir George and then back to me.

'May I reply to that?' I asked the clerk and he nodded his assent. 'I was not referring to our sweet and dear Lord. I was looking to his example in the raising of Lazarus over whose death Jesus wept.'

The room went completely silent then the clergyman started again.

'How can a simple soldier know the scriptures so well? This man must be possessed by a devil. Don't forget that even the devil can quote the scriptures.'

'I have read the bible in the English language as translated both by Wycliffe and Tyndale,' I hastily replied.

'Tyndale was executed. As you will be,' the clergyman looked venomously at me then turned to the bench. 'Could the soldier Appleshanks read?' It was not a rhetorical question as the black clad crow continued… 'We can use Sir George's witnesses to answer that.'

*

Drip-splat, drip-splat, drip-splat

Yes. I had woken up during the operation. I remembered it clearly. I was wide awake but unable to move a muscle and they were going to operate on my back so I was lying on my side. The anaesthetist had roughly thrust a tube down my throat and attached me to a ventilator. The machine had inflated my lungs then deflated them. "Skaaa" was the sound on the inspiration and "shkeeee" on expiration. Skaaa - shkeeee, skaaa - shkeeee, skaaa - shkeeee. On and on endlessly and I had no control over it, whilst the surgeon prepared to operate.

'Where's the scrub nurse?' asked the surgeon.

'I sent her to get me a sandwich,' replied the gas man. 'She won't be long. Hell of a looker isn't she?'

'Damn it!' replied the surgeon. 'I'm ready to start now.'

'She'll only be five minutes. Don't fret yourself.'

'Then she'll have to scrub up again. It's all too trying.'

'You can help me with my next difficult clue.'

'Read it out,' replied the surgeon in a resigned voice that spoke volumes about his feelings with regard to the anaesthetist.

'Ugly pixie quickly eating the top of the range.'

'Let me think. Ogre. No......goblin. That's it,' replied the surgeon, busily swabbing my back again. 'The answer is hobgoblin.'

'Why?' asked the hapless gas man.

*

'Yes your honour,' replied Appleshanks' cousin when asked the question. 'My cousin wert a good reader and a good scriber.'

'Then why was the man only a bugler,' asked the thin, gaunt priest.

'Tis an honourable position, your honour,' replied the cousin. 'And John was proud of his talents, he was. He could play many a good tune and all, your honour.'

I could see that the clergyman was furious.

'Then I bring forward evidence that the bugler was in cahoots with the Catholics. Not only was he supping with the devil, he was consorting with the enemy also.'

The man put his hand in a leather bag and pulled out a

document.

'We found this in the bugler's house just before Sir George arrived.'

The priest handed a piece of paper to the clerk. The court scribe read out the first lines. They were in French and I could tell from my schoolboy knowledge that they were an incitement to treason against King James.

'What do you have to say about this?' asked Sir George, directing the question at me.

'It is a lie,' I replied. 'The priest did not even enter the house.'

'I can bring witness to the effect that I didst enter the house and find the document there,' countered the priest. 'Note that John Appleshanks is mentioned by name at the end of the document.'

The clerk and Sir George again examined the paper.

'It does indeed appear that thou art implicated by the wording,' said Sir George.

'May I see the document?' I asked.

I could not tell whether or not John Appleshanks had been a conspirator or not although, given the man's advanced age, it seemed highly unlikely. My mind was inhabiting the man but his memories were not open to me.

Sir George walked across the floor of the temporary court room and held the document in front of me. I could immediately see that the name Appleshanks had been added by a different hand. The writing was similar but not the same.

'My name has been added by somebody other than the writer of the document,' I pointed out to Sir George .

'I don't quite see how you can be sure of that,' answered Sir George, disturbed by this sudden turn of events.

'And the priest has given his sworn word that he found the document in your house and it is a very grave thing to accuse a priest of lying,' added the clerk.

'Yes,' agreed the clergyman triumphantly. 'You have condemned yourself by your own base accusations. You are clearly a conspirator and a witch. You must burn.'

The few other people in the room, perhaps ten, murmured in agreement, led by the priest's false logic.

'Wait, wait,' admonished Sir George, worried about the way that the proceedings were going and the vicar's addition of new evidence. 'Let us make not haste in our judgement.'

But the room had gone against Appleshanks and everybody knew it. The clerk called for a vote and it was only now that I realised that the senior clergyman and his sidekick were also being allowed to be party to the decision. The clerk, Sir George, the clergymen and two men sitting in the front row filed out only to return five minutes later.

'Appleshanks has been found not guilty of being an impostor but guilty of being a witch or having been in a pact with the devil,' stated the clerk. 'By a vote of five to one it has been decided that Appleshanks must burn. This will be done in accordance with the law at dawn tomorrow or near after.'

So the poor old bugler had been resurrected with my mind in control only to be condemned to death by half a jury, none of it properly constituted. It hardly seemed fair and unless I managed to escape my supernatural jaunt to the early seventeenth century would soon be at a very painful and grisly end.

*

'Mixed up goats wear roman skirts,' said the anaesthetist, reading out another line from the crossword.

For God's sake can't you get any of the clues yourself? I remembered thinking that, appalled that the gas man couldn't even get the answers to the easiest clues.

'It's obviously Togas,' replied the surgeon, without a moment of hesitation. 'Are you sure this guys alright?'

He was referring to me.

'Of course he is,' replied the anaesthetist, still not looking at my face.

I got the distinct impression from the surgeon's voice that he was less than happy with the anaesthetist. Perhaps he was not the person he usually worked with?

Skaaa - shkeeee, skaaa - shkeeee, skaaa - shkeeee went the machine and my lungs inflated and deflated to order.

I'm OK until you start cutting, I thought, totally petrified. *Then I'll probably die.*

*

- *The Queen has been taken to a safe retreat. Prime Minister Darcy Macaroon has asked Brigadier Spencer Blenkinsop to take charge of emergency services and administration. All parliaments and assemblies, local governments and statutory bodies have been disbanded during the duration of the emergency.....*

Chapter 4

Skaaa - shkeeee, skaaa - shkeeee, skaaa - shkeeee went the machine. The drip-splat, drip-splat, drip-splat on my head was making me relive the terrible experience.

'The scrub nurse has still not returned,' complained the surgeon.

'Yes and I'm still waiting for my sandwich,' answered the anaesthetist.

'Blast your sandwich,' replied the irate surgeon, swabbing away at my skin once more. 'If you hadn't sent her away we could have finished by now.'

My feelings exactly.

'No need to get upset, old boy,' retorted the gas man, my bête noir. 'Try this next clue while we wait. Black liquids in silo.'

Oils. I wanted to scream this out loud but I was still paralysed, able to watch everything, feel everything, even smell everything but not move a muscle except involuntarily.

Skaaa - shkeeee, skaaa - shkeeee, skaaa - shkeeee. The machine kept inflating and deflating my lungs.

'Oils,' the surgeon was beginning to despair. 'Where did you get the crossword, the Beano?'

'I don't think they publish the Beano anymore,' replied the gas man, unabashed. 'I never was much good at crosswords, I have to admit it.'

You're no good at anything, you buffoon, I wanted to yell. *I'm still awake and the guy is about to drill into my spine. And it's the Dandy that they've stopped publishing not the Beano.*

'Ah good,' said the surgeon, ignoring the anaesthetist's confession. 'The scrub nurse has returned.'

*

'I'm sorry it has come to this,' said Sir George. 'You will be well looked after tonight but in the morning I regret to say that you will have to die. I will try to make sure that the fagots are dry so that the pain is brief.'

'That is cold comfort but a very hot prospect,' I answered. 'And the priest definitely did not enter the house.'

'I don't doubt you, old bugler, but the die is cast.'

Then he was gone and I was blindfolded again and led away to the cellar. Sometime later they brought me a full cooked meal of meat and potatoes. The latter were perhaps considered a luxury as they had not long been introduced into England? Or maybe they just fed them to the animals as I had read somewhere when preparing a history lesson for the twelve year olds.

At midnight the two priests entered my cell each carrying a lit candle. Three burly guards remained outside, the door was locked after they had entered and there was no chance for me to escape.

'You are going to die, bugler. Wouldst thou like to confess your sins to a man of the cloth?' asked the leader of the two.

'Papist blasphemy,' I replied, the answer coming unbidden to my lips.

'Yes. I was right,' stated the priest in a sibilant whisper. 'I was convinced that thou hadst discovered our little plot which is why my colleague and I administered poison to thee when we visited thee at thine home. I was sure that thou hadst died but poison is very unpredictable. It can provide a semblance of death as I am sure happened in this case. But there will be no second miracle. This time thou shalt surely die and in great agony. Farewell and good riddance, bugler.'

'Your plot is not that clever, priest,' I answered angrily, having no idea what he was talking about but hoping to goad him into further indiscretions. 'It's only a couple of months since Guy Fawkes and they will be looking out for co-conspirators.'

'Your mind is befuddled, bugler,' replied the second priest. 'It is a twelve month plus two since the man bungled his mission.'

'Quiet,' hushed the more senior clergyman. 'He must learn nothing from us.'

'You won't get away with this,' I challenged them. 'History does not lie.'

'Your boldness does you credit, old bugler,' laughed the elder priest. 'But history is written by the winners and worthless fairy tales by the losers.'

'The Catholics are the losers in England,' I answered. 'They will not come back into power in parliament or on the throne.'

'You cannot know this, bugler, and thou dost not frighten me,' replied the senior priest. 'And if you want to have dry tinder you must tell me where you hid the document.'

Document? Which document?

'So you haven't found it?' I replied, still trying to squeeze information from the black clad form.

'Clearly not or wouldst I ask thee?' answered the priest.

I suppose not but I have to keep hammering at the man.

'You might be trying to fool me into revealing something that you don't know,' I countered.

'Curse you bugler,' the priest answered. 'I hast not found the document and I need it to prove my loyalty to the cause. I need to know exactly what you know. Give me the letter!'

The man stepped forward and shook me vigorously. When the shaking had stopped and the priest had regained his normal supercilious and superior demeanour I replied.

'It would be silly to let me burn tomorrow when I still have something you need,' I retorted.

'Hah,' answered the priest. 'If the threat of fire dost not make thee reveal the whereabouts of the letter when you were on trial then I can suppose further threats from me will do no good.'

He stared at me closely.

'Or perhaps thou dost not really have the letter?' he shook his head. 'Mayhap, but that cannot be the case or how couldst thou have confronted us with the knowledge of the contents of the letter when we came to berate thee for not attending church?'

He stood looking at my calm appearance.

'Or maybe thou knowest something that I do not?' he suggested.

Now he was talking. I was convinced that there were many things I knew that he did not. Einstein's theories of relativity for example or the winner of the FIFA world cup in 2014. But there was one fact I had recently remembered stimulated by this clergyman's argument and I was certainly not going to reveal it to this raven of a figure, this priestly crow.

'I shall speak to thee just before you burn and there is just a chance that I will arrange for thine freedom if thou givest us the letter,' said the crow.

The man turned round and beckoned for the other priest to follow him. They marched to the door and hammered on it. A guard let them out and the door was slammed shut locking me into the darkness.

I lay back and thought about my predicament. Locked in a cellar, hungry, tired and unable to sleep. No mattress, no bed, a hard cold floor. January and it was bitterly cold outside. Even if I got away I had nowhere to go. I was in the wrong century, the wrong place and the wrong body.

The whole thing was inexplicable but at least I was alive.

Or was I? Was this some kind of Purgatory? Was I already dead? Was any of this real?

If this was a dream it was surprisingly self-consistent.

*

Drip, drip, drip. Something was leaking onto my head as I lay immobile on the bed.

Skaaa - shkeeee, skaaa - shkeeee, skaaa - shkeeee.

Was I in a bed, on an operating table or in the steel cabinet?

Drip, drip, drip.

'Now the nurse is here can we please get started?' asked the surgeon.

'Just one last little clue before we start?' pleaded the hapless gas man.

'OK, OK,' agreed the surgeon, resignedly. 'Go ahead if you must.'

'Backwards rodents from far distant star.'

I silently screamed the answer exactly in time with the surgeon. *Rats.*

'Rats,' the man who was about to cut into me screamed.

'Rats?' cried the scrub nurse and ran out of the operating theatre.

I could hear her shouting from the preparation room.

'I hate rats. I'm not coming back until you get rid of them,' her voice was very clear. 'Whatever next? First the relief anaesthetist is leering at me, then I have to get sandwiches for him and now you are shouting about rats. The management are going to hear about this Mr. Fishguard. Oh yes they are.'

You're damn right, I silently agreed with her. *When I get out of here, if I ever do, I will tell everybody about this unbearable farce. I shall sue all of you. I shall tell the GMC. Aaaaargh.*

The surgeon had pushed the scalpel into my back and it was extremely painful. Unbearably painful. I could think of nothing but the pain.

'His blood pressure must be a little high,' murmured the surgeon. 'He's bleeding rather a lot.'

What do you expect? I silently screamed. *You are all monsters torturing me. Your blood pressure would be up if someone was stabbing you in the back..... and is it any surprise that I am bleeding? Aaaaargh!*

Then I realised that in a way they were stabbing the surgeon in the back as well as myself. The anaesthetist had so far ruined everything and that was no good for the surgeon's reputation.... or my sanity.

I was definitely cracking up. I wanted to laugh like a hyena, let out a mad cackle. But I couldn't.

Drip-splat, drip-splat, drip-splat. Skaaa - shkeeee, skaaa - shkeeee, skaaa - shkeeee. Aaaargh! The Chinese water torture continued and my memories and flashbacks bounced around intermingling with the ongoing strange adventures in Jacobean England.

*

It was early and the pale glimmerings of the false dawn were just lighting the sky. I could see this through the small gap by which they had fed me.

The senior clergyman, the Reverend Theodore Dean, thin, gaunt and treacherous, slipped into the cell on his own.

'We are going to kill the star of the King's Men,' whispered the black-clad priest. 'And thou canst do nothing to stop us, Hippocampus.'

'You are going to kill the playwright William Shakespeare?' I was horrified, Shakespeare was not due to die for another ten years at least.

Why is he telling me this? And why did he say hippocampus? That's part of the brain.

'No, not him. Though we may do that yet,' hissed the clergyman. 'We are going to kill Richard Burbage. The actor.'

'But why?' I was confused. Why would anyone kill an actor?

'The man is extremely popular and the public wilt miss him,' replied the crow. 'He taketh all the lead parts in Shakespeare's plays and hath no equal in the land.'

'That does not explain why you wish to kill him!' I protested.

'The outrage will be extraordinary methinks. Dost thou not agree?'

'Obviously,' I nodded vigorously. 'But how will that benefit you and the other Catholic conspirators.'

'We shall make it look as if extreme English Protestants arranged his murder,' laughed the priest. 'They do not believe that people should enjoy the theatre. We will frame friends of the Marian exiles, active clergy of the Anglican Church who remained here in England. The backlash against the Protestants will be exciting to behold paving the way for the Prince of Wales to take over from James when the king is executed by us. The prince will be controlled by Catholics.'

'Prince Charles?'

'No,' the priest looked at me quizzically. 'Not the younger son. I'm referring to Henry Frederick, Prince of Wales and Lord of the Isles, who is almost thirteen years of age.'

'But both the sons are Protestants,' I parried.

'Prince Henry Frederick has been in secret talks with his mother,' responded the priest. 'And we have reason to believe that he is not so enamoured with the breakaway English heretics as thou might believe. We can win him over and we shall make sure that the Regency is in our control.'

'It won't work,' I said in a confident voice.

'Oh but it will,' whispered the priest. 'And if the prince will not help us we will kill him and use the princess.'

'That's ridiculous!' I exclaimed.

'Not at all, old man,' laughed the priest. 'It is an idea of true genius. So clever that I wish I had thought of it, Corpus callosum.'

'I still don't understand why you are telling me this information.'

And did he really say corpus callosum?

'Because I need thine help,' replied the priest. 'I'm sure that thou wouldst like to assist the one true church rather than be damned for eternity. It will be easier on thee if thou wert to tell me where thou hast hidden the letter of introduction and explanation.'

The crow-like man put his face very close to mine. 'I may even be able to arrange a full pardon.'

'I won't help you change the destiny of England,' I replied

pompously, my mouth saying the words before I could properly think. 'England shall remain a Protestant land. The greatest of all Protestant lands. It will build a great empire and rule much of the world whilst the Latin countries will slip into decline.'

'Latin countries?'

The term was clearly not in general use in the Seventeenth century.

*

Drip-splat, splurge. Drip-splat, splurge.

Brrrrm, brrrrm, brrrrm.

The dripping was once again forcing me to remember and relive the agonies of the surgery and the breathing machine.

Skaaa - shkeeee, skaaa - shkeeee, skaaa - shkeeee.

Suffer, Chambers, suffer.

'See,' said the anaesthetist, unaware of how much I loathed him. 'The delay has done no harm.'

The nurse had been placated and the surgeon had explained, with a wry smile, that the only rats in the hospital were the managers. She was standing holding some sort of retractor. If the circumstances had been more favourable I would have enjoyed the view of her legs. They were only exposed from the knee downwards but they were undoubtedly shapely.

Skaaa - shkeeee, skaaa - shkeeee, skaaa - shkeeee.

Arrgh. Another silent scream as the knife plunged in.

Bzzz, bzzz.

There was a horrible smell of burning.

'Just a little diathermy. The fat's bleeding a little.'

That's my fat you're burning! I wanted to shout this in his face but all I could do was lie still and suffer.

I must have been particularly bad in a former life to deserve punishment like this.

Skaaa - shkeeee, skaaa - shkeeee, skaaa - shkeeee.

Drip-splat, splurge. Drip-splat, splurge.

*

The priest had gone away dissatisfied. I had no idea where his document was or whether John Appleshanks, the rightful owner of the body, knew where to find it. In fact I knew almost nothing about Appleshanks and perhaps this lack of knowledge was taking his body to the funeral pyre.

They provided no breakfast and as I lay down to take a few minutes rest a plump rat decided that it would try to bite my hand. As quick as a flash I caught the animal and bit it back in return. This seemed to give me added strength and, feeling completely parched, I drained the rat of its blood.

I did this without thinking and then threw the dead carcass to the floor of the cell, disgusted with myself. I would never have dreamt that I could ever have done such a foul deed. If anyone had told me that I would kill a rat and eat it cooked I would have laughed in their face even though I knew that in some countries a fat rat was a delicacy. So to suck its blood uncooked would have seemed absolutely impossible.... But that is what I did, just like some kind of huge human leech, and it gave me strength enough to greet the day.

The dawn had now arrived properly. The day before had been fine but today was very overcast and I could tell that a storm was brewing. This was what I had hoped for although I was keen not to be left in the cellar for too long. That could be catastrophic.

The soldiers came and took me out of the basement, forgetting to put on the blindfold. I could see the house in which I was incarcerated for the first time.

I was led out of my place of imprisonment into a fair sized hallway. The interior was dark but I could look around as my eyes were already very well adapted to gloom. The walls were panelled with dark carved oak, the hall furniture was covered in rough sheets. I tried to dally to look into the rooms as I passed the doors but the soldiers pulled me forward and out of the building. It was a semi-timbered structure on three floors, plus, of course, the cellar. I recognised where the building was standing. In modern day Burnham there was a house right there called Tregunter: a beautiful Georgian house painted pink, housing the offices of a legal firm. I knew that it had previously been the site of a large farmhouse owned by the Roper family and that in the year of 1685 they would be deported to America for taking part in the Monmouth uprising.

I knew all this but it would do me no good nearly eighty years earlier.

The men pulled me towards a large heap of dried tree branches stacked up like a wigwam. This was situated on the outskirts of the village near the sea banks. I struggled in vain as they placed me on top of this collection of wood and tied me securely to a pole. This had been rammed down into the centre of the pyre and roped to several other beams.

By my reckoning it had to be about half an hour after dawn, perhaps 8.30 am. The priests were standing some distance away, halfway to the church, watching and gloating. I could see Sir George on his horse even further away.

'Dost thou have any last requests before we burn thee?' asked a wizen looking man with a burning brand held firmly in his hand. He had climbed up onto a form of temporary wooden scaffolding set near to the wooden tepee on which I was perched.

I stood shivering with the cold and could see in the distance the relatives who had talked in my defense standing near Sir George. They were weeping silently.

'I would like to have a last word with the squire,' I asked.

'Dost thou meanest Sir George?' asked the fire maker.

'Of course,' I replied. 'Sir George, the commander of the militia.'

'I'll ask him if he wishes to speak to thee,' answered the man with fire but I could see that he was sorely tempted to just set fire to the wood. 'He probably won't wish to speak to a condemned criminal, especially not a witch like thou art.'

'Please try,' I asked in a very reasonable voice.

'Most of the witches we've burnt were screaming by this stage,' he continued, ignoring my plea. 'I'm a'wondering why thee isn't.'

'Perhaps because I'm not a witch,' I replied, not actually sure quite what I was but still getting stronger by the hour. 'Or maybe because I am. Now Sir George? May I speak to him?'

'I suppose I better ask,' replied the man, twitching with impatience to get on with the burning.

'Please do,' I added.

Very slowly and with considerable reluctance the man climbed down from his vantage point and ambled over to the leader of the militia. Sir George listened to him for a moment and then climbed off his horse, giving the reins to my cousin to hold. The baronet then walked briskly over to me at the fire.

'If you wish to plead for your life there is nothing I can do,' said Sir George when he had climber onto the wooden scaffolding. 'King James is very keen that we exterminate all witches and I cannot be seen to disobey the king in this matter.'

'I was not going to request anything for myself,' I replied. 'What I wanted to do was to ask whether you could take my cousin and nephew away from here before they set this bonfire alight.'

'Really?' the soldier raised his eyebrows in surprise. 'No last words of pleading or confessions?'

'None,' I replied. 'Just a warning. Please take my relatives and make for higher ground. Do this as fast as you can.'

I paused.

'Oh yes.... and the priest called Theodore Dean is involved in a plot to kill the actor Richard Burbage.'

'Is there some reason that you say this?' he asked warily.

'Which? The warning to flee or the information about the priest.'

'The warning to flee,' replied the militia leader.

'There's going to be a flood,' I answered.
'And when abouts will this happen?' asked Sir George, intrigued.
'Any minute now, if I'm right,' I replied.
'Appleshanks,' he answered staring at me. 'You are a disturbing man. If you are right it probably is proof that you are in league with the devil but also you will have saved our lives.'
'Go,' I answered. 'Go immediately and persuade my relatives to go with you. Go on. Go!'
Sir George looked at me again.
'And why do you make these absurd accusations about the priest?' he asked. 'It cannot help your cause.'
'I agree that it sounds absurd but he told me himself that he planned to kill Burbage and that I had stolen his letter of introduction.'
'To whom was this letter addressed?' asked Sir George.
'No idea,' I replied. 'But if you don't go soon you will be too late and this conversation will all be irrelevant.'
He was clearly not used to taking instruction from the likes of Appleshanks and to be told to go by a man about to be burnt made it doubly odd. Nevertheless he climbed down and walked briskly over to my relatives and, after a moment of conversation, they started to walk away from me. My cousin turned round to look back but was hurried on by the baronet.
'Now you burn,' said the wizened arsonist with glee. He had been carefully keeping his brand alight. The whole conversation with the militia leader could only have taken a couple of minutes judging by the extent that the wood of his brand had burnt down. The man leant over and touched the flames to the dry timber of my pyre. My arms were fastened tightly behind the pole but my legs were free. I struggled against the stake but although I could slip up and down on the piece of wood I could not reach high enough to get away.
The flames started to lick around the outskirts of the bonfire

and I could already feel the heat. It would not be long before it became unbearable. I may have miscalculated and the fire was burning up very quickly. Very quickly indeed.

*

Drip-splat, splurge. Drip-splat, splurge.
Skaaa - shkeeee, skaaa - shkeeee, skaaa - shkeeee.
Arrgh, arrgh, arrgh.
More silent screaming!

The surgeon drilled into my spine with a pain that started as a stabbing sensation, then a moderate burning, developed through a toothache-like sharpness to unbearable agony. And all the while I could do nothing about it. I just lay there trying to bear the pain until the power went off, the lights went out and the respirator gave up the ghost with a dying wheeze.

The anaesthetist, taking his time and in the dim light filtering in from the high place windows, idly switched to the ambi bag and hand-inflated my lungs. He had only just noticed that my heart rate had risen.

He had then injected something into a cannula in my arm and I started to go unconscious. As I did so the surgeon, still operating in the gloom, hit a nerve and unbearable pain shot down my leg and up my spine.

'The osteophytes are bigger than I expected,' said the surgeon. 'I may have to chisel them off.'

Drip splat splat. Drip splat splat.

I was still in the metal confinement and still reliving the operation over and over again, every little agonising detail.

*

- Brigadier Spencer Blenkinsop has declared martial law and will be running the United Kingdom from his headquarters in Maidenhead. Prime Minister Macaroon has temporarily retired to Chequers. Asked

to comment on the State of Emergency he replied... "This is for a short time only. I have all confidence in Brigadier Blenkinsop. In times like this it is important to have a safe pair of hands in charge of the tiller.".......

Chapter 5

Drip-splat-splat, drip-splat-splat. Splat!

'Chisel!' ordered the surgeon and the nurse clearly handed it to him for I felt the cold metal passing into my back and then a truly dreadful sound as a hammer hit the end of the tool.

My body jerked under the pressure of the blow and the unbearable pain passed up and down my entire body then right down to my toes.

'Strong bones,' murmured the surgeon and so saying he swung the hammer again, thumped the chisel and sent more pain down my legs.

I mercifully blacked out but came partially round again.

My consciousness started to fade once more as I heard the sound of the anaesthetist saying rather loudly and in a measure of panic "cardiac arrest, cardiac arrest."

Then the fellow was pounding on my chest and screaming blue murder.

'The defibrillator's not working because the power's gone out. Where's the ruddy back up generator? Bring me some adrenaline. Has anybody got a torch?'

The anaesthetist had thrown me onto my back and I could feel the retractors and forceps poking into the incision in my dorsum. Another sharp pain shot down my legs and up into my thoracic spine.

'What are you doing?' cried the surgeon. 'You can't just chuck him over like that you'll contaminate the operation site.'

'Rather irrelevant if he's dead,' replied the gasman as he continued to thump me very painfully on the chest and intermittently inflate my lungs with the bag. He continued to do this until I blacked out completely.

Drip-splat-splat, drip-splat-splat. Splat!

*

The heat was increasing and the flames were getting closer. I was sweating profusely and I was exhausted from trying to loosen my bonds. This I had succeeded in doing to the extent that I could move my arms much more freely but they were still tied together and I could still not get free.

If I was wrong about my calculations the end of Appleshanks was near for the second time. If I was right things could change dramatically any moment.

I heard a distant roaring sound that was gradually becoming louder. From my vantage point on top of the funeral pyre I could see a grey smudge on the horizon. It looked, mercifully, as if my suspicions and my calculations were correct. The smudge rapidly came closer, approaching at a speed of about forty miles per hour. The wave hit the sea bank and continued straight over it. If I had realised how big it was going to be I am sure I would not have been so sanguine for the wave was huge, perhaps twenty feet in height or even more and it swept everything in front of it with a great roaring sound. It crashed over my bonfire of the vanities putting it out instantly and lifting the pole up with myself attached. I had taken a great deep breath before the wave hit but even still I found that the air was knocked out of me. I was struggling disoriented and still attached to the stake. I was turned over and round, over and round and I swallowed large gulps of revolting salt water.

Then my face broke to surface. Somehow the attachment to the post had been a blessing. I was still alive and floating along with the wave. The post had heavier wooden beams to which it was attached and these were weighing it down at one end. It kept crashing into trees, houses, people, cattle....I was still tied to it by my arms. My head hit a branch on a tree and I passed out.

*

I awoke again in the metal drawer or tube.

Drip-splat-splat, drip-splat-splat. Splat! Drip-splat-splat, drip-splat-splat. Splat!

I could not work out why blood or something like it should be dripping on me. If I was in a mortuary drawer it should be refrigerated and airtight. There should certainly not be anything dripping on me from the drawer above. It was simply unfair and a nasty turn in my repeating nightmare. And the previously cold drawer I seemed to be confined in was warming up. It no longer felt refrigerated.

I tried to think what I had done to deserve this. I was not a perfect person....nobody is. But this was very bad.

If I get out of this I shall try to lead a better life, I told myself.

I tried praying but it felt false. I had never been a church goer and it seemed too late to learn.

Oh sinner man where you goin' to run to?

Drip-splat-splat, drip-splat-splat. Splat!

Drip-splat-splat, drip-splat-splat. Splat!

Oh sinner man where you goin' to run to?

In the Jacobean world I knew that I had hit my head. My clever ideas had probably come to nothing. I had realised that January 1606 on the Julian calendar was equivalent to 1607 on the Gregorian.... and that one had to add ten days to the date. So they were trying to burn me on the 30th of January 1607. That was the date of the fabled Bristol Channel Tsunami .... or possibly tidal surge. Whichever it was it had become a purely academic question. It made no difference as I was unconscious in the water then or dead in a metal box now........

Drip-splat-splat, drip-splat-splat. Splat!

There *is* something in here with me.

*

I came round gasping for air. I must have been out for only

seconds and I was being carried along attached to the pole. The contraption that had been constructed to kill me had now, by pure chance, saved me by twisting round and pulling my head above the surface. I wriggled up and along the pole and was able to get my arms over the end of the stake. Balancing precariously on the wooden structure and squeezing tightly with my legs so that I would not fall off I gradually worked my hands loose from each other. I was free but I was still effectively surfing along on this, the biggest Severn Bore that had ever been recorded. Eventually the makeshift raft crashed into the roof of a house and stayed there. Holding onto the chimney was a man holding a dog.

The man took one look at me and screamed.

'Hey, weren't 'ee the fellow that was supposed to burn.'

'No, no,' I replied. 'That was my brother. He looks a lot like me.'

'Nah,' gasped the man. 'Thee is the witch. I knows that Appleshanks hath no brother and I'll set me dog on 'ee. Go get 'im, Toby.'

The dog growled and jumped at me, teeth bared and slavering. I kicked the brute in the stomach and it flew off into the still surging waters.

'Oy,' cried the man, taking a swing at me with a knife that he plucked from his belt..

It's either him or me, I reasoned and pushed him into the water also.

'I can't swim,' cried the man as the waters washed him away.

'Should have thought of that before you attacked me,' I shouted back. 'I could have given you lessons!'

*

Drip-splat-splat, drip-splat-splat. Splat!

Was any of this happening? Was I already dead and if not why not?

I had never been a callous person and I had just pushed a man into a raging flood and gloated over it. Was this what happened to people after they had died and returned to life?

I was back in the metal drawer and feeling hot. I was beginning to get some life back into my limbs and my toes were twitching convulsively. In fact I could not stop them from moving and now my legs were jerking. Despite the dim or almost non-existent lighting I could see quite well and I was imagining a goblin's face staring back at me. Why?

I was feeling mortified that I could have treated a fellow human being in the way that I had even if it was only a dream.

Was it only a dream?

The Chinese water torture continued.

Drip-splat-splat, drip-splat-splat. Splat!

Was it really the dripping that was turning me crazy?

Am I awake even now?

Drip-splat-splat, drip-splat-splat. Splat!

*

I am a good swimmer, or at least I was. But was the bugler a swimmer? If not it might be dangerous to try to swim away from the rooftop.

I had been swept miles away from Burnham. By some freak of the current I had undoubtedly been taken way up the valley of the Severn River and away from my persecutors. Now I had to consolidate my luck and get away from this house. The man on the roof had recognised me so I was not yet completely safe but I was free and that had to count for something.

Why was I here? Was this some form of cosmic time travelling Quantum Leap situation where I had to accomplish a task before I could return to my reality or was I dreaming this in some form of intermittent coma?

I sat on the rooftop waiting for the floodwaters to abate but they did not appear to be doing so.

I had to get out of this army uniform...it was surely the reason that the man on the roof had recognised me so quickly. Eventually I snagged a body that was floating past me and, with great difficulty stripped all his dirty clothes off and put them on myself. I had to resist a temptation to bite into his flesh ..... I was certainly hungry enough.

I clad the man in the bugler's clothes and set him off again, floating face down in the still moving flood waters. I reasoned that somebody might find the body and think that it was that of Appleshanks and the hue and cry for me would die down.

The two priests who had instigated the proceedings against me may already have perished in the flood though I doubted it. The last I had seen of them they were near the church and I reckoned that they would probably have got into the building and climbed to safety.

Of Sir George and Appleshank's two relatives I was less sure. They had moved away but were not on high ground when the floods hit. I had tried to warn them but I was not certain that the warning had been sufficiently heeded.

*

Drip-splat-splat, drip-splat-splat. Splat!

Flashback..... they were starting the operation all over again and I knew that the anaesthetist was going to muck it all up. The surgeon was swabbing my back with the pink spirit, the gasman was mouthing crossword clues and the nurse was screaming at imagined rats.

My whole body was convulsing and contorting and suddenly my arms were thrashing around and pushing the end of the cabinet to no avail. I now tried pulling against the drawer above and pushing with my body but the uncontrolled convulsions made this difficult. Was there slight movement? Was the drawer shifting? Was I even in a drawer or was I just moving phantom limbs?

Drip-splat, splurge. Drip-splat, splurge.

Skaaa - shkeeee, skaaa - shkeeee, skaaa - shkeeee.

*

Living two lives almost simultaneously or perhaps three was very difficult. Was this what schizophrenics experienced or people with multiple personality disorder? I remembered reading an article that disputed whether MPD had ever existed despite its popularity as a diagnosis, particularly in North America. I had heard of many cases where people claimed to have led former lives as famous people such as Napoleon, Queen Elizabeth the First or William Shakespeare. I had never heard of a single case in which the person had alternatively been still living the life of an unknown ancestor and also in the present world. But what is time? Physicists had great difficulty explaining it. Einstein had moved people away from believing that it was just the movement of things, or even the medium that allowed things to move. Scientists now accepted that time could be considered as a dimension of the continuum known as space-time and could be treated as such in equations.

Some people still believed that there was no other time but the Now and that this encompassed everything. Einstein had concluded that the flow of time was just a very persistent illusion.

So maybe I could alternate existences.

Maybe I'm not completely insane. Maybe.

*

- Brigadier Blenkinsop has put out the following statement .. "The emergency is nearly over. The Government is actively seeking the whereabouts of James Scott and his family. We are asking anybody who has information related to the Scott family to get in touch with us via this telephone number ...0800......"

Chapter 6

I was shivering and shaking as I stood on the almost submerged house. Eventually a tree started to drift by that was so large I decided that I could risk travelling with it. I do not normally fear water, however this was bitterly cold and subject to difficult and unpredictable currents. I realised that I could not stay on the roof for ever and I was freezing. The day was fairly good considering it was January but the chill factor of wearing sodden clothes and standing in a brisk wind was bringing my body temperature right down. I was inhabiting the body of a very old man and I had no idea why I had not already succumbed to hypothermia.

I jumped into the branches of the tree and it drifted with the wind away from the house and over towards some distant hills. It eventually grounded in a forest perhaps two miles further on and I was able to dismount and climb down. The waters were still waist high and now started to recede but I waded against the current towards higher ground and right out of the flood.

So far so good. I had survived but had no money, no food, nowhere to sleep. Add that to the knowledge that the body was not my own and I had no aims or objectives and you might have thought that I would be despondent. For some reason I wasn't and I was feeling considerably stronger than when I first awoke in the wooden coffin.

I was almost elated. I had, after all, escaped from being burnt to death. That had to be a good thing.

A small cottage was visible about a mile distant. Smoke was drifting from the chimney and I decided to throw myself on the mercy of the householder. I stumbled along a rough path through the sparse wood and reached the house. I knocked hard on the front door but there was no reply. I ran round the house calling out but still received no response so decided to try the door. It opened immediately. It was clear from the mayhem in the main room that the waters had reached this far but retreated and in the small kitchen I found who I took to be the homeowner, a little old lady who had drowned next to her sink. So where had the smoke come from?

I climbed up the stairs. An old man was lying in a wooden cot, roughly sewn blankets over him and a fire burning in the grate.

'Is that you Maud?' asked the man.

He was looking towards me but I could tell that he was completely blind.

'I'm sorry to say that it is not,' I replied.

'Who are you sir?' asked the man. 'And where is Maud?'

'I'm a very wet and weary traveller by the name of Peter Chambers,' I replied, having decided to shed the dangerous Appleshanks name. 'I'm sorry to say that Maud has died.'

'Died?' asked the blind-man. 'How very selfish of her, dying before me.'

'Selfish?' I was stunned by his reply. 'She didn't mean to die. She was drowned.'

'That would explain it,' said the blind man. 'Maud doesn't usually do silly things like dying.'

'No, I don't suppose she does,' I answered. 'Most people don't make a habit of it.'

'Except the undead,' replied the man. 'Those who die and then return and then die again. I understand that there was a case like that in Burnham. Maud told me about it.'

'Really?' I tried to sound interested but nonchalant.

'Apparently so,' nodded the blind man. 'But I don't believe a word of it. What am I going to do if Maud is dead?'

'Do you have any other relatives?' I asked. 'Is there anyone else who can help you now that your wife has died?'

'Oh, Maud wasn't my relative or even my wife,' replied the man. 'She was my housekeeper. My wife died years ago. I employed Maud.'

'Maybe someone else will work for you,' I suggested.

'Cobbins the woodcutter should be here soon. He keeps my garden,' said the blind man, apparently unconcerned about Maud except for the inconvenience of her passing. 'Unless he's stupidly got himself drowned as well.'

'I don't think that anybody wants to be drowned,' I remonstrated gently. 'There has been a terrible flood and it actually entered your house to a level of over six feet in height.'

'Lucky I was upstairs don't you think?' replied the man. 'And I keep my money here too. I'll pay you if you'll stay and look after me until Cobbins returns.'

'I am rather busy,' I started to say this but stopped. What was I busy doing?

'I'll pay you handsomely,' said the blind man. 'I do have money. I live in this hovel by choice....it is cheap to maintain.'

'I will stay until Cobbins turns up,' I agreed. 'But how much will you pay?'

'One penny a day and your full board and lodging,' quoth the man. 'You can't say fairer than that.'

No, I suppose I can't, I pondered. *At least I now have a bed for the night.*

*

The flashback was slightly different this time. The anaesthetist was bending low and whispering in my ear.

'I know you can hear me, Chambers. How do you like a taste of your own medicine? Do you like a little bit of torture?'

What the heck does the man mean? I've never tortured anyone!

'You tortured my daughter and now you shall suffer in return!'

No, no. You've got the wrong man. You can't mean me! I was screaming this silently.

'I've been letting you suffer the pain but the power failure has given me an excuse to break a few of your foul ribs.'

'What are you whispering to the patient?' asked the nurse, suspiciously.

Perhaps she can save me?

'Trying to keep the patient calm, Staff Nurse Bohn,' replied the disingenuous doctor. 'He is coming round which is good news.'

'But he has a great hole in his back,' cried the nurse. 'So you are supposed to keep him anaesthetised.'

'That as well,' smiled the mad doctor. 'But at least he is not dead.'

'Have you finished playing with the patient?' asked the surgeon sarcastically as the lights came back on and the respiratory machine once more made its peculiar inspiratory and expiratory noises: skaaa - shkeeee, skaaa - shkeeee. 'If so can we have him on his side again so that I can finish the operation.....and do make sure that he is properly under this time.'

So the surgeon had been suspicious. But why did the anaesthetist think that I had tortured his daughter?

'I'm going to addict you to heroin like you addicted my girl,' whispered the gas man.

Now I might have three girlfriends but I neither take drugs nor am I a pusher.

'I detest you and your so-called physical education, Roger Chambers,' whispered the anaesthetist.

Roger?

'Stop whispering to the patient and get him ready. I'm starting again,' declared the surgeon.

Roger Chambers was the PE master at the academy just up the road. Same surname but no relation...and he did leave under a cloud if I'm not very much mistaken.

'You're lucky,' whispered the gasman. 'This time I will give you a proper GA.'

He injected something in my arm and I did pass out...... and woke up in this metal drawer and there is now a glimmer of light. My legs are still bound up but my arms are free.

Drip, drip, splat. Blood and other bodily fluids falling onto me from above and covering me in gore.

I cannot understand it but I was somehow sure that my returning strength was related to the constant dripping. Or perhaps I was completely bonkers.

Probably the latter.

Drip, drip, splat. Drip, drip, splat.....

Skaaa - shkeeee, skaaa - shkeeee, skaaa - shkeeee.

*

'I'd like a mutton and parsnip stew,' said the blind man. 'And you can have a slice of bread for you supper.'

'That doesn't sound particularly fair,' I protested. 'If I make you a stew I would like to have some too.'

'If I smell the stew on your breath I will know that you have eaten it and broken the terms of engagement,' whined the rich blind man. 'Then I won't have to pay you. Heh, heh.'

'But you say you have money and can afford to pay for the meat,' I was indignant.

'I only have money because I don't give meat away to every waif and stray who arrives at my door,' replied the blind man.

'I'll make the stew,' I replied walking down the stairs.

And I'll have to bury Maud, clear up downstairs and then start to make plans for the future.

'Hurry up with that stew,' shouted the blind man. 'I can't wait all day.'

He really is unpleasant, I thought. But I'll have to stick it out for a while.

'You can sleep downstairs,' said the blind man. 'Don't want you up here.'

Thanks a bunch. I'll have to bury Maud before I can sleep there and the room is all wet from the flood.

'OK,' I said, hiding my feelings.

'Push Maud into the pig enclosure,' ordered the sightless tyrant. 'They'll get rid of the body.'

'I didn't see any pigs,' I replied.

'They'll have floated off in the flood but they'll come back,' the man giggled in a horrible manner. 'They know who feeds them.... Maud, of course! Heh, heh, heh.'

He is seriously unpleasant.

*

If you've had a whore the thing to do
Is to dip your wick in the chemical loo

The chorus of the old rugby song was going round and round in my mind as the drips continued to hit me square on the forehead.

If you've had a whore
Drip-splat
the thing to do
Drip-splat
Is to dip your wick
Drip-splat
in the chemical loo
Drip-splat

Singing the songs was one thing, actually enacting them quite another.

I live an exemplary life. At least, I did until now. No whores, drinking a bit too much on a Saturday night but otherwise abstemious. Three girlfriends? Did I say three girlfriends? Two of them are my dogs, Gemma, a Labradoodle, and Lizzie the greyhound. My real girlfriend and I are due to marry in three weeks time. We've been together for five years. Five years!

Roger Chambers was a completely different matter. There were rumours that he had become too friendly with the students....girls and boys indiscriminately. Then finally there was a drugs scandal.

The anaesthetist is torturing the wrong man.

Drip-splat, Drip-splat, Drip-splat.

*

'When you come round you won't remember any of this.'

It was the anaesthetist whispering in my ear. The surgeon was drilling away at my spine and I was silently screaming in agony.

'But I,' continued the gasman. '....Will have the pleasure of knowing that you suffered just like my daughter.'

What in the heck did Roger Chambers do to this man's poor daughter?

'Chambers,' the anaesthetist was still whispering and clearly answering my unspoken question. 'You addicted her to drugs then left her to overdose. Dead, Chambers, she's dead. I bet you wish you were dead, don't you Chambers?'

If I survive this I will look for this Roger Chambers and confront him with what this anaesthetist is telling me. Aaaargh, that was a very painful jolt.

'I've almost finished here,' said the surgeon. 'Have you stopped tormenting the patient, Gransbury?'

So that's the anaesthetist's name. Gransbury. Definitely not the Great Gransbury. No that should have been Gatsby. The man's clearly deranged but I understand his angst. Aargh.

'Done,' pronounced the surgeon. 'Now to get him sewn up. More extensive op than I expected but despite all the delays and interruptions it has finally worked out OK.'

Owww. Stitches in my skin. Not the worst of the pain but still uncomfortable.

I seem to have survived this so what has killed me?
Stupid question. I'm thinking, so I can't be dead. Cogito ergo sum, I think therefore I am. Descartes has to be right.

'I've given you Rohypnol. You won't know what hit you,' whispered the gas man so that only I could hear. 'And I've mixed it with tetrodotoxin from the puffer fish. That's a zombie drug from the West Indies.'

Unless, of course, something supernatural has happened and I am dead. Or a zombie.

Drip-splat, Drip-splat, Drip-splat.
Or maybe none of it has happened?
'Try the seven Tesla.'
What?

*

- *The Commander-in-Chief of the United Kingdom, Brigadier Blenkinsop, has asked us to broadcast the following statement.* "*The reported sightings of one-eyed giants, ogres, fairies and werewolves must stop. These reports are the hysterical outpourings of damaged minds……*"

Chapter 7

The sun has gone down and it is too cold to go outside. I will have to bury Maud tomorrow. Tonight I am to sleep in this freezing cold downstairs room. The blind man has a fire in a stove upstairs and I had to cook his stew on it. I did sneak a little of the stew for myself but I found I was not hungry or that my appetite had changed.

I was unable to light the stove down here…everything was too wet. I am now lying on a sodden kitchen table, albeit a large one. This has taken me above the wet floor and I have found a few clothes and a single blanket upstairs. I had to look for them very quietly as the blind man was listening to my every move.

I'm on the table and the woman called Maud is lying on the floor. I am finding it very difficult to go to sleep as I keep imagining that Maud is moving. She is dead…stone cold dead.

Now I am wide awake and the blind man is standing next to me with a hideous grin on his face, his white marble eyes staring at me. In his hands he is carrying the corpse of Maud and he is pushing her towards me. Her eyes have gone completely and there are only raw sockets where they had been, her face is a ghostly green.

'Kiss her,' he whispers. 'You know you want to. Go on, hold her tightly. Do what you really want to with her. '

I sat up in shock. The room was lit by the light of the moon and the corpse was still lying on the floor. There was no sign of the blind man but I could hear him upstairs snoring gently.

A nightmare. A hideous nightmare within a nightmare.

All of this horror had to be a hideous nightmare.

Now a dripping of water had started from the ceiling of the kitchen and inevitably it was landing on my forehead.

Drip, drip, drip.....

*

Drip-splat, Drip-splat, Drip-splat.

'Push him into the drawer,' said a disembodied voice. 'Hippocampus.'

I could not see anything and the voice was etching patterns on my eyelids.

'We'll do the postmortem when we return,' continued the voice and this time I could feel the sound as an itching all over my body and I could see swirling patterns of iridescent colour.

Synesthesia! That's what it is!

A neurological condition when stimulation of one sensory nerve pathway leads to involuntary experience in another. I could read the definition as if from a dictionary.

How did I know this? I have no idea but I do know that it is correct.

Was this due to a psychedelic drug like LSD? Was this a result of the surgery?

I felt my body being lifted but simultaneously it was dropping and turning into a falling leaf, tumbling from a tree in Autumn, fluttering down to the floor of the forest. Concurrently and impossibly the surgical procedure was starting all over again.

'What was that bit on the news about bad weather coming this way?' asked the voice, more distant now and smelling of cheese. I could not hear the reply.

The dripping started. A distant bugle was playing the Last Post.

Drip, drip, drip.

I lay in the metal drawer going over all the experiences of my life, judging them. Had I spoken too harshly to that useless boy at Sports Day? Was I too slow at appreciating the Head Teacher's efforts? Was I a dangerous driver? Did I drink too much alcohol?

Was swearing a deadly sin? Was ogling a woman's legs tantamount to adultery? Was touching a leg a mortal sin?

I lay in the box and judged myself, weighed myself in the balances and found I was wanting.

*

I was up before dawn and pulled Maud into the garden.

Come into the garden, Maud
I am here at the gate alone

I keep singing this to myself as I haul away at the cold body. I can see the pig enclosure but I have no intention of putting the poor old lady into it.

There has been a frost overnight and as the sun comes up I am hacking away at the ground with a mattock and then digging a hole with a shovel.

Eventually I have a shallow grave dug and put the body into it. I stand and mutter a little prayer which bubbles up from somewhere deep inside me. That is not one of my own memories, I am sure of that.

Then back inside to make breakfast for myself and the blind man. It is going to be porridge for both of us whatever the sightless one says.

*

'She was only sixteen, Chambers. Sixteen!'

The anesthetist whispered in my ear again. He was giving me more details about my transgressions with his daughter. Except it was not me....it was my namesake at the other school. I tried to scream silently.

'Rogered her in your bedchamber,' he hissed. 'You've certainly got the right name, Roger Chambers.'

You're wrong. That's not my name. I'm Peter Chambers, not Roger

Chambers.

Drip, drip, splat. Drip, drip, splat..... skaaa - shkeeee, skaaa - shkeeee, skaaa - shkeeee.

My neck was still painful where the rugby player had bitten me and there was a notch out of my ear. Why was it hurting me now?

*

'Porridge?' screamed the blind man. 'What do you think I am paying you for? I want more than this.'

He is seriously nasty.

'Get me some cured meat and a mug of ale. Do it now!'

The blind man was still ranting. But where could I get meat and ale from? I thought I had done well to find some unspoiled oats at the top of a tall cupboard. There was no more meat and no ale. That which had not been washed away by the flood had gone into the stew.

I tried to explain this to the man but he would not initially listen. Eventually he stopped his tirade and pulled out a leather purse from under his pillow.

'Here is a silver shilling,' said the man. 'Take it, go into town and bring back some food. Do it now.'

I looked at the coin he had passed me and realised that it was a gold coin of some sort, a noble or an angel or some such thing.

The man was seriously horrible but I did not wish to cheat him. Perhaps I would have been just as nasty if I was blind?

'That's a gold coin,' I told him. 'I'm sure that I will not need so much.'

'Heh, heh, heh,' laughed the blind man. 'I knew it was gold. I was just tempting you and I bet you wish you had not told me it was gold. Heh, heh, heh. Stimulate the Limbic System.'

I stared at him.

What was he playing at ?

*

'I'll get you Chambers,' the cousin of the Queen was sledging me in the scrum. 'You're a weak old man, Chambers, and I'll definitely get you.'

And he did. He bit me on the neck and ear and minutes later someone tried to break my back.

Drip-splat-splat, drip-splat-splat. Splat!

Skaaa - shkeeee, skaaa - shkeeee, skaaa - shkeeee.

Bang-crunch, Bang-crunch. The chisel was removing my bone and the pain was shooting down my paralysed legs.

Drip-splat-splat, drip-splat-splat. Splat!

*

'You say your name is Peter Chambers,' said the blind man, staring at me with white marbles. 'I bet you would like to rob me, Peter Chambers.'

Why was the blind man telling me this? Why was he trying to incite violence against himself?

'Did you roger the dead maid last night, Peter Chambers?' the old man pointed a shaky index finger at me as he accused me of necrophilia.

He turned over on the cot and started to bare his buttocks.

'Is this what you want, Peter Chambers?'

I looked in horror at the moon-like appearance of the blind man's naked bottom.

Was this really happening? It defied logic. I made no comment.

'Come on Peter Chambers,' exhorted the blind man. 'Do what you want to do.'

Once again I considered what a horrible creature this blind man had become.

Horrible.

*

Drip, drip-drip, drip. Drip, drip-drip, drip. Drip, drip-drip, drip.

The rhythm had changed and whatever was dripping on me

had started to smell bad despite the formaldehyde.

Bang-crunch, Bang-crunch. The surgeon was still chiselling bone out of my back. Why did he need to remove so much or was it just a small piece that felt huge?

Drip, drip-drip, drip. Drip, drip-drip, drip. Drip, drip-drip, drip.

*

- Speaking on behalf of the Interim Government a spokesman today said "There is no truth in the rumour that the Isle of Skye has revolted against Martial Law. The entire UK is as peaceful as it has ever been and the State of Emergency has been overcome." When asked if that was the case when would the elected democratic government be put back in charge the spokesman replied "No comment."

Chapter 8

I had to get away from the blind man. He had a strange psychological hold over me and I had stayed there for three days already. To my surprise I had found more food in a cupboard in his room and had managed to feed both of us. Still the blind man grumbled and protested and he was getting right into my psyche.

I should leave today but I owned nothing. I should leave right now but the blind man had not paid me even the penny a day he had promised.

'And I won't pay you until the end of the month,' cackled the creature as he lay in his cot. 'If I do pay you now you'll just get up and leave me.'

I stared at the blind man. He was right. I would not rob him, he had discovered that, but if I was paid even a few pennies I could leave. A penny would buy me a night in a featherbed in Bristol, something I knew from my knowledge of history.

I could not sort out what was going on by staying here in a hovel somewhere up country.

Where exactly was I? This question was constantly on my mind but the blind man would not tell me a straight answer.

'You're where the bakers all live or come from,' he had wheezed and dribbled.

This had been followed by his usual mad cackling laugh.

I had asked him to explain but he had replied that I should work it out for myself. I had tried but it made no sense. There were no wheat fields around here and I was yet to see a mill.

I had just about decided to leave, money or not, when the blind man climbed out of his fetid cot and grabbed me with a skinny, age-marked hand.

'You want to leave,' he whispered, spit dribbling from his mouth and his sightless eyes staring at me. 'I shall come with you and then you will come back here.'

I tried to shake him off but it was impossible. He clambered onto my back and hung on like the old man of the sea.

'I have my gold and we shall go to the nearest town to buy more victuals,' ordered the blind man as he moulded himself into the shape of my dorsum.

'I would like you to let go and climb off my back,' I said to the sightless burden.

'Of course you would,' giggled the blind man. 'And you would like to murder me and take my money. Heh, heh. But you won't. You'll do just as I say.'

So here I was tramping through the mire trying to get to the road with a blind man clinging tightly to my back urging me onwards whenever I stopped. Which road? I still did not know. Where did I get the strength from to carry the man? Again, no idea.

*

Drip, drip-drip, drip. Drip, drip-drip, drip.
Drip, drip-drip, drip.
Put you lipstick round my dipstick
And open up the choke
Fire my sparking plugs
Don't put my piston off its stroke
We were singing after the rugby game again.
My engine isn't Wankel
Or horizontally opposed
It's an A series in-line OHV
With standard rubber hose.

The very game before the one in which I was injured and I had scored a try by bulling my way over the line with pure strength.

Perhaps I had been too vigorous?

*

Drip, drip-drip, drip. Drip, drip-drip, drip.
Drip, drip-drip, drip.
Skaaa - shkeeee, skaaa - shkeeee, skaaa - shkeeee.
Into the operating theatre again...the ceaseless drip, drip, drip was pulling me back.... the anaesthetist was whispering into my ear.

'You'll wake up as a zombie which is more than you deserve,' he hissed. 'My daughter died, Chambers, and you know why.'

No I don't, I screamed silently as the hammer came down again onto the chisel.

Skaaa - shkeeee, skaaa - shkeeee, skaaa - shkeeee.

*

I know where I am! I recognise that church. It is St.Mary's, Lydney, on the edge of the Forest of Dean. The Vice Admiral of England Sir William Wynter was granted the manor of Lydney in 1588 for his services against the Spanish Armada and that is where we are. Or did he buy it in 1561? It is a hamlet rather than a town but maybe we will be able to obtain food here.

'This is William Wynter's place, isn't it?' I asked.

'Was,' replied the incubus clinging to my shoulders. 'It now belongs to Edward but all of us are rich.'

'So you are a Wynter?' I asked.

'Yes and I spell it like the season,' replied the blind man. 'My brothers still use the Y. My name is also William like my father. I am William Winter.'

'Now is the winter of our discontent,' I murmured, quoting from Richard III.

'That's right,' the disagreeable burden concurred. 'William Shakespeare at his best.'

Why did everything keep coming back to Shakespeare?

'Are your family royalists?' I asked Winter.

'That depends on the royal, don't you think?' retorted the blind man, speaking rather too loudly in my ear. 'I didn't like Bloody Mary but then nobody did. I liked Elizabeth a little more. Capricious.'

'And James?'

'King James the First of England and the Sixth of the Scots?' wheezed the blind man. 'I have no quarrel with him and he hath no quarrel with me.'

That makes a change, I thought. *This blind man seems to be the sort who would pick an argument with anyone.*

'My brother, Sir Edward, is a staunch royalist and so is his young son, John,' muttered Winter. 'They march up and down together at Raglan Castle.'

'Raglan?'

'Yes. Sir Edward is married to Anne, daughter of the Earl of Worcester.'

'Are you married?' I asked and received a clout round the ear by way of partial reply.

'You forget yourself, Chambers,' hissed the blind man. 'It is enough that I speak to you and use you as a beast of burden. But no, I am not married. I take what I can when I can. Like you.'

He started laughing again with his horrible wheezing cackle.

'Heh, heh, heh. Just as you would like to do, Peter Chambers, if you were given even as much as half a chance. Just as you would like to do.'

We walked into the manor house at Lydney and the servants hurried round to fill up a bag with food for the blind man. They all seemed extremely scared of him. I was glad to get the burden off my back and to put him down onto a chair. When the retainers had finished collecting the supplies together the blind man handed over a gold coin and they all stood gawping at the sight of the money.

'Bring the change, bring the change,' hissed the man. 'That coin could pay for five times this amount of supplies.'

There was consternation amongst the servants then the boldest of them, a man perhaps in his thirties, spoke up.

'We do not have sufficient change for this coin, sir,' he explained. 'We shall have to ask Sir Edward and he is away at Raglan.'

'Playing soldiers with his son, John, no doubt,' cackled the blind man. 'Then give me a receipt and a promissory note for the remainder. I will collect the remainder as further supplies and you will be able to mark off as I do so.'

So saying the blind man brought out two pieces of paper from his dirty tunic and passed them to the man who had spoken up. Clearly Winter had expected this and had come prepared.

The man stared at the notes long and hard.

'I do not read so well, sir,' he said hesitantly. 'But I can sign my name.'

'It just obliges you to repay me the change and supply the food I need,' cackled William Winter. 'Just sign at the bottom on both. I will take one copy and we will be gone.'

The man tried hard to decipher the long words but eventually gave up and signed the documents.

'Heh, heh, heh,' cackled the blind man as he hid his copy back inside his tawdry tunic. 'Now we must go before it gets dark.'

Not for the first time I realised that I had been carrying this monster all day.

'I've a good mind to find a whore. Do you think you could carry a whore as well as me?' he cackled this in my ear as he swung himself back onto my shoulders, proving himself to be even more agile than I thought and driven by base desires.

'Of course I couldn't,' I replied.

'You're a young, strong man,' he remarked. 'You could do it. I'd let you have her for half of the night.'

I looked at my legs. They had thickened out and looked more like the legs I remembered than those of the old bugler. I examined my arms. They had also beefed up.

What was really happening here?

'Move,' ordered Winter. 'We do not want to get caught in the dark by the half-formed creatures of the forest.'

'The Forest of Dean?'

'Of course,' replied the blind man. 'I told you that they were bakers. They are all inbred.'

So saying he cackled away, laughing so much at his own joke that he almost fell off his perch on my weary shoulders.

'I wouldn't have thought that you would have been too upset by the dark,' I answered in measured tones.

'I'm not inconvenienced by it but you would be,' replied the incubus, the devil riding on my shoulders. 'And you are the one carrying me.'

We set off back along the path that we had come by. As the forest swallowed us up the light did begin to fade and I sped up and eventually found myself trotting. In the distance I could hear wolves howling and I knew that the blind man was right. We had to get back before it was completely dark or we would have problems.

'Don't worry about the wolves,' hissed Winter. 'It is the ogres, hobgoblins and sprites that you should worry about.'

'They don't exist,' I protested.

'Really?' replied the blind man. 'Little do you know, steed. Little indeed.'

*

'This one is responding differently.'

'In what way?'

'At least three different areas are activating.'

'Simultaneously?'

'No, sequentially.'

'And you've not seen that before?'

'Not exactly like this.'

Drip, drip-drip, drip. Drip, drip-drip, drip.
Drip, drip-drip, drip.
Brrrm, brrrrm, brrrrm.

*

- A spokesman for the armed forces ruling the country under Blinkers Blenkinsop stated today that the troops gathering around Stonehenge are necessary for crowd control and to stop the ancient monument being desecrated on mid-summer's day. Our reporter is on the scene...
- Thank you Julian. Yes, the atmosphere here is quite extraordinary. There are thousands of new age followers but in addition a large number of concerned "silent majority." The army are very noticeably keeping to themselves at present and there has been no violence but as we near mid-summer we are all hoping that nothing untoward will happen. Back to you in the studio.
- Thank you Crispin. Other news... the tsunamis and earthquakes that have been affecting the majority of the world...

Chapter 9

'You told me that you did not believe in the supernatural,' I protested. The blind man had become so much part of my back that I could hardly imagine an existence without him whispering into my ear.

'I said no such thing,' countered the encumbrance.

'You didn't believe in the undead.'

'I just said that I did not believe that the case in Burnham was an example of the undead,' explained the blind man. 'Burnham is not that sort of place.'

'So where is that sort of place?' I queried.

'Right here, in the Forest of Dean,' retorted the incubus, the devil on my back. 'But you are making me change my mind.'

'So now you don't think that there are ogres, hobgoblins and sprites here in the woods?'

'Of course there are,' replied the blind man, holding ever more tightly around my neck. 'It is the case in Burnham I am referring to.'

'Why?'

'Because of you, Peter Chambers. Because of you.'

'What about me? In what way have I made you change your mind?' I was alarmed. I knew that I was the reincarnated or at least revivified version of the bugler John Appleshanks but I had purposely kept that information from the blind man.

'You are changing, Chambers, and you know it,' replied the sightless man clinging to my back. 'When you arrived you were old and skinny, weak and aimless. Now you are taller, stronger and your libido is returning.'

'How do you know this, Winter?' I demanded. 'Tell me how a

blind man can know such things.'

'It's Mister Winter to you,' replied the weight on my shoulders. 'And blind men can use all their other senses and see things the sightless cannot perceive.'

'So what do you now believe about Burnham?'

'That you were the revitalised man from that small town and that you are growing stronger by the day, Peter Chambers. Or should I call you John Appleshanks, the witch of Burnham?'

I was about to deny his accusation when we were suddenly stopped in our tracks by a small mob carrying pitchforks.

'What do we 'ave 'ere?' asked the leader of the mob. 'A man carrying a blind man on 'is back and the sightless man looks a lot like that rich 'ermit known as William Winter!'

'What would you have with us, peasant?' asked Winter in an imperious tone.

'Peasant, is it?' replied the man. 'Then I shall call you monster, you and your usury.'

'Usury? I make fair loans,' replied the blind man.

'Your family has never been fair,' snarled the leader. 'Taking over the ironworks at the whim of the king, displacing us from our rightful land. No. All of you Winters are too long and too cold.'

It hadn't occurred to me until now that the blind man was actually rather tall when he stood up. I had thought him to be small because he was curled up in a cot but he was indeed long and he was definitely of a cold nature.

'You take what you like and then tell us that we are in debt,' muttered someone else in the crowd.

'I take only that which is rightfully mine,' retorted the blind man.

'Not so,' responded the second speaker from the mob, a small man with bright red hair and a heavily freckled face. 'We have already heard what you did today.'

'And what did I do?' asked Winter. 'And how could you know?'

'A horseman preceded you,' replied the red head. 'And you unfairly indentured George Trescothic.'

'He owes me money!' protested the encumbrance.

'Only because you insisted on paying with a large gold piece,' countered the red head. 'You knew he would not have enough change.'

'He has that gold piece and can make money with it,' answered the blind man.

'Not at the rate of interest you made him sign up for,' replied the first speaker, the leader of the mob. 'But we reckons that he won't have to pay nobody if you are dead, William Winter, parasite of the Forest of Dean.'

The leader made a signal and the mob jumped at me and my burden. I waved my hands wildly trying to ward them off. The blind man clung ever tighter to my neck squeezing the blood from my veins and half strangling me.

'Don't wave your hands like a pansy,' cried the blind man. 'Bite the bastards. They deserve no better.'

That was not the way that I normally fight but when I found that three of the mob were pulling at my arms and legs and dragging me down I did what he said. I bared my fangs and bit the first of the assailants. He screamed with agony and let go of me. The others in the mob also pulled back, muttering, then melted into the forest.

'We'll be back for you, Winter,' cried the leader as they retreated. 'And we'll get your pet guardian monster too.'

It was all quite inexplicable.

'That stimulated the Limbic,' laughed the blind man.

*

The bugler had been poisoned, the actor was to die and the king was to be executed. There was a pattern here and I was the only person able to do something about it. But here I was with a blind man stuck to my back scurrying through the woods back to the small hovel of a cottage that the man called home. Presumably the mob did not know exactly where Winter lived or if they did they were too scared to raid it. What sort of creature was this parasitic blind man and for that matter what was I? Rising from the dead is not unheard of when the person was not actually deceased but what if I had been truly dead? What manner of creature could rise up from death? Mythologically perhaps one could name a few... zombies, vampires, witches, wizards and spiritual beings such as ghosts.....and those in league with the devil. That was about it. I was too substantial to be a ghost and perhaps too aware to be a zombie. I was certain that I was not in league with the devil for if I had been I would not have been a mere bugler, a horn wielding foot soldier. So maybe the court got it right and I actually was a witch?

The blind man was asleep and was murmuring away, talking in a somnambulist manner. What he said was weirdly anachronistic but then so was I....a twenty-first century rugby player in a seventeenth century body.

'Stimulate the limbic again and run the FMR sequences,' muttered the man. 'With the feedback loops? Yes, including full immersion.'

I thought that I recognised some of the terms. The man was referring to the brain again when he mentioned the word limbic. FMR could be the acronym or initials for many things. Perhaps it was Frequency Modulated Radio? Full immersion? Was that some form of hydrotherapy?

So this is not real. It cannot be real.

Of course I knew that all along but it felt so real and I was convinced that I had to achieve something to proceed. Maybe something that the priest had told me was important? Perhaps I had to save the actor and the king by riding to London?

That was too impossible. I was still penniless and had no horse.

If I did get to London and tell the players at the Globe about the plot against their star actor would they believe me? No way!

So it had to be something closer to home.

At last I was beginning to think.....

*

Drip, drip-drip, drip. Drip, drip-drip, drip. Drip, drip-drip, drip.

Bang-crunch, brrrrm, Bang-crunch, brrrrm.

Damn....just as I was beginning to cogitate logically I'm dragged back into the metal tube.

This time it is just noises.

Drip, drip-drip, drip. Drip, drip-drip, drip. Drip, drip-drip, drip.

Bang-crunch, brrrrm, Bang-crunch, brrrrm.

This is definitely a variation on the Chinese water torture.

*

'You can't leave here without me, heh, heh,' cackled the blind man as I tried to decamp from the poor apology for a cottage. 'We are inseparable. We cannot be apart. We need each other.'

'So how did I manage before we met?' I asked, hand on the door knob.

'I was always there,' said the blind man, inexplicable as usual.

I opened the door and stepped out into the surrounding countryside.

'See,' said the blind man.

I looked round at the sound of his evil, hissing voice. He was on my back again. How he had got there I had no idea but he was certainly in his now accustomed position, clinging tightly to my throat, long fingers in a vice-like grip.

Had he hypnotised me? It seemed the only explanation.

'So where are we going?' asked the encumbrance.

'I have no idea,' I replied truthfully. 'I was just trying to get away.'

'That's fine,' replied Winter in a cold, frosty voice. 'But we will need to eat and drink. Then we can do whatever you want to do.'

'We will take the provisions with us,' I was determined to leave the house but I could see that food was needed. In fact I already felt hungry.

'Gather the food and we'll go whilst it is still light,' replied the blind man. 'If light it still is. You are my eyes. I am relying on you.'

'I know that,' I answered. 'What I don't understand is why you say we have always been together when in fact I found you by chance.'

'The bodies are irrelevant,' hissed the blind man in my ear as I gathered the food. 'Surely you have realised that by now?'

'No I haven't,' I replied angrily.

'Good, good,' cackled Winter. 'You are showing some emotion. The limbic stimulation is working. I wonder whether the FMR will show the usual pattern.'

What is he talking about?

I was finding this blind monster very irritating and I resolved to remove him from my back. Try as I might I could not shift the blind man. It was as if he was grafted on, adhered to my very skin, one with the deep muscles of my back, fused to my spine. I struggled and struggled to no avail.

'Stimulate the claustrum,' whispered the blind man. 'He is becoming dangerously agitated.'

I slowed my struggling and then stopped completely. I became overwhelmingly tired and sleepy. I knelt down on all fours with the blind man still attached to my back then gradually buckled over into unconsciousness.

*

'You are a monster, Mister Chambers,' whispered the anaesthetist in my ear, stressing the mister sarcastically.

I realised for the first time that this anaesthetist was much like the blind man.

'I shall make you suffer for what you did to my daughter,' the gas man was still whispering. 'You won't remember what is happening to you except in occasional nightmares. Maybe not just occasional.'

'Have you finished whispering to the patient?' asked the surgeon. 'I want to continue the operation in peace.'

Bang-crunch. Bang-crunch. Peace for him, maybe, but agony for me. Bang-crunch. It was as if the surgeon was trying to remove the blind man. No, that was wrong. That was happening in a different century to a different person.

*

- We are in the midst of a pitched battle, Julian. The word went out that Blinkers was about to sacrifice the two innocent Scott boys and the crowd surged forward to prevent it from happening. The army stepped in and would have been overwhelmed by the mob but were supported by supernatural creatures.

- What exactly do you mean by supernatural creatures, Crispin?

- One eyed giants, dragons, griffins. That sort of thing, Justin. The crowd surge was quelled and then I saw with my own eyes a gigantic figure pluck a central stone from Stonehenge and replace it with a throne. Ooops. Must go now, I'm being crushed by the crowd.

- We've temporarily lost contact with Crispin but we will be back with him as soon as possible. Other breaking news.... the experimental neuroscientist Professor Pugh Cruikshanks stated today that his latest work has shown that the human brain can be maintained in a viable state out of the skull so long as sensory input is maintained and vital blood vessels supplied with oxygenated blood and glucose. He has declared that the experimental work conducted by El Cadaver did not go far enough. More of that later. Now a report of a man who bites dogs for a living........

Chapter 10

I awoke in an uncomfortable position on the ground outside the cottage. The blind man was standing staring at me with white sightless eyes. I was relieved to find that he was no longer attached to my back but the relief was short lived.

'Now you have collected the victuals we should leave,' he said in his hissing tones.

'I would much rather go without you,' I replied.

'Of course you would,' sneered Winter. 'But you have no choice.'

I stared at the man and he met my gaze with eyes of marble. The man's appearance had changed. He was filling out, growing younger and broader. He was looking a lot like myself.....my twenty-first century self. Pete Chambers not John Appleshanks.

Then he was on my back again and I was walking.

'I'm going to Burnham,' I stated. 'I'm going to find that letter of introduction or whatever it is that the priest wanted.'

'You could do many other things,' moaned the blind man. 'You could hire a whore. I've plenty of money.'

His long bony hand came round in front of my face holding a fistful of gold coins.....double crowns, angels, unites and laurels. How I knew what they were I had no idea.

'I've no interest in whores,' I answered truthfully.

'A boy then,' he replied. 'Whatever takes your fancy.'

'I'm going to Burnham.'

'Don't go to Burnham. Go gambling instead,' the blind man was pleading with me and trying to tempt me at the same time. 'Buy a slave. Beat up an old lady. Purchase some opium.'

'No, no, no and no,' I replied and walked steadily down towards the river. I reckoned if I followed the river I was bound to reach somewhere I recognised and we could take it from there. Maybe I would find a rowing boat and we could row to Burnham? It was a long distance to row or to walk but we had provisions and we could stop on the way.

Quite how long I had stayed at the cottage I could not tell but the weather had become very mild for the time of year and I wondered whether Spring was in the air.

'I do not want to go to Burnham,' stated the blind man.

I continued to walk as I replied. 'Then you can get off my back and look after yourself.'

The weight remained on my dorsum and the bony fingers still gripped me round the neck.

My mind was so preoccupied by the struggle with Winter that I did not notice we had company until I heard a low, croaking voice.

'Well, well. What have we here?'

I turned round sharply at the sound. It was not a man who had spoken. It was some kind of hobgoblin, fully man-size but with a much larger head than a normal human being. This creature had distorted facial features that included a bulbous turned up nose and huge, low slung, pointed ears. I was reminded of Big Ears from the Noddy books of Enid Blyton.

'An old man carrying an old blind man?' the hobgoblin was staring at us. 'Or maybe a much younger man carrying a burden of guilt?'

He was staring at me intently as if reading my very soul.

'Or perhaps a dead man who doesn't know that he is dead?'

I returned the stare. This miscegenated goblin creature was too close to the truth for me to afford to ignore it despite the comic overtones of its appearance. The distorted gargoyle suddenly pursed his lips and whistled sharply. Out from the trees came a ragtag of hideous monsters, some with missing limbs or part of a limb. One had very short stumpy legs with no feet. Two had missing hands. There was even one fiend with two heads and another with a conjoined twin growing from its stomach. These were the more human looking of the beasts. In addition there were werewolves, snake-men and large snarling cats all on short chains being led by one-eyed giants. Cyclops!

'Maybe you would like to join my menagerie?' asked the malevolent creature with the big ears. 'I would feed you well.'

'No we would not like to join your misshapen zoo of misfits!' screamed the blind man. 'Go away and leave us in peace.'

Not for the first time I wished that the blind man could have kept quiet. Maybe he had said what I wanted to say myself but it was madness to speak out like that when we were in a position of such weakness, outnumbered by the menagerie, each of which looked perfectly capable of dealing with the two of us on its own. The blind man on my back was just a hindrance and I was still weak from the ordeal in the flood....and, presumably, from the poison administered to me by the evil-minded priest.

'The encumbrance has a mind of its own,' laughed the hobgoblin as he turned and waved instructions to one of the cyclopean giants.

The one-eyed creature rolled its hideous globe, its seeing apparatus, around in its socket and stared balefully at me. It then took two strides and picked the two of us up with one massive hand.

'Do you want me to eat them?' asked the cyclops.

'Not yet,' laughed the goblin. 'Just bite the head off one of them. That should give the other one something to think about.'

Large, smelly teeth came over in my direction and I tried to wriggle out of the brute's grip before we could be devoured. It missed me and crunched down on the blind man. The old fellow let out a wailing cry that was cut off as the cyclops tightened its bite. Then the massive one-eyed giant let go with a cry of anguish.

'Acid!' the giant screamed. 'The old blind man is full of acid.'

I could have told you that, I murmured to myself.

*

Drip drip drip drip.

I lay in the metal cabinet, or was it a tube? I was still being bombarded with drips which landed on my forehead, or where my forehead ought to be. I now had no true sensation of my limbs or my body. I realised now that the previous perception of myself, even the spasms, were not real. However I was still not sure what was real. From below my neck there was no accurate data...I was sure that the sensations were those of phantom limbs and body. I seemed to have real sensations from around my head as if my skin was pierced in a hundred places and the head was held firmly in a crown of thorns. Could this be possible?

My hearing and sight were intact in a partial way. Even my sense of smell was present and there was an acrid taste in my mouth. I could move my eyes and wiggle my tongue very slightly.

'Stimulate the olfactory bulb.'

That disembodied voice giving commands... who did it belong to?

'Now!'

*

I could no longer feel the blind man on my back. This was strange as I had expected to feel a dead weight but I looked around and saw no body. After the performance of the cyclops I was not going to put up any protest. The monsters led me towards a deep cave. The smell inside was fetid. It reminded me of an unclean public lavatory crossed with a dog poo bin and then covered in vomit for good measure. Absolutely foul!

A hideous woman, a witch who had sightless eyes like the blind man, sat on an old wooden chair. She sported a tall black hat, long talons for fingernails, spiky encrusted hair and no clothes over the sagging skin of a very ancient naked body.

'Why the hat and no clothes?' I asked the crone, intrigued and disgusted in equal measure.

'Because that is the way that I like it,' laughed the witch. 'And you still don't know what is happening, do you?'

'No idea,' I replied and it was true. Apart, of course, for the fact that the beasts were wrapping ropes around my limbs and pinning me out on the floor.

'We have to go to Burnham, as you suggested to the blind man, but we are taking reinforcements, heh, heh, heh.'

The witch climbed onto the back of the giant one-eyed man.

'I shall ride on Walter's back,' she wheezed. 'He is more reliable than you, Peter Chambers.'

She looked at me lying painfully on the rocky floor of the cave, hands bound, limbs extended.

'What has happened to Winter?' I asked, summoning the remaining strength for further futile resistance.

'It's giving way to Spring,' replied the crone.

'No,' I replied. 'I meant William Winter, the blind man from the cottage.'

'Of course you did,' said the witch. 'And that is for you to find out.'

'Why do you wish to go to Burnham?' I asked.

It was very odd. I was the one who had wanted to go to the little hamlet but now this witch also wanted to get there.

'I want to go, so we shall,' screamed the witch, stamping her feet. 'And you will come with us whether you want to or not.'

'But I was the one who wanted to go!' I protested. 'Of course I shall come. But I can hardly do so tied up like this.'

The witch nodded in resigned agreement and signalled to her followers who instantly released me. The crone led us to the entrance of the cave. The outside world looked strangely different and the air smelt fresh. The scent of Spring flowers was on the breeze.

'Disgusting!' screamed the witch. 'Give me the smell of decay any day, not this fresh air.'

I looked at the witch. *You are as perverse as the blind man,* I thought. *You really are. Totally perverse.*

*

Drip-splat, splurge. Drip-splat, splurge.

'If you had been a better person you would not be in this plight,' a voice whispered this in my ear.

Was it the anaesthetist?

'I've stimulated the hippocampus in the same place as before,' remarked another voice.

'You're a monster,' whispered the gas man in my ear. 'And I shall make you suffer.'

It had started all over again. The surgeon was scrubbing up and the anaesthetist was purposely paralysing me but not anaesthetising.

'We'll soon have you squealing like a stuck pig,' murmured the gas man and then he chuckled. 'Except, of course, you can't squeal because you can't breathe and you can't breathe because of the muscle relaxant. What a shame!'

Drip-splat, splurge. Drip-splat, splurge.

'Did I tell you the one about the patient who told his GP he was a pair of curtains?' asked the surgeon.

'Yes you did,' replied the anaesthetist.

The whole scenario was playing out once again and I was suffering as the surgeon chopped away at my back.

Drip-splat, splurge. Drip-splat, splurge.

Silent scream.

*

One of the monsters, a misshapen dwarf with an absent nose, decided that he would climb onto my back and very soon he was riding me like a jockey. He had a small whip which he brought down onto my side whenever I slowed down and tiny spurs that dug into my flank. I tried to dislodge the creature but I was no more effective than I had been with the blind man. The witch, riding on the cyclops, would let out a screech of insane glee every few yards but this did not upset the one-eyed giant in the way that it would have done me.

Where the body of the blind man had gone I had no idea at all.

We reached the river and very quickly found an abandoned rowing boat with the oars floating inside it. The oars were floating because the boat was ninety percent submerged but between us all we very soon had the thing afloat again. The oars were immediately passed to me.

'Why doesn't the giant take a turn at rowing?' I asked, peeved that I should have been given the task.

The misshapen dwarf had jumped off my back and he now hit me with his whip across my chest.

'Because our queen wishes you to row,' he replied. 'And you will or you will suffer.'

I set to, placing the oars in the rough notches which served as rowlocks and pulling hard. The boat went nowhere.

'Heh, heh,' laughed the crone. 'Walter was holding onto a tree. Naughty Walter. He doesn't like going on the river, do you Walter?'

The huge one-eyed monster shook its shaggy head.

'Tell him to let go if you want me to row you towards Burnham,' I retorted.

Walter very reluctantly let go of his hold on the overhanging branch and we moved away from the bank. I heaved and I pulled and gradually made some headway.

'Move over to the other side of the river,' ordered the old witch.

'Why?' I responded.

'In order to catch the current. You'll never get there if you continue on this side.'

I did what the crone told me to do and very soon we were spinning along and I was just using the oars to keep the boat pointing in the right direction.

'Soon be there,' muttered the witch. 'And then we'll see what this resurrected bugler is looking for.'

*

- I'm near the front of the crowd now, its nearly dawn and I have a good view of the proceedings. The huge creature who moved the stone was apparently a ruler from Faerie known as Parsifal X. He has our ostensible leader, Brigadier Blenkinsop, crawling on all fours and wearing a dog lead. Wait …. a new development….Oh my gawd. A massive, truly massive, apparition has appeared. No it's more than an apparition, it is the full embodiment of no less than Lucifer, the devil incarnate. He has to be at least one hundred feet in height and dwarfs everybody, even the giants. No wait….Parsifal X has enlarged to the same size and they are greeting each other. The crowd is horrified by the appearance of these monsters and is trying to get away. They are being hampered by the army who are just as terrified of the creatures.

- Did you say Devil?

- Yes Julian. The hundred feet tall monster that just appeared is undoubtedly the devil. Red skin, horns, tail, cloven hoofs, the lot. Classical appearance of Satan, or Lucifer if you prefer……

- We seem to have lost contact with Crispin. In the meantime we have some music performed by the School of Oriental Studies Philharmonic Orchestra.

Chapter 11

Drip-splat, splurge. Drip-splat, splurge.

Skaaa - shkeeee, skaaa - shkeeee, skaaa - shkeeee.

I had been placed on the breathing apparatus once again and the entire operation sequence was replaying. I was now convinced that it was indeed a sequence that I was doomed to repeat for some reason. It was almost as if someone was turning a switch.... now you'll be having the operation. Switch.... now you'll be in the seventeenth century. Switch..... now you'll be in a metal tube or filing cabinet. In addition there are whispers of current news programmes and disembodied voices interspersed with the action sequences.

It was hard to believe that all of this was real. In fact it was hard to believe that any of it was real and along with the repeating of the sequences I had the "groundhog day" experience of remembering having undergone the experiences before. Except that the sequences did not last a day...... the surgical operation took at most an hour, the seventeenth century escapade was taking weeks, the experience of time in the metal tube was indeterminable. Of all these the latter was strangely the most persuasively real.

*

I was rowing the boat again and steering it in the fast current. Several times we almost tipped over but on each occasion I just about managed to correct the small craft. We had almost reached Burnham. The witch was right. Without the current the journey would have taken for ever but with the flow we had reached the hamlet in a matter of hours although it did seem as if I had been rowing throughout the night and that another day was dawning.

At the instigation of the witch I started to steer the boat to the shore but I was finding it hard to battle against the tide which was trying to pull us onwards and away from the muddy bank.

'I need an eye,' screamed the crone when I complained about the problems. 'I could steer through these currents blindfold when I was a lass.'

'Why can't you do it now?' I asked.

'The flood has changed the flow. It must have scoured the river bed of the Parrett,' she grumbled. 'But what I need now is an eye. Without it I can't save us.'

The giant cyclops stretched his arms out and for a moment I thought he was going to pluck his single huge eye from the centre of his head. His hands quivered in hesitation then he grabbed hold of my head and plunged his strong fingers into the socket of my right eye and grabbed the globe. An agonising pain shot through my head as he ripped the vile jelly from its accustomed place. The giant let go of me and I fell into the row boat in a quivering heap.

I held onto my face weeping and blood pouring down between my fingers. I could just see with my remaining eye as the cyclops passed the round object to the witch. She pushed it into her left socket and muttered a few words.

'Yes,' she cried exultantly. 'I can see. Peter Chambers get back to your rowing and pull hard to your left. The channel has changed and you have only minutes left to take the correct direction.'

I ignored the witch and lay quivering in the floor of the boat.

'Do it now,' she screamed and the misshapen dwarf with the absent nose hit me with the small whip.

'I'm in pain, I'm losing blood and you have stolen my eye,' I cried.

'Stop fussing,' muttered the witch. 'I'll give it back to you when I've finished with it.'

'But it won't work then,' I sobbed.

'It did not work properly anyway,' cried the witch. 'Or you

would have noticed who I was.'

With my one eye I stared at the crone. Who was she? As I looked her features melted into those of the blind man who I thought had been killed.

'Heh, heh, heh,' the now-sighted man laughed. 'Thought I'd gone away, did you?'

'I don't understand,' I wept. 'How can you do these things?'

'I do just whatever I want to do,' replied the creature. 'Whatever I desire. Now row or die.'

I refused to row and the boat drifted out to sea, was swept into a faster current, buffeted by huge waves. The boat overturned and I was sinking into the deep waters. I tried to swim but my heavy clothes were dragging me down and the water was bitterly cold. My chest had gone into spasm and my limb muscles would not work properly. Suddenly I gave a great gasp as my head was momentarily above water but as I did so another wave swamped me and I got a deep lungful of salt water. The indescribable pain eased rapidly as my life flashed before my eyes in a kaleidoscope of images. My hands grasped at the water unsuccessfully trying to find even a straw....

*

Drip, drip-drip, drip. Drip, drip-drip, drip. Drip, drip-drip, drip.

Brrrm, brrrrm, brrrrm. Rat-a-tat, Rat-a-tat, Rat-a-tat.

Got it!

I have remembered what the latter sounds reminded me of. An MRI scan. The sound was a sequence on a Magnetic Resonance Imaging machine. I remember when I had a scan on the magnetic scanner. They were scanning my knee when my cartilage was playing up and the sound is just the same. Not the dripping but definitely the brrrm, brrrrm, brrrrm, rat-a-tat, rat-a-tat, rat-a-tat.

If it were an MRI scan the radiographer would now be saying … "This scan will take just two minutes, please lie still." Then the sound would start and, judging by my pulse, the scan would take three or four minutes. I am sure that they lied to me.

Nobody is telling me to stay still but perhaps they don't need to. Perhaps I can't really move around.

'Almost lost him. Deep stimulation of the Hippocampus.'

The disembodied voice. I've heard it before.

*

'On this the XVII day of January 1606 it has pleased the Lord to take unto himself His servant John Appleshanks of Burnham'

I could read this on a piece of rough paper pinned above my head on the inside of the coffin. The lid was off and nobody was in the room. The sun was only just up, a weak and watery sun and if the date was right it must be about eight o'clock. I felt very cold, almost frozen.

What???

Exactly this happened before. I got out of the coffin, walked over to the door and scared the middle-aged woman. No… that was last time. No, don't do it again. Stop!

I have stopped at the door of the room. Good. You can change what is happening.

I looked down at my body expecting to see that of an old man.

No. It was the body of Pete Chambers, solid strong and a pair of damaged knees.

So this time you must try to sneak past the sleeping servant and get away. There is something you must do. Something you must find out here in Burnham.

The secret the old bugler was hiding. A letter of introduction, if that is really what the priest was looking for.

I know it was not in the house or the priest would have found it.

It must either be in the farmer's house, where I was incarcerated, or in the church. Otherwise it would be lost in the flood. Maybe it was indeed lost in the extraordinary flood.

What has happened to the alter ego of the witch, the blind man who took my eye…?

Do they still exist?

I have a strange feeling that I generated them and the monsters and that this time it will be different.

I am creeping past the sleeping woman but I have an almost overwhelming desire to bite her on the neck.

Stop!! Do not do it.

OK.

I'm out of the house. There is not really a street, just a muddy path.

Appleshanks was poisoned by the priest and I think I know why. He had hidden the document in the tower of the church.… the famous leaning tower of Burnham.

So that is where I must go.

For some reason I can remember more about Appleshanks than I could last time but I don't have his body. Weird or not?

I wish I had bitten the woman on the neck. It looked so inviting.

Oh dear. The woman has awakened and has entered the room.

She has come running out, right past me and ignoring me, presumably because I look nothing like Appleshanks. She is now shouting that the dead body has been removed and has run over to the church.

I shall hide behind the yew tree and wait for a chance to enter the church.

I am rather conspicuous in these clothes and anything else might be of assistance.

There she goes with the priest and his curate.

Now I must seize the opportunity. I step forward to enter the house of worship.

'Who are you?' a man has grabbed me and is asking me questions roughly. It is the local militia leader, Sir George Merriford.

'I am visiting the church,' I improvised. 'I was staying at the farmhouse.'

'Then why are you in your night shirt?' he enquired.

'I overslept and someone has taken my clothes,' I answered. 'And the priests have run off somewhere. It's all very confusing.'

'What is the name of the priest?' asked the militia leader.

'His name is Theodore Dean,' I replied. 'And you are Sir George Merriford. I'm staying with the Ropers.'

'Fine,' said the militia captain. 'That rings true. But why were you about to sneak into the church, right now?'

'Sneak?' I queried. 'I don't think I was sneaking in, apart, of course, for my embarrassment about my absent clothes.'

'You were definitely sneaking.'

'Well, I didn't trust the Reverend Theodore Dean,' I replied. 'I think he may have been the person who stole my clothes.'

'You did not trust the vicar?' he queried. 'You think he might be up to no good?'

'I'm pretty certain of that,' I replied. 'I was sent down here to investigate the man.'

'Then who sent you?' demanded Sir George.

'I work expressly for the king,' I answered. 'I am one of his witch-hunters.'

'Then you had better get on with your work,' replied the militia man in a voice heavy with contempt. 'But I shall make no bones about it. I do not believe in witches.'

The man turned heel and stomped off. I went into the church. In the small vestry I found several long black cassocks and two white surplices.

I took one of the cassocks and threw it on over my night shirt. Then I started to search the tower of Saint Andrew's church. If the document was going to be anywhere safe it should be here.

I could not find it.

*

- Today on Hard Talk we have the experimental neuroscientist Professor Pugh Cruikshanks. Sitting opposite him is medical ethicist, Dr. Jeremy Blandford and at the desk, John Quick. Over to you John.
- Thank you, Julian. Our main topic of discussion today is the announcement by Professor Pugh Cruikshanks that it is possible to keep the human brain alive as an isolated specimen out of the skull. Is that correct, professor?
- Not quite, John. Doctor Blandford will be pleased to know that we have not actually carried out the experiment. My press release has been widely misquoted. I stated that we have good reason to believe that the human brain could be maintained indefinitely as long as it was serviced not only with blood, glucose and oxygen but also appropriate sensory input and motor output with feedback. Assisted also, of course, by judicious use of the fifth force
- Thank you for clarifying that point.... and by the fifth force you presumably mean magic?
- Of course.

Chapter 12

Drip-splat, splurge. Drip-splat, splurge.
Damn. It's the operation again. Just when I thought I was getting somewhere back in the reign of James, First of England, Sixth of Scotland.
Skaaa - shkeeee, skaaa - shkeeee, skaaa - shkeeee.
'Have I told you how time flies like an arrow?' asked the surgeon.
'You have,' replied the non-compliant anaesthetist. 'And the rejoinder is that Fruit flies like a banana.'
'Oh,' replied the surgeon, deflated by the gas man.
'And I did not laugh the first time either,' said the anaesthetist. 'It's just a pun. Only groan-worthy.'
'It's one of the Marx Brothers best lines,' protested the surgeon weakly. 'It's a double pun.'
'So you didn't even make it up?'
'Well, no. Groucho Marx did.'
'I prefer Karl Marx.'
'Karl Heinrich Marx, 1818 to 1883?' riposted the surgeon instantly. 'Developed the theory of dialectical materialism based on the earlier work of Hegel..... And was thus the founder of Communist thinking. Fine ideas but never really worked in practice because of human nature. Groucho Marx was closer to the truth in my opinion.'
How's that for a put down? I thought as I lay there, paralysed but breathing with the aid of a respirator. *This anaesthetist could do with a few more slaps to his ego......*

*

'We shall now try the link-up,' came a disembodied voice. 'First increase the glucose levels and then inject the endorphin enhancer.

Now make the link.'

*

I had been left in the church of Saint Andrew looking for the supposed letter of introduction. It was certainly not in the tower. As I climbed out of the inclined structure I heard a rustling noise in one of the high wooden pews. A well-scrubbed female face, maybe thirty years of age, poked very tentatively round the end of the seat.

'Do you have any idea where or when this is?' asked the bewildered lady.

I stared at her. Her speech was modern English, slightly upper class, possibly even finishing school.

She saw my hesitation and continued.

'Because I was somewhere near Guildford when the tsunamis and hurricanes struck then I woke up here which I do not think is Surrey.'

'No,' I replied guardedly. 'It is certainly not Surrey.'

The girl, I realised now that she could not be much more than twenty, clambered out of the pew somewhat gauchely. She was tall and just a little heavy around the hips but had an intelligent look about her face.

'You look like the priest. Are you in charge here?'

'Not exactly,' I answered. 'I think you had better come with me.'

I had heard voices approaching the church and thought it better that we beat a hasty retreat. I knew how these people responded to strangers and this young lady would definitely be considered to be a witch.

I took her by the arm and led her to the side of the church where I had spotted a small wooden door. The large wooden portal at the sea end of the church was just opening as we exited but the priests entering saw us leaving and started to walk down the church towards us. I left the building but was still looking over my shoulder towards the priests as I was grabbed very firmly by a strong grip. I swung round to find myself confronted by a large soldier.

'I've caught him, Sir George,' cried the armed militia man.

'Well done,' replied the baronet. 'And I have caught his accomplice.'

Sir George had his arm round the waist of the young woman who was struggling furiously.

'Let me go, you foul smelling creature,' cried the woman. 'I'll make you pay for this. I'll sue you for assault. Just get off me.'

'If you keep struggling I'll hit you very hard,' said the baronet.

'No you bloody won't,' she answered and promptly brought her knee up into the crutch of the militia leader. She then put her hand into a pocket and pulled out an aerosol which she sprayed in the face of her assailant. Sir George, already doubled up, screamed with pain and put his hands over his eyes in agony. His face and clothes were covered in a red dye.

'Legal alternative to pepper spray,' she shouted. 'And it doesn't wash off easily so the police will be able to identify you.'

I, meanwhile, had executed a neat judo throw on my own attacker, leaving him gasping on the floor. The entire sequence had taken only seconds.

'Time to run,' I said to the girl as she stood there looking triumphant. 'The priests will be here any moment.'

'But I want to call the police,' she argued, taking out a small mobile telephone.

'No time to explain,' I cried taking her arm. 'Just come with me.'

'You're as bad as them,' she cried, trying to pull my hand off her.

'I assure you that I am not,' I answered. 'And if you don't come with me immediately you will find out that I am right.'

Reluctantly she followed me and I led her into a small thicket.

The priest saw us leaving but seemed amazed by the sight of the baronet with his eyes firmly shut, face covered in red dye. They made no immediate attempt to follow us.

The thicket was only small but a path from it led down to the River Parret. As I hoped there were several tiny craft moored at the edge of the river.

'Quick,' I exclaimed. 'Get in here and take an oar.'

'What is this all about?' she cried, hesitating at the river bank.

'Either help now or I'll leave you behind,' I replied. 'I'll do my best to explain as we row.'

She jumped in next to me and started to row quite competently. Better than myself, in fact.

Definitely independent sector schooling, I thought as I sat next to her heaving on my own oar. *No UK state education teaches rowing.*

We were about half way across when I saw the priests on the river bank, looking towards us. They did not get in a boat but turned back up the path that took them towards the church.

'I think that has bought us some time,' I remarked and saw that the girl was holding the oar with one hand and was trying to ring a number on her cell phone.

'No damned signal,' she swore, putting her phone back into a pocket and taking up the oar again in her proficient manner. 'Toss, toss, toss!'

'There wouldn't be any signal in the seventeenth century,' I sighed. 'And no policemen. That's why we had to run.'

'Seventeenth century?' she replied scornfully. 'Is that your idea of an explanation? Some form of abortive time travel?'

'I don't know about the abortive bit,' I answered pulling hard on my oar to stop her better stroke from turning us in an arc. 'But a form of time travel, yes.'

'Bollocks,' she answered. 'I just don't believe it.'

'Believe it or not we are better off out of the hands of that lot, I'm telling you.'

'How do you know all this?'

'They've tried to burn me at the stake once already,' I retorted. 'And it was no joke.'

The girl went silent and pulled harder on her oar. I struggled, just about keeping us level, and we reached the distant shore. I then saw why the priest had been in no great hurry. It was deep mud with no immediate place to moor.

'We'll have to go further upstream,' I remarked. 'This mud is too dangerous to walk on.'

'Where exactly are we?' she asked.

'Burnham,' I grunted as we turned upstream.

'Burnham on Crouch?' she questioned.

'On Sea,' I replied. 'Burnham on Sea.'

'Never been there,' she stated. 'So I have no idea why I am there now.'

'Nor have I,' I added. 'But we must make the best of it. And I assure you that this is some form of seventeenth century England, not the twenty-first century.'

She nodded as we slowly progressed upstream, fighting against the strong current which included a powerful tidal flow as the tide went out. She was silent for several minutes, putting considerable skill and power into her strokes, then she spoke again.

'This will be something to do with the supposed supernatural attack at Stonehenge,' she concluded after the long pause.

'I'm sorry,' I replied. 'I know nothing about a supernatural attack.'

'The appearance of monsters and fairies at Stonehenge?' she asked almost scornfully. 'They passed you by somehow? Tsunamis all over the world? Hurricanes? Billions dead? You just didn't notice?'

'I was in hospital having an operation and that is the last thing I remember,' I explained. 'Perhaps this all happened whcn I was unconscious.'

I told her the date of my operation and she looked blank for a moment.

'That was the day before it all happened,' she was working backwards through the calendar. 'You missed a heck of a lot.'

'So how long ago was this in your reckoning?' I enquired.

'A couple of weeks,' she answered.

'Did anything untoward happen to you?' I queried.

'I was in a head-on collision on the A3 near Guildford,' she answered immediately, still pulling on the oar.

'Then perhaps this is some kind of after-life?' I suggested. 'Perhaps it is Purgatory?'

She thought for a moment then replied.

'I suppose the alleged appearance of the devil at Stonehenge does make the afterlife more likely.'

'The devil appeared at Stonehenge?' I was incredulous. Despite my experiences with the blind man, the witch and the various other Forest of Dean monsters I was not expecting that.

'Yah,' she replied, her stroke beginning to falter a little. 'I saw it on television. The devil incarnate. Lucifer in person....but it may have been a publicity stunt for a film. It's impossible to tell with the special effects they can do these days.'

'And what happened?'

'Difficult to be precise but the story is that a guy from Bristol named Jimmy Scott appeared to defeat him with the help of his mother-in-law.'

'Not the electrician?' I gasped, it was my turn to falter. 'Used to be a physicist?'

'Sounds like the same person,' she nodded. 'Lived in Bristol at somewhere called Redland. Another place I have never visited.'

'He wired my new kitchen,' I was sweating as I pulled. 'How could he possibly defeat the devil?'

'I have no idea,' panted the girl. 'But then nor do I have any idea how the devil appeared in England in the first place or why we are now in the seventeenth century and my phone does not work.'

I could see that we were reaching a better, firmer part of the far bank of the Parrett and I indicated this to the girl. She nodded in agreement and we pulled gratefully towards the shore.

'Do you have any particular place that we are heading for?' she asked.

'Afraid not,' I answered. 'Just a good distance away from the pursuers.'

'Who do not appear to have taken to the river,' she commented.

'But then I did tip the oars out of the other row boats,' I smiled. 'So they would not have found it very easy to do so.'

*

- The Prime Minister Darcy Macaroon has taken charge of the UK again under the benevolent watch of the Head of State her majesty, the Queen. His first act has been to sack members of the government who did not support him during the crisis and to bring in James Scott to assist. James Scott, known to his friends as Jimmy, is credited with defeating the tyrant demon Parsifal X and the demigod Lucifer. We hope to interview him later in the programme.....

Chapter 13

- On Hard Talk today we have the Very Reverend Erica Portis, Provost of Saint Dunstan's College. We are asking her the significance of the apparitions of Lucifer and its relationship to the orthodox Church of England Christian theology. Sitting on the settee with us is Donald Fluxhead, the well known atheist. I shall start with Donald. Mister Fluxhead, this appearance at Stonehenge of Lucifer, the devil incarnate, does rather upset the applecart for atheists, doesn't it? Surely the existence of Lucifer also proves the reality of God?
- I'm sorry Julian, but I don't believe that. I would rather think of this creature as a very powerful and evil alien, thus not automatically implying any further supernatural beings. It is foolish to assume such a thing.
- Thank you Donald. Erica, you have a very different view of this?
- Good afternoon, Julian. Yes, you are right. We do believe that the evidence before our eyes of an evil demon and other supernatural creatures supports our theology. If there is a devil there must be a God.
- Nonsense, that's the simplistic thinking of a medieval intellect, if you don't mind me saying.
- I think that Erica might indeed mind you saying that, Donald, and before we come back to you I would like to hear a few more words from the Provost.............

*

We pulled up as close as we could to the bank but there was still a stretch of muddy shore before we could reach really solid ground. Feeling chivalrous I stepped out of the boat holding the rope and promptly started to sink in the brown glue. The young woman looked on with an annoying smile all over her face.

'Try to step on the grassy tussocks,' she announced. 'That is usually firmer ground.'

I managed to lift my left foot out of the mire and place it on a nearby patch of longer, thicker grass. It was just in time...I was already down beyond my knees and I had the devil's own job pulling the right leg out.

She was correct. The tussock did provide support and I hopped from the tiny grass island to the next and thus made progress towards the solid land, pulling the row boat behind me. When we reached the harder ground I heaved the boat up onto the shore. The girl gingerly stepped out, completely clean and pristine.

I stared at her properly for the first time. She was in sling back shoes, brown legs with no tights, short pleated skirt and a frilly cotton blouse. She looked beautiful but her smug expression made me boil.

'You made it,' she said in a condescending voice. 'Well done. Perhaps you will now be able to prove to me that we really are in the seventeenth century.'

She was beginning to grate on me.

'Not immediately,' I growled, trying to keep my cool. 'Anymore than you can prove to me that Satan appeared at Stonehenge.'

'No need to get stroppy,' she countered as she fiddled with her mobile. 'Damn. There's still no signal.'

'Of course there isn't,' I replied. 'They hadn't even discovered electricity in 1607 let alone invented cellphones.'

'You're serious about this, aren't you?' she was somewhat deflated.

'Why else would I make you row like stink?' I retorted.

'No idea. I just did what you said because I thought you were a madman and it was safest to go along with you.'

I sat down heavily on a rotten tree stump. So she hadn't believed me at any point. I put my head in my hands and shook it from side to side.

'We've got to trust each other,' I eventually said as I looked up at her. 'And whether this really is the reign of James the First or not we have to act as if it is. It's cold, the day is getting on and we must find shelter.'

'Fine,' she replied. 'I'll go along with whatever you say, just don't expect me to be too enthusiastic.'

She paused for a moment and then continued.

'And, by the way, I'm a Roman Catholic and the Pope has cancelled Purgatory so you can forget about that one.'

'How can the Pope cancel Purgatory?' I was perplexed. 'It either exists or not irrespective of the Pope's view on it.'

'I don't think that he would agree with that,' sniffed the good Catholic girl. 'And what makes you an expert on the subject?'

That stopped me in my tracks. What did make me an expert?

'Has he really decreed that Purgatory does not exist?' I asked.

'Pope Benedict stated that Purgatory was a process not a place,' replied the girl. 'And he had already decided that Limbo did not exist either.'

Move off the subject, I told myself.

'I'm a schoolteacher from Bristol,' I stated, holding out my hand. 'My name is Peter Chambers, most people call me Pete.'

She reluctantly took the proffered hand.

'Fiona,' she replied. 'Fiona Makepeace-Smythe.'

Her handshake was unenthusiastic.

We stomped across the salt moor moving inland as quickly as we could away from the banks of the river and as we went I tried to tell Miss Makepeace-Smythe my theories about our situation. I explained that I had been here before and that a tsunami was coming. She did not want to know.

'This all has to be bullshit,' she stated vehemently. 'Someone is organising this.'

'I don't deny that is a possibility but it still means we have to act as if it is real,' I batted back at her. 'Last time when I was hurt it was extremely painful and you must have found the rowing tiring.'

'Virtual reality can be tiring,' she remarked. 'Doesn't prove it is real.'

'If we don't move quickly we will be caught out in the open tonight and we could die of exposure. And if we don't then move on to higher ground tomorrow we will be caught in the flood.'

'How do you know that you have woken up on the same day this time round?' she asked. 'And what does it matter if we drown if we come back to life like you have done. From your story you must have drowned in the Bristol Channel but you are still here.'

'It was a very unpleasant experience,' I countered. 'And I'm convinced that we have to find out some information or change things here before we can progress.'

She laughed out loud with a stentorian guffaw that was very aggravating.

'So this is just a feeble Quantum Leap impersonation?' she hooted. 'Do me a favour!'

'It did occur to me that it was like Quantum Leap,' I replied. 'But I have not come up with a better explanation.'

'Random time travel, hallucinogenic drugs, virtual reality, holographic imprinting, memory stimulation, purgatory, fairy magic. There's a few,' she replied scornfully. 'But Quantum leap it is not.'

'OK, OK,' I replied, stopping in my track and waving my hands around. 'Whatever this reality is we have to try to be civil to each other. I'm pleased that you have so many other ideas. I did not think of them all and I have never met you before…..'

I wish I hadn't now, I thought but continued politely…..

'…So let's call it a truce and work through some of the suggestions you have made. Memory stimulation is a good idea but how could I have remembered the Seventeenth Century?'

'You taught history as well as PE and geography,' she answered. 'And then your imagination filled in the gaps.'

'So you are just a figment of my imagination? A figment that somehow comes up with new ideas?'

'I am most certainly not imaginary!' she was most indignant. 'I can tell you my entire personal history, all the details about my school and college, what my aspirations are, my parents, my dog. Oh yah!'

'And how can I check them out?' I asked. 'You see the difficulty?'

She calmed down and we walked on, hurrying the pace to catch up time.

'I don't know of any virtual reality that is anywhere near as good as this,' I was still working through the ideas.

She shook her head.

'Nor do I.'

'Hallucinogenic drugs could also be involved but they usually break up reality into disjointed crazy sensations….you can smell the music, taste the light. Things like that. Not a completely different continuum.'

'I tried Acid just once,' added Fiona. 'Bad trip. Nothing like this.'

In the distance I could just make out a small cottage. Miss Makepeace-Smythe spotted it at the same time as I did.

'We'll head for that place,' I remarked.

'I knew you were going to say that,' Fiona replied. 'I could tell your exact words before they came out of your mouth. How weird is that?'

'Banana split!' I said randomly. 'Did you know I was going to say that?'

'Yah, oh yah,' she answered.

The way she said yah instead of yes was really irritating me. I could put up with the rest of the way she talked…it was just a little posher than myself. But the yahs!

'Now you are thinking that the way I say Yah is annoying,' she said accusingly.

I looked at her in embarrassment wondering how to get out of this one.

Mushroom, I thought.

'Why mushroom?' she asked, clearly reading my thoughts.

'Because I'm usually more of a fun guy than I am today,' I replied.

She had the decency to laugh even though she had clearly read the reply in my thoughts before I had vocalised it.

We had reached the cottage and I knocked rather cautiously on the old wooden door.

*

Drip, drip-drip, drip.

Drip, drip-drip, drip.

Drip, drip-drip, drip.

Skaaa - shkeeee, skaaa - shkeeee, skaaa - shkeeee.

'You won't even wake up as a zombie,' whispered the anaesthetist. 'They are going to use you for illegal medical experimentation.'

The surgeon hacked at my back with his hammer and chisel. The pain was a little dull compared with the ten previous occasions.

'This torture will never end in your mind,' sniggered the psychopathic gas man.

'Diathermy,' stated the surgeon and electric shocks rippled through my body followed by an acrid smell of burning flesh.

'Clamp,' said the surgeon calmly. There was no immediate response.

The surgeon spoke more urgently….

'Clamp!'

He then looked up.

'Where has the scrub nurse gone?' he asked in a loud voice, directing the question at the insane doctor who was turning this into the sophisticated torture of yours truly.

'I sent her to get me another sandwich,' answered the

anaesthetist.

'Damn it!' exclaimed the surgeon. 'She is my scrub nurse not your chambermaid.'

'No need to lose your temper, old boy,' replied the gas man. 'Bad language won't help. Get your own clamp. It's lying on the side.'

He pointed to a table covered in green sterile cloth and an array of clips, scalpels and clamps.

'That is not the point,' answered the surgeon. 'There are times when I cannot stretch out to get things and I need her assistance.'

'She'll be back soon,' the anaesthetist was nonchalant. 'You'll do fine without her till then.'

The surgeon growled to himself then spoke.

'He's lost a lot of blood. We'll have to transfuse him with at least a pint.'

'Not yet,' answered the gas man. 'His haemoglobin is still fine and his circulating volume good. A little blood goes a long way.'

*

- Science Now, the programme that looks at controversy in the world of science. We have with us a representative who claims to be from Faerie. She looks like a rather beautiful young lady but is said to be a dragon one hundred and fifty feet long. Lady Aradel, that does stretch the imagination somewhat. Conservation of matter and energy hardly permits a slim figure like yourself to be a monster many tons in weight and more than forty-five metres in length.

- One of the reasons we were able to hide before your very eyes, Julian.

- But surely you are not saying that you really are that big?

- Not in these dimensions right now but if I manifest my total multi-dimensional nature, yes, I am that big.

- Makes a joke of people who ask if their bum looks big in something.

- *It certainly does, Julian, and I am pleased that you are taking the subject seriously.*
- *Yes, but can you change into anything else?*
- *Only if I want to.*
- *Could you make a quick change for us now?*
- *If you like. What about this?*
- *Oh God. Security…somebody. There's a giant rat in here, help. Help!*
- *Was that convincing enough?*

Chapter 14

The door opened silently at my knock, swinging back against the internal wall with a slight bang. At first I thought that there was nobody in the front room and then I made out two dark wooden beds in the far distant corners. There were occupants in the cots but I could see no details. Then one of the occupants sat up.

'I see you have more control of your morphic projection this time,' said the blind man.

'How did you get there?' I asked. 'I thought you had died….. and how can you see me?'

'I've still got one of your eyes,' cackled the previously blind creature.

I felt my face and closed my eyes alternately. Both seemed to be working.

'As I said,' wheezed the apparition. 'You have better control of your body this time.'

'But how did you get back?' I asked this again.

'You got back so why can't I?' enquired the parasitic creature. 'Now let me climb onto your back again. We need to get away from here if we are to avoid the tsunami.'

This was the stuff of nightmares. I stared in horror at the creature.

'What is this place and who is this monster?' asked Miss Fiona Makepeace-Smythe.

'Who are you calling a monster?' groaned the once-blind man.

'You, obviously,' replied the young woman, brazenly.

'Then, Miss Makepeace-Smythe, you had better reserve

judgement until you have met your own monster.'

The creature I had known both as Winter and also as the witch indicated the huddled mass under the skimpy bedclothes of the other bed. This large mass slowly turned and pulled the sheets down. It was hideous. Whereas the old blind man had looked simply haggard and ill, this creature was obese and bloated with sagging, ulcerated body flowing over the edge of the bed. It had to be at least thirty stone in weight, if not more, but under five feet in height. Well over four hundred pounds, probably greater than two hundred kilograms. This was adipose tissue gone wild and the face was difficult to discern amongst the billowing excrescences of extra tissue. However one feature I could make out was immediately apparent…. where the eyes should have been were hollow orbits.

'Hello dear,' gargled the fat fiend. 'Welcome Fiona. I've been waiting for you. Come here and give me a cuddle.'

'No, no,' cried the young woman in horror and fright. 'No. Don't make me do that.'

She hid behind me, all of her bravado evaporated in an instant.

'Keep her away from me,' she pleaded. 'I don't even want to feel her touch.'

'So who is the monster now?' asked Winter in a supercilious manner.

'There's no way that your companion can ride on someone's back,' I remarked. 'So if we are to get out of here we must find transport. We probably have time as the wave is not due until the day after tomorrow.'

'You're wrong Pete Tong, you're wrong,' chuckled Winter. 'You are a day later than you think. The tsunami will hit tomorrow at eight o'clock.'

'But we're tired, cold and miserable,' I answered. 'We can't go any further this evening.'

'Then you will have to wake very early tomorrow,' said Winter. 'And you shall have help with carrying Susan.'

'Where from?' I asked.

'Remember me?' came a voice from up the bare wood stairs.

A huge foot appeared, followed by another. The person who now appeared could not stand up straight in the low-ceilinged room. It was the one-eyed giant from the woods. The cyclops called Walter had also returned.

*

Tic, tic, tic.

The dripping was more reminiscent of a clock than it had been before but I knew instantly that I was back in the metal tube.

Brrrm, brrrm, brrrm. Brrrm, brrrm, brrrm.

The sounds of an MRI machine.

Where the hell was I and what form was I in?

My sight was blurred but I could just make out a dim light and a surface that was steel or perhaps grey plastic. It was very close to me and if I could only move my arms I could reach out and touch it.

Not only could I not move my arms I could not feel them either. Or my legs. Or my body.

Was I paralysed from the neck down? Was that the problem?

I seemed to be looking through murky fluid, a milky opalescent liquid. It was the fluid that was blurring my sight.

I could not move my eyes or close them.

Brrrm, brrrm, brrrm. Brrrm, brrrm, brrrm.

'Hippocampal stimulation,' said a disembodied voice.

*

Bang, bang, bang.

There was a persistent knocking at the door of the small cottage. I had crept into a corner of the room as far away from the monsters as possible and Fiona had hidden behind me.

'How do they know who I am?' she demanded to know. 'I've never been here before so how do they know?'

I had no answers and I had persuaded her that we should try to get some sleep.

The knocking came in the dead of night.

'Open up or we will burn the place down,' came a roar from outside.

The cyclops hobbled over to the door and swung it open with his huge fist.

'Did you want me?' he grinned at the small posse of clergy and militia outside.

They were lit by moonlight and the one-eyed giant's oil lamp. The shadows cast were horrific but the monsters were inside the house already.

'We have no argument with you but we are searching for witches and hobgoblins,' answered the leader of the group, Sir George Merriford.

'And I'm not goblin enough for you?' leered the giant, holding the lamp under his face so that they could see the one eye.

The small mob all pulled back in horror then Sir George plucked up his courage.

'We need to speak to the black-clad clergyman who claimed to be a witch hunter,' the baronet said firmly.

'Yes we do, indeed we do,' gabbled the Reverend Theodore, standing way back behind Sir George.

'The two clergyman and Sir George can come in,' announced the cyclops. 'But the rest of the mob must stay outside. Or go away if they want to.'

The giant let out a mad chuckle and stood at the door waiting for their reply.

Eventually, after some to-ing and fro-ing amongst the gathered mob, the baronet spoke up again.

'We accept your terms if we can bring one other with us.'

'Name him,' ordered the cyclops.

'He is my brother, the magistrate, Sir Edwin Merriford,' answered the baronet.

'Deal,' replied the cyclops, opening the door wide. 'Just the four of you and no more.'

The two black clad clergymen entered followed by the baronet and his brother. They recoiled with horror when they saw Winter and then even more when they made out the shape of Susan, the hugely obese blind woman.

'We have come to apprehend the witch hunter and the witch,' stated Theodore Dean, the clergyman I had encountered before with such a bad outcome.

Fat Susan let out a gleeful chuckle.

'There are no witch hunters here,' she wheezed, her huge body shaking with mirth. 'But plenty of witches, male and female. Take your pick. Four witches and a cyclops.'

'Don't forget me,' came a reedy voice from the small room upstairs and the misshapen dwarf with the absent nose clattered down the steep and slatted wooden stairs. 'I'm not a giant or a witch. I'm a dwarf….and I'm suffering from the condition the Turks call the Christian disease, the Italians and Germans call the French Disease, the Dutch call the Spanish disease and which has recently been called Syphilis. So why not embrace me also?'

*

- Lord James Scott, welcome to Breaking News, the Breakfast TV show for the discerning viewer. May I call you Lord James?
- Call me Jimmy, everybody does. Well, nearly everybody.
- Probably not Lucifer or Parsifal X, hah hah.
- No, Julian, probably not.
- Now I wasn't there but they say that Lucifer tried to kill your two

boys at Stonehenge but was thwarted by yourself?

- That's correct but I was considerably assisted by my mother-in-law.

- Your mother-in-law?

- Yes, indeed. You see my mother-in-law is a witch.

- People commonly say that their mother-in-law is a witch. How does yours differ?

- She differs by actually being a witch.

- Come now, we're intelligent people here. You can't really believe that your mother-in-law is a witch, do you?

- I don't just believe it, I know it to be so.

- Does she agree?

- She does now. But I thought you had asked me on the programme to talk about my new job?

- Yes, of course. You have been appointed as a roving ambassador to Faerie, which I understand is spelt FAERIE. How does that differ from Fairy, FAIRY.

- The latter is only a small part of the Faerie realm. Strictly speaking FAIRY refers to the Fairy Kingdom and its inhabitants, FAERIE to the whole world.

- So you really believe that there is a Faerie realm parallel to our own?

- Listen Julian, I have been there and if you wish we could arrange for you to accompany me to the tamer parts of the Faerie Realm.

- Tamer?

- Some parts are distinctly not tame. Hades, for example, or the Southern Dragon Mountains.

- You are just making this up, aren't you Jimmy?

- Not at all…. and the offer is genuine. I would be pleased to take you with me to Faerie.

- Well, I might just take you up on that offer. After this short break we shall be talking further with Jimmy Scott, roving ambassador to Faerie for the UK government.….

- Magnificent Magical Muscle Stain Remover makes Mighty Light Work of those hard-to-shift stains. Available at all high class stores Magnificent Magical Muscle ....

Chapter 15

'A pretty bunch indeed,' said the priest who I knew as Theodore Dean. 'Not a Christian amongst them.'

'I beg your pardon,' Fiona Makepeace-Smythe spoke up loudly. 'I object to that. I'm a practising Roman Catholic and I think that qualifies as Christian.'

'Not in England under good King James,' growled Sir Edwin Merriford.

'No, indeed not,' muttered the evil crow-like priest called Dean, rubbing his hands together and clearly pleased.

His compatriot, the curate, looked on with his mouth gaping open and Sir George stared at Fiona as if she were mad. I hid my head in my hands. She could hardly have said anything worse apart from directly suggesting the king be murdered...... which, I suddenly remembered, was the intention of this evil priest. Maybe that knowledge could give me leverage I could use?

'You must arrest all of these people,' stated the priest aggressively. 'They are enemies of the State.'

'Now, now dearie,' the grossly obese creature sat up in bed. 'There's no need to be so angry. Come and give Susan a cuddle.'

Theodore Dean looked over towards the bed and shuddered.

'Methinks there is little in the world that I would rather not do,' he replied stiffly. 'Your very presence is an abomination.'

Fiona looked towards Susan and I could see a similarity in the appearance of the two women in their response to the priest's rebuff.

'Harsh words to direct at a little girlie,' simpered the fat creature.

She started to cry tearlessly, her sightless orbits remaining dry as she whimpered. Fiona looked upset and the dwarf was furious.

'Now look what you've done!' exclaimed the syphilitic dwarf. 'You've upset my friend Susan and she's never nasty to anyone.'

'Never nasty?' queried the priest. 'She is nastiness personified. To suggest that I should besport myself by taking her into close proximity! Why...the very thought is an anathema.'

'I notice you are not wearing a wedding band,' hissed the "my-eyed" blind man that I knew as Winter. 'Perchance you are not married?'

'No,' answered the Reverend Theodore Dean. 'And I have no desire to marry either.'

'What of your clergyman sidekick. Is he of the same persuasion as yourself?' asked Winter suggestively.

The curate went a bright red colour that was obvious despite the dim light inside the lowly cottage.

'I'm not married either,' he said in a slightly broken voice.

'Is that because you are both sticking to the old Catholic ways?' queried Winter.

Dean looked annoyed and his sidekick murmured something about the right girl not having come along.

'Never mind, dearie,' warbled the gross Susan, having cheered up. 'You'll find someone I'm sure.'

'This is all irrelevant,' stated Dean. 'We have come to apprehend the two fugitives and we are more than happy to take all of you.'

'Even me?' asked the cyclopean giant, rolling his one eye. 'You might have quite a job if I object.'

'Which I am sure you will,' said Winter. 'Peter Chambers and Fiona Makepeace-Smythe are staying with our company and we are about to leave to go to higher ground.'

'Why?' asked Sir George, the conversation had been confusing the baronet as he tried to understand the hidden meanings and innuendo behind Winter's remarks.

'Because we shall otherwise drown,' replied Winter. 'There is a high tide coming and it augers badly.'

'There!' exclaimed the elder priest. 'He is predicting the future! Devilry in front of our very eyes. Witchcraft for our ears.'

'Hardly that,' sneered Winter, rolling my eye in his loose socket. 'An understanding of the tides is well established amongst the educated.'

'He has a point, Dean,' nodded Sir George Merriford. 'Sailors know the tides well.'

'That is certainly true,' added his brother. 'And he is right. This morning is high tide.'

'But we are on dry land,' protested Dean.

'Yet it is the flood plain,' wheezed Winter. 'And we are moving out soon.'

'If we let you,' countered Dean.

'You would be well advised to move to high ground too,' I added. 'It is a spring tide and I believe it will coincide with a storm surge.'

'There is no storm,' hissed the Reverend Dean.

'Tell that to the cows and the birds,' I remarked.

I had no idea whether the cows and birds had predicted a storm but I knew that country folk believed that they generally did.

'Right,' said Sir George, clearly coming to a decision. 'We shall allow you to move out but we shall accompany you.'

'We are not at all sure that you are not up to some mischief,' explained his brother, the magistrate.

'And I'm of the belief that Peter Chambers is wearing my second best cassock,' stated the priest.

'Come now Reverend,' responded Sir George. 'Cassocks all look the same. Can you be sure that it is yours?'

'Not in this light,' the priest reluctantly acknowledged. 'But when the sun is up I shall be able to tell.'

When the sun is up there will be a mighty great wave over this land, I thought.

How do you know? replied Fiona.

*

Drip, drip, drip. Brrrm, brrm, brm.
'Hook up the electrode interplay. I am going to partake…..'

*

'You are an evil man, Chambers,' murmured the anaesthetist in my ear.
'Why are you muttering to the patient?' asked the surgeon.
'I have found that talking to the patients calms them down,' replied the gas man.
'Talking to patients who are under GA?' queried the surgeon scornfully. 'You might as well be talking to plants.'
'Prince Charles doesn't think that talking to plants is such a bad idea,' answered the anaesthetist.
The surgeon guffawed.
'Hardly a role model for a science based discipline such as medicine,' he laughed. 'You'll be saying next that homeopathy works and that Chinese medicine is next to godliness.'
'Homeopathy does work,' sniffed the anaesthetist. 'Even if it is only via the placebo effect. And osteopathy is very useful.'
'OK, I accept that they have their place,' agreed the surgeon. 'But talking to patients who are under general anaesthetic does seem rather daft.'
Not when the gas man knows you are fully awake, I thought. *And his whole objective is to punish you.*
A silent scream issued from my mind as the surgeon started chipping away at the osteophytes once more.

*

There was a loud knock at the door. Sir George Merriford was standing next to the wooden portal and he opened the thin plank.

'Is everything alright, sir?' asked a man in a soldier's uniform.

'I think so Sergeant. We are all about to move out.'

'Even the rather large lady?' asked the sergeant, pointedly.

'All of us, I believe.'

'Do you have a horse?' asked Winter.

'We have several horses,' replied Sir George.

'One that is used to pulling a cart?'

'I believe so. Or at least it is conditioned to pulling a gun.'

'We have an old cart out the back and we could put Susan onto it,' suggested Winter. 'That will speed us up.'

'Is speed important?'

'Yes,' replied Winter, pulling at the stolen eyeball and then squeezing the globe on its stalk between the index finger and thumb of his right hand.

Mysteriously I could feel the pain in my own head as if he was squeezing my own eyeball.

'We must not forget Maud,' dribbled the nasally challenged dwarf.

'Oh yes,' agreed Winter. 'I suppose we had better bring Maud.'

The dwarf clattered back up the short flight of wooden steps and returned with a bound and gagged woman over his shoulder. At first sight I thought the prisoner was an old lady but when she straightened up I could see that she was only the age of Fiona, early twenties or so. Her hair was also the same auburn colour as the girl. But this young woman was thin and spiky. Too thin for my liking.

'Take the gag off the poor woman,' ordered Sir George. 'This is appalling behaviour.'

'If you say so,' grinned the dwarf and immediately ripped the greasy rag out of Maud's mouth.

'At last I can speak,' she screamed. 'You are all sinners and you are damned to an eternity of hell. Get on your knees and pray. Beware the temptations of the flesh. Confess to your sins. Lay aside worldly goods. Follow the paths of righteousness. Forego the pleasures of this bleak world so that you can lay up treasures in the next…'

On and on she ranted until eventually the dwarf roughly pulled the gag back into her mouth.

'Would you have liked me to have left the gag off for longer?' grinned the dwarf lasciviously.

'Take it off permanently,' ordered the baronet.

'If you say so,' slobbered the noseless midget, pulling at the gag again.

'Prepare ye the way of the Lord,' screamed the woman as soon as her lips were free. 'You have been weighed in the balances and found wanting. Many are called but few are chosen. Take the narrow hard path of salvation and beware the broad path that leads to destruction. Hell awaits the unwary. Oh sinner man where are you going to run to? Let it be soon Lord, let it be…..'

'Perhaps you should keep the gag on her for a little longer until the shock wears off and she comes to her senses,' suggested the militia leader. 'And by your reckoning it is time that we moved out from here so let us do it.'

*

- *Professor Ralph Breadstein, the eccentric Nobel prize winner, is with us in the studio today.*

Professor Breadstein, welcome to Science Watch.

- *Thank you Crispin.*

- *Professor, during the recent cataclysm you stated that alpha, the fine-structure constant, had shifted by one half of a percent. You argued that this is just within the limits that permit the sun to continue functioning. Do you still hold to the same view?*

- *I certainly do Crispin but may I first say that I am delighted to see that you have recovered from the injuries you sustained at Stonehenge.*

- *Thank you Professor. But other people are claiming that the* problems occurred due to a clash of realities between this, the normal world, and the Faerie Realm.

- My measurements showed that the constant had changed and that is unequivocal. The reason for the change is more vexatious but a clashing of adjacent branes is a distinct possibility.

- Brains? Do you mean functioning human brains, computer brains or something different?

Very different. The branes I am referring to are spelt BRANES, and the term is loosely derived from the word membrane. Nothing to do with grey matter or cognition.

- Go on..

- The central thesis is that the four dimensional universe, our reality, is restricted to a brane inside a higher dimensional space called the bulk. This model explains the weakness of gravity, a perplexing problem in most cosmology systems.

- I think you've lost me Prof. Surely gravity is very strong or we would not be kept here on the world? We would be whirling off into space.

- Not so, Crispin. Compared to the other three forces gravity is surprisingly weak.

- How does this relate to the cataclysm and the Stonehenge incident?

- Within the bulk there may be many branes and they can influence each other.

- Could this cause a disaster?

- If they clash, certainly.

- And you think that this is what happened?

- I do. I believe that the Faerie Realm is a separate brane universe.... like a slice of bread in a loaf.....and it is next to ours.

- What sort of loaf are we talking about?

- Probably thin-sliced, white, small tin, Crispin. Or maybe wholemeal.

- Wholemeal?

- That was a joke. The bread is a metaphor, Crispin. A metaphorical *loaf.*

    - *And that loaf represents the universe?*
    - *The whole multiverse...... and two slices, two universes, came together to make a sandwich....*
    - *Thank you Professor. There we have it. The latest inexplicable view from science is that our reality is a slice of bread in a complex sandwich. Tomorrow we shall hear more from Professor Pugh Cruikshanks and his controversial experiments on animal brains. That's brain spelt BRAIN...*

Chapter 16

The giant cyclops picked up the huge obese woman who called herself Susan and carried her outside to the cart. The first lights of the false dawn were just appearing in the distance. I reckoned that we had about thirty minutes before the wave struck us. To my horror the once-blind man grabbed me with one skinny hand and swung himself onto my back before I could protest.

'Why are you letting him do that?' asked Fiona Makepeace-Smythe. 'He's horrible and he's evil.'

'I can't stop him,' I tried to explain.

'Of course you can,' she countered. 'You just have to tell him to get off you.'

But the creature had once again got his grip on me. His thin bony hands were tightening around my neck and his feet were working into my back. He was grafted onto me in some non-biological manner.

The baronet had instructed one of the men to put a horse into the shafts of the cart. It was a huge carthorse that had no difficulty in pulling the vehicle but it lumbered along at less than walking speed. I reckoned that at best we might make one or two miles inland before the wave struck and I was not at all sure that it would be enough.

I spoke to Sir George and he tried to speed up the equestrian contingent but even then we were going at less than a proper marching pace.

We stumbled over muddy bogs and then along a makeshift path. This was not a commonly used route and I marvelled that a house had been built there at all. As we went along in the gradually lightening gloom a hideous desire came over me to murder all of the company, one by one, and suck blood from their necks, or even from their toes. Anything for the blood.

'You know you want it,' whispered the blind man in my ear.

I looked round at him as he peered over my shoulder. He was indeed totally blind once more. Presumably he had discarded the stolen eye somewhere.

'It was anomalous,' he noted.

'What are you talking about?' I demanded, trying to shake him off my back.

'I firstly meant that you desire blood and secondly that I no longer have your eye,' he answered sharply.

'How do you know what I am thinking?' I asked.

'How do you know what I am replying?' he retorted.

'Because I can hear you, obviously,' I batted back the answer.

'And yet I am not vocalising it,' he replied.

I looked closely at his wrinkled old lips.

'…And you can still hear me,' he added.

'It's ventriloquism.'

'No it's not,' he disagreed. 'I'm still not moving my lips, breathing out or wobbling my Adam's Apple.'

All that was true.

'…You can hear me because of telepathy. Makepeace-Smythe was doing the same with you earlier. You are easy meat for a telepath, Pete Chambers. Easy meat.'

*

'Fiendish live backwards,' said the anaesthetist.

'How many letters?' asked the surgeon.

'Four,' replied the gas man.

Evil, I cried silently.

'The answer is evil,' replied the surgeon.

'But still tell me,' prompted the hapless anaesthetist.

'I just did,' sighed the surgeon as he hacked at another of my osteophytes and I silently screamed in response. 'Evil, EVIL. Live backwards.'

'Oh yes, got it!' smiled the gas man.

*

'Ow!' I exclaimed. 'You bit me!'

I looked at the rugby player accusingly. The tall saturnine opposition prop stared back.

'Only because you bit me first.'

Had I done that? Why would I have bitten him? He certainly had a mark under his left ear. In fact several puncture marks. How could I have done that?

Aaargh. Someone has jumped into the small of my back in a maul. The pain is dreadful.

Why? Why?

*

- Professor Pugh Cruikshanks joins us today in the studio. Professor Cruikshanks, welcome to Science Watch. May I call you Pugh?

- If you must.

- Pugh, your experiments with isolated brains are causing controversy. Can you explain a little more about the science involved?

- Certainly Crispin. We are taking the brain from an animal, usually a mammal, and keeping it alive in a bath of artificial CSF and blood.

- CSF is cerebrospinal fluid?

- Correct, Crispin.

- And is that real blood or artificial blood?

- We are using artificial blood. Perfluorocarbons or PFCs to be exact.

- Are they the same as used in refrigerators?
- Sometimes that is the case.
- And do they harm the ozone layer?
- Strictly speaking we are using organofluorine compounds and these only contain carbon and fluorine. They are very inert and non-toxic and are not ozone depleting as they contain no chlorine or bromine atoms. We use them as a blood substitute.
- Why don't you use blood?
- For a number of reasons, Crispin, including availability. But don't lets get bogged down on the intricacies of the blood substitute. There are far more exciting developments to talk about.
- Such as ?
- We are mending nerve damage with liquid metal.
- I thought that was something imaginary from the Terminator? Surely the only metal that is liquid at room temperature is mercury and that is highly toxic.
- We are using an alloy of gallium, indium and selenium. We believe that it is non-toxic and it can be removed after use as it is easy to find on X-ray.
- So no mercury?
- No mercury.
- And how does it work?
- We followed the example of Jing Liu from Beijing who tested the alloy on bullfrogs. Nerves reconnected with liquid metal conduct electrical signals about as well as healthy nerves. That is only one of our innovations.
- What is your final aim?
- To re-implant the brain into a healthy donor body.
- Isn't that what El Cadaver did? The madman who murdered the American Vice-President?
- No, Crispin. He took whole heads. We are experimenting on isolated brain. A completely different situation.
- Well, on the line today we have Dwight J. Freedman. It will be

interesting to hear his views on the ethics of your experimentation. He, as you and the viewers will recall, was the man who received one of El Cadaver's cast off bodies and the madman took his. Dwight is the last remaining survivor from El Cadaver's murderous medical spree. Dwight, are you there?

- Yes Crispin. Thank you for asking me to join your programme.

- So what do you think about the experiments by Professor Cruikshanks.

- My worries are surely that of most viewers and listeners. The suffering of animals and the possible transfer of the techniques to human beings. If these techniques are misused they could be horrendously harmful just like El Cadaver's evil surgical transplants.

- Professor?

- I can assure Dwight that these techniques will not be misused. We are only developing them to help people.

- But if they are used in people doesn't it mean that you would have to take the brain out of the person's skull before the person was brain dead or there would be no point in even trying?

- Good point Dwight but we would only consider doing that if the person was damaged beyond repair and we do believe that we may be able to salvage dead brain.

- And then where would you get the spare body to implant the brain into? Body snatching like El Cadaver?

- That is unfair, Dwight. Crispin, you surely don't agree with Mr Freedman.

- I'm not sure, Professor. I can actually understand Dwight's point. In the wrong hands these techniques would be highly dangerous. What if they kept somebody's brain working outside the body for months or even years. …Wouldn't the isolated brain go mad?

- Hopefully not. That is the whole point of the sensory and motor hook ups.

- And are there any problems so far?

- Many, Crispin, of course. But we are overcoming them in our rat

specimens.
- Dwight, do you have any further points?
- Just to remind the professor that even rats can feel pain.

*

'Hurry, hurry, hurry!' cried the blind man, sticking like glue to my back.

'We can't leave the others behind,' I replied.

'They are unimportant,' hissed the blind man and I could not tell whether it was a telepathic message or not.

'Don't you dare go without me!' exclaimed Fiona Makepeace-Smythe. 'I know that you are thinking of doing so.'

'Then come with us,' I shouted back to her. 'Come with us!'

The priests and the militia stared at us as we conversed but peculiarly seemed disinterested. Then I realised that they could hear none of the exchange. It had all been in our minds.

'I can't,' she confessed, tearfully telepathic. 'For some unknown reason I cannot move far from the fat girl and the skinny harridan. They are attached to me by some unseen force. Bound to me by cords I cannot break.'

I thought to myself that she had berated me for not getting rid of the old blind man.

'Don't remind me,' she was chagrined.

'Evil bitch,' groaned the blind man in my head.

'So we try to hurry them up,' I remarked.

'Too late,' stated the blind man. 'Look behind you.'

I turned and saw a darkening on the seaward horizon. The wave was approaching.

'How did you see that?' I asked. 'You have no eyes!'

'I look through the eyes of others.'

The wave was approaching at twenty or thirty miles per hour, maybe faster. The whole sky was darkening and the atmosphere was troubled. We had reached a line of trees and had started to scramble up a steep bank but the horse and cart could not enter so fat Susan was wobbling with fear and the large horse was rearing with apprehension. Suddenly it bolted and turned sharply round a corner, tipping over the cart and contents. The hugely obese young woman was flung to the ground just as the wave hit and broke against the trees.

I clung on to a large branch but the water came up over my head. I struck for the surface, trying not to inhale but the rush of brine impelled me through the forest. I held my arms over my head to protect myself and eventually came to rest in the branches of a large yew tree. The blind man was still on my back but I could hear no word from him, either orally or in my mind.

Just as I thought I had survived unscathed a large mass settled on me, enveloping me, engulfing my very being.

'Hello dearie,' it said. 'Give Susan a big cuddle.'

'Certainly,' said the blind man on my back. 'If you give me a kiss.'

Chapter 17

The branch I was clinging to was bending. It was not equal to the task of supporting the weight of the three of us and dipped alarmingly until it finally snapped and we were all flung back into the water.

The current was now weak but would soon be flowing back down the hill and the wave had brought with it mud and muck. This welled up around my neck and I thought that I would be sucked under. The huge bulk of Susan, however, was mainly adipose tissue. She was considerably less dense than water so she floated and pulled Winter and myself up out of the mire. We were floating like so much flotsam and jetsam on a raft of conscious fat. The smell of the flood waters was absolutely foul and the touch of the woman was equally bad.

'There we are dearie,' she smiled. 'I knew you would like a cuddle.'

If it had not been for you we could have moved fast enough to avoid the wave, I thought.

But you had better not tell her that, argued Winter.

Susan did not appear to be able to hear my thoughts in the way that Fiona had done. Where was Fiona? Where were all the rest of the company?

I looked around from my position of relative safety but could not see them. The water was bitterly cold and having initially shivered violently I was now beginning to feel very sleepy. I realised that this was something I would have to fight as it was a sure sign of hypothermia. If I allowed myself to sleep I would not wake up.

But on the other hand when I had drowned I had returned in a stronger form.

Wake up, wake up! demanded Winter. *You have to find the instructions.*

The letter! I had forgotten all about it. Supposedly a letter of introduction. But from who to whom?

*

'This is a good one,' a disembodied voice was talking.

'Well preserved?' came a question from an equally invisible woman.

'Take a look for yourself.'

There was a clattering sound and the sensation that a drawer had been pulled violently open.

'Not bad at all,' agreed the woman. 'We can take this one's grey matter. The professor will be pleased.'

'He will.'

'Will anybody miss him?'

'No relatives. A few friends but mostly sporting chums. Rugby players.'

'Girlfriend?'

'Yes and two dogs. Bitches.'

'Will she be a problem?'

'Not at all. She's asked that he be cremated and we will be sending him directly to the crematorium.'

'No inspection of the body before the ceremony?'

'She has already done that but we will leave him looking perfect.'

'But no eyes?'

'Glass. Very much like his own. If she does insist on seeing him and complains about his eyes we can tell her that it is due to unexpected deterioration. He is, after all, dead. You can't hurt dead people.'

'With all this supernatural stuff going on I'm not so sure.'

'You may be right but that is what I shall tell her if she wants

to look.'
'What does the locket around his neck have in it?'
'A picture and some incomprehensible writing.'
'Is that to be burnt with him?'
'The girlfriend did not want it.'
'I like to keep a souvenir.'
'Take it. You're welcome.'

*

- Today on Talking Back we have a follow-up on the programmes of the week that have most influenced or vexed the viewers and listeners. We have received the most emails, phone calls and letters about our programme Science Watch introduced by Crispin Dangerfield. Several letters complained about Crispin's stupidity in asking obvious questions. In reply to that we would point out that not every viewer has a Nobel prize in physics or physiology and Crispin tries to draw out the information in a way that is understandable to all . We feel that he does a jolly good job in a hard situation. More vexing for most of the viewers was the attitude of Professor Pugh Cruikshanks. The viewers were all in agreement that Dwight Freedman, the chimera man as he is sometimes called, had some very good points to make and was not given long enough to express them. The RSPCA have also been in touch and commended Dwight for his comment that even rats can feel pain. Dwight will be joining us on the programme later and a member of the professor's team will be here. The professor is apparently too tied up in his research to make it to the studio today and Dr. Diana Bones will be taking his place and will be telling us about her role in the research and may mention one of the aspects that was not properly covered..... the use of the fifth force, loosely known as magic.....

*

I was beginning to despair.
'Cheer up,' cried our conscious raft. 'Someone will come and

save us soon.'

'Who?' I asked, irritated by the adipose one's unbearably happy attitude and belief that everybody would do things to look after her.

'Don't know,' she confessed, a little more morosely. 'But it always does work out well and then we can all sit down and have a cream tea!'

'We could sing a song to keep ourselves happy,' suggested Winter as he hung onto my back and I clung onto the raft of fat. 'And it may serve to keep Chambers awake.'

'Good idea, dearie,' cried Susan. 'Here's one we all know…Pack up your troubles in your old kit bag.'

'Never heard of it,' retorted Winter. 'I was thinking about Greensleeves.'

'Pack up your troubles is a much better one, dearie,' replied Susan. 'You'll soon pick it up. Peter Chambers definitely knows its.'

I had to agree that I knew the song well. Susan started singing in a surprisingly pleasant contralto.

> *Pack up your troubles in your old kit bag*
> *And smile, smile, smile*
> *While you've a Lucifer to light your fag*
> *Smile boy that's the style*
> *What's the use of worrying?*
> *It never was worthwhile. So!*
> *Pack up your troubles in your old kit bag*
> *And smile, smile, smile.*

I joined in and after a while so did Winter, the evil old blind man who was still clinging to my back.

I was beginning to feel my mood of black depression lifting when I felt something else attaching itself to me. Something was wrapping itself around my dangling left lower leg. Something big.

Something from the depths thrown up by that massive wave. I faltered mid-verse but the other two kept singing.

What's the use of worrying?
It never was worthwhile. So!
Pack up your troubles in your old kit bag
And smile, smile, smile.

I tried to shake off whatever had its hold on me but I could not do so. Then I felt a pull on my back. The creature had also got its grips on Winter. Finally Susan faltered also. We were being pulled down into the murky salt water but as yet I did not know what was doing the pulling.

*

Zzzzing, zzzzing. The buzzing of a small rotating saw. Then it was biting into my skull.

Cremation? My girlfriend had asked for my body to be cremated? No way! I'm sure we had discussed this and I had said that I did not want to be incinerated. She knew about my recurring nightmares about waking up in a coffin but that did not mean that I wanted to be cremated. I was sure that I had told her that.

What was happening now? There was no pain but I still had awareness. I could see! They were doing something to my eyes….. they were breaking the bone around them, taking out my entire brain, optic nerves and eyes intact.

No….this was just another very disagreeable nightmare. Such things did not happen and even if they did there was no reason for me to be aware of it… I would be dead.

*

- Dr. Bones in what way will the fifth force, loosely known as magic, be used in the neuroscience research?

- Only very slightly Julian, mostly to determine what is happening in the mind of the isolated brain.

- What can you learn about a rat's brain using magic?

- You could call it telepathy rather than magic and it is really an extreme form of empathy. Just like the viewers we do not want the animals to suffer and we can determine the emotional state of the isolated brain using telepathy.

- Dwight, your take on this?

- Stop the research and stay away from forces which we do not understand. Calling magic the fifth force is all very well but the way in which magic works is so poorly understood that we should not use it in experiments such as this.

- Diana?

- I disagree entirely. Without the magic we would not be able to successfully interrogate the isolated brain specimens.

- Then stop the research....

*

Food? Foe? Friend? Filth?

I could hear the thoughts of the creature holding onto my leg. But what sort of beast was it?

The creature's head broke through the surface. Two huge eyes stared at me above a powerful looking beak. The head of a huge octopus. Its tentacles were wrapped around Susan, Winter and myself. Then the other tentacles broke through the surface. Two were wrapped around a tree but the others had struggling occupants in their coils. Fiona Makepeace-Smythe was in one of them, the struggling woman, Maud, in another. Then two more coils appeared on the surface wrapped round the limp bodies of Sir George Merriford and the priest, the Reverend Theodore Dean.

That made nine tentacles and I knew that an octopus only had eight. I was not, however, intending to argue with this creature.

Food? Foe? Friend? Filth?

I could not hear any more detail in the monster's mind-talk and its large round eyes were staring straight at me. The beak was a cruel object that was obviously capable of tearing me to pieces. I hoped that it would decide I was "friend" rather than, foe, food or filth.

To that end I mouthed the word "friend" and then tried to say it louder to no avail.

'You are so useless,' growled Winter from within the next coiled tentacle. 'We are your friends.'

The blind man shouted this very loudly at the octopus and the squeezing lessened as if it understood what he was saying. I could still feel the large rubbery suction pads drawing blood up into the skin of my legs but the pressure on my chest and abdomen diminished. I could breath.

Pulpo gallego, I recalled. One of my favourite Spanish meals, usually as Tapas.

Sounds like a good dish, agreed the blind man.

Was this retribution?

Susan appeared totally happy with the turn of events. She liked a hug and the huge coils squeezing around her body were right up her street.

'I told you someone would come and save us.'

'You fat fool,' cried Fiona, who was, in contrary to Susan, furious and scared in equal measure. 'This isn't someone. It's an aberrant octopus with nine arms.'

'Must be an Nonapus then, dearie.'

'Or maybe Enneapod,' added Winter. 'If you prefer Greek.'

'And we are stuck in its coils,' I reminded them. 'Does anyone have any idea how we can get out of this?'

There was no reply except the ranting of the skinny Maud.

'The devil will take you if you do not confess, your sins. The day of judgement is nigh. You must be baptised. Repent and be saved or wallow in sin and suffer for eternity…..'

Sentient? Sea creatures? Surface dwellers? Subtlety? Salvage? Scintillate?

I could hear the words in my head as English but I could not understand what the creature's thoughts meant. They were as alien as if the creature was from Mars.

Friend? Food? Friend?

The choice was narrowing.

Communicate, confiscate, coruscate, copulate?

I bloody hope not, I thought. *Not with me.*

It could try the blessed Susan, wheezed the blind man. *I'm sure she wouldn't mind.*

'You friend? asked the nine-tentacled creature.

'Yes,' I cried out loud. 'Definitely friend.'

When you're not eating him, wheezed the blind man in my mind.

Shut up, I mind-spoke in response.

Together shall work we. We work shall together. We shall work together.

'Fine,' I agreed. 'But we would feel better on dry land.'

You are water dwellers not?

'No, we are from dry land.'

The monster's understanding of our own speech pattern was improving rapidly. Perhaps it was able to read our thoughts?

Yes. I your thoughts read. Understanding better becoming. Soon full comprehension.

The speed of its acquisition of our speech patterns was amazing and it was definitely understanding me. The creature placed me onto a branch of an adjacent tree then sat Winter next to me. Fiona was sat on another stout branch with Susan and Maud on either side.

I am sorry, thought projected the aberrant octopus. *The other two are non-functioning units.*

'Did you kill them?' asked Fiona angrily.

They were non-functioning when I appeared and I am unable to reverse the deterioration.

'What about the rest of the company?' I asked. 'Have you seen them?'

You are the only units, replied the huge cephalopod mollusc.

'You mean that you did not see the other people,' stated Fiona.

No, replied the octopus. *I meant that you are the only units.*

'So,' surmised Miss Makepeace-Smythe. 'The others must have drowned.'

There are no others, replied the octopus. *You are the only units.*

*

I was lying in a very expensive wooden coffin and I was scratching at the wood with my fingernails. Then I was screaming and banging hard. Nobody came. There was no light and relatively little air.

'Breathe slowly and calm down,' came a voice. It was the disembodied voice of Winter, the blind man from my back. 'You have been buried alive but you can survive if you do what I say....'

*

I was lying in a cheap coffin. The woodwork was poor and the finish shoddy. There was a very dank and musty smell plus a distant whiff of bonfire. I pushed open the lid. I was in an ancient crypt under a church.

*

I was lying in a peculiarly shaped stone sarcophagus. Fluid was being dripped onto me and I could feel its warm glow energising my body and revitalising me.

The top of the tomb was already pushed back and I could feel a draft from the stone stairwell. This was a very old castle or house. Very old indeed.

*

The nightmares had returned. The psychotherapy was not working, it had just made things worse. This all had to be nightmare but why could I not wake up?

*

- Today on Talking Back, Mary Atwell, the woman credited with defeating the devil. Mary, may I call you Mary?
- You just did Julian and I am happy for you to continue doing so.
- Is it correct that you are a witch?
- That is what a person like me would normally be called.
- And do you believe that you beat the devil?
- The devil is very devious, Julian, and I would not like to take too much credit.
- But you did defeat him?
- Yes, OK, I did defeat Lucifer.
- And is it true that you claim to have dated Lucifer when you were young?
- That's correct. I went out with Lucifer when I was just eighteen and lived in South Croydon.
- Ha, ha. Do you really want us to believe that Lucifer dated you when you were a young lady in Croydon?
- No Julian, I don't.
- You didn't date him?
- I did date him but I do not care whether you believe me or not. Therefore I don't really want you to believe that Lucifer dated me nor do I care whether any other members of the production crew believe

me either.

- You have confused me now, Mary.
- Of course I have, Julian, because you are not very intelligent.
- Sorry?
- I expect you are…probably you are sorry that you invited me onto the programme.
- Well.…
- And next you will ask me whether or not I am on speaking terms with my son-in-law, James Scott.
- I wasn't going to ask you that but since you have suggested the question perhaps you will tell us?
- Tell you what?
- Whether or not you are on speaking terms with your son-in-law, James Scott, given that he makes no compunction about calling you a witch?
- So you have asked me.
- Well yes, but only because you prompted me to do so.
- That is how my witchcraft works.
- That's how it works?
- Yes…mostly by persuading people to do things they would not otherwise do. And the answer is yes. We are on good speaking terms. Perhaps you would now like to ask me what I think of the use of magic in Professor Pugh Cruikshanks' research.
- So what are your views on the use of magic in Professor Pugh Cruikshanks' research.
- The man is meddling with dark magic that he does not understand. He should be very wary about taking the research any further and particularly careful when he invokes the use of the so-called fifth force.

*

I climbed out of the stone coffin and onto a cold slate floor. I looked back into the sarcophagus and could see my body-shape outlined by blood. It was nighttime and the only light was that of the moon filtering down through a grilled window set high in the solid granite wall. The window was set at ground level, for some reason I knew that without needing to look. This was a cellar room below a huge house or castle. I stretched my arms, cracked and popped my joints and then set off towards the worn slab stairs.

Cobwebs hung in festoons from the ceiling, brushing against my face. There was a dank, coldness in the air and a musty smell of mould.

At the top of the steps a strong wooden door was closed. I pushed on it and it swung open easily. I walked through and looked appreciatively at the oil paintings hanging on either side of the broad corridor. The eyes were painted with that clever trick of perspective such that they appeared to follow me wherever I stood. Or perhaps they actually did follow me as I walked past.

Baroque music was coming from a room at the end of the passage so I hurried towards these signs of life. I pushed open the portal and saw a servant sitting at a harpsichord playing a piece by Johan Sebastian Bach. I stood watching without moving and he started a piece by Antonio Vivaldi. The man played very well which surprised me as one of his hands was distinctly larger than the other which I imagined would be a considerable handicap. He must then have noticed a change in the airflow, a slight breeze from the corridor for he stopped playing, swivelled on the stool and saw me standing in the gloom of the doorway.

'Sir,' he said. 'I did not realise that you had already risen or I would have attended you. Please forgive me.'

'I was enjoying your playing, Ivan,' I remarked, somehow knowing his name automatically.

'Thank you sir, but not as well as yourself. After all, you did teach me to play. Will you be caressing the pipe organ? I would love to hear it. You usually do play when you arise.'

'Yes,' I heard myself agree.

Could I play?

The servant, Ivan, stood up and I could see that he had severe kyphoscoliosis. He was a hunchback.

Ivan stumbled to the far side of the room and took hold of two huge velvet curtains, both of a deep reddish-brown, a burnt sienna. Emblazoned on each curtain was a bright green dragon.

He pulled the curtains apart revealing the console of the organ and, behind it, an array of huge pipes rising fully thirty feet or more.

I looked up. The room was very large and the ceilings stupendously high and halfway up the righthand wall ran a gallery, presently empty.

A chandelier lit with candles swung in the slight breeze and candle-wax dripped constantly onto the hard stone floor.

I walked over to the organ with some trepidation. I could not remember ever trying to play the piano beyond the level of chopsticks so how could I possibly play an organ? There were three manual consoles, several rows of stops and a full deck of foot pedals.

I threw my black cape over my shoulder and climbed onto the studded leather organ stool.

Then my muscle memory took over. My hands raced over the stops, pulling out more than half, and my feet hovered over the pedals.

Na ne na, de didlydede na na. Na ne na, la la la la.......Bach's Toccata and Fugue in D minor and I was playing it magnificently.

I looked up and could see myriads of ghostly figures in the gallery, paired spectral bodies clasped together in stately dance.

Ivan stood entranced his unequal hands clasped behind his back.

The sound of the organ filled the room and infiltrated the entire castle.

Na ne na, de didlydede na na. Na ne na, la la la la

Chapter 18

The sucking tentacles of the giant octopus, or more pedantically nonapus, coiled around my body and I was convinced they needed to be there in order to communicate. It was as if they were in actuality electrodes connecting directly to my very soul, arrows piercing deeper than my heart.

'Do not be troubled,' warbled the octopus. 'There is nothing to be afraid of.'

'Nothing to be afraid of?' I queried. 'Are you serious?'

'Of course,' trilled the creature. 'I am here to protect you.'

'That's just great then,' I replied. 'I'm lost in the wrong century or I'm dead in a metal coffin but there is nothing to fear, nothing to worry about because a misshapen octopus is going to look after me.'

'Be happy. Everything will be alright,' sang the aberrantly nine-armed cephalopod.

'Look what happened to him!' I retorted. 'He's not alright. He's dead.'

'Who dearie?' asked Susan. 'Who is dead?'

'We're all dead, of course,' wheezed Winter. 'That is the only explanation.'

'Don't think like that,' responded the over-tentacled octopus. 'It does not lead to happiness.'

'No, I don't suppose it does,' I retorted. 'But what if it is true?'

'How can we all be dead and still thinking, speaking, breathing?' asked the mollusc.

'That is, of course, the million dollar question,' put in Fiona. 'This could all be a dream sequence but you don't dream when you are dead.'

'So act as if you are alive,' ordered the octopus. 'This has been an unpleasant experience for you but nothing more than that.'

At least we are no longer being chased by psychopathic clergy and murderous militia but why and where was I playing the organ?

*

'Your breakfast is ready, sir,' intoned the hunch-backed servant.

I was still sitting at the organ consoles and had been daydreaming momentarily. I looked up at the gallery and the last remaining spectre waved goodbye.

I followed the lurching flunky into a large dining room where just one place was set. Two equally deformed servants helped me to my seat. I recognised them as Boris and Mikhail.

A pale black-clad serving maid, Maggie, entered carrying a tray on which there was a single large bowl of soup. Mikhail handed me a plate of roughly hewn bread.

I picked up the silver soup spoon and dipped it into the liquid.

'It is slightly heated, sir, as you like it to be,' Boris bowed his head as he spoke.

'Thank you Boris,' I replied.

I studied the soup carefully.

What type of soup is it? Cream of tomato? Borscht? More beetroot red than tomato.

I put the spoon to my mouth. Unusual taste. No! It couldn't be! *No! No! No!*

Blood. A plate of fresh blood, slightly warmed, steadily congealing. I dipped the bread in the blood and ate it then started to greedily drink the fluid. Blood in my throat, blood dribbling down from my mouth, blood in my cold stone tomb.

Blood.

Human blood.

*

It was a relief to be back in the swampy waters of the drowned Somerset levels and away from the gothic horror of the castle. I had thought that nothing could be worse than the deformed octopus, the blind man and fat Susan. But I was wrong. The castle was certainly worse.

'I think we should sing another song,' suggested Susan.

I was so shaken by the castle episode that I hastily agreed.

Susan started to sing an old folk-blues from the prisons of USA.

Let the midnight special shine its light on me
Let the midnight special shine its light on me
Let the midnight special shine its light on me
Let the midnight special shine its ever-loving light on me

I realised that the sun was going down and that we were perched on tree branches, in the cold, surrounded by swampy flood while a giant deformed mollusc was telling us it had come to protect us.

If you ever go to Houston
You better walk right
You better not stagger
You....

'If we do not get to shelter soon we shall all die,' I interrupted the singing. 'We cannot stay out here in the freezing cold.'

'Why not?' asked the octopus. 'It is going to be a warm night.'

I then noticed for the first time that the flood waters had gone and in their place were spring flowers. The cephalopod did not seem at all perturbed to be out of the water and for the first time I could see its entire bulk. It had to be at least thirty feet across and its body was resting in a shallow stream whilst its tentacles were still wrapped around the five of us. There was no sign of the bodies of the clergyman or the baronet and I had the distinct impression that the octopus had eaten them.

'Was that wrong?' asked the cephalopod, answering my thoughts. 'They were already dead. I could not revive them.'

'From your aspect I suppose it was not wrong,' I replied. 'But we tend to venerate the dead, burying them or burning them.'

'If you do that are the essential essences of the creature not wasted?' asked the nine-limbed mollusc.

'We would prefer to waste them than eat them,' I replied.

'Do you not eat cows and pigs?' asked the octopus.

'I'm basically a vegetarian though I do eat seafood,' I replied without thinking. 'I do not eat pigs and cows. Too much like a human being.'

'But the other units were not like me,' stated the octopus. 'I do eat fish and land mammals but not other octopodes.'

'I expect the others eat cows and pigs,' I remarked.

'Except on a Friday or during Lent,' stated Fiona Makepeace-Smythe.

'I eat anything,' stated Susan simply. 'The more I get the better.'

'Repent your greed and turn away from the evil life you lead,' preached Maud.

'Saved a funeral,' laughed the blind man. 'If the octopus eats the dead bodies we don't have to bury them.'

The sun had gone down completely now and we were still sat on the branches.

'How are we expected to sleep?' I asked the octopus.

'Can you not sleep on a perch?' asked the multi-limbed creature.

'I fear you are confusing us with birds,' I replied. 'We do not normally sleep in trees or roost on perches. We stretch out in a nice warm bed.'

'Then you will probably be more comfortable lying on me,' replied the mollusc, drawing us towards its body, the long tentacles still wrapped around us.

Oh my god, I thought as I was dragged closer to the fishy smelling mass. *My big mouth. A perch would surely be preferable.*

I was wrapped in coils lying on the huge pulsating body close to the cruel looking beak and with the blind man, Winter, to one side and the hugely fat Susan to the other. Fiona was next to the obese girl and beyond her was the skinny Maud who was still mumbling about damnation.

It was surprisingly comfortable and I was soon soundly asleep.

*

'Do you know who we are?' asked a disembodied voice.

'Of course I do,' came a female voice. 'We are mortuary attendants.'

'Not just that,' the first voice, a rougher, masculine voice. 'We are the latter day Burke and Hare.'

'The murderous body-robbers from Edinburgh?'

'That's right.'

'We are nothing like them. For a start they were both men.'

'That's not the point.'

'And they murdered their victims. Ours are already dead.'

'Are you sure?'

'Of course I'm sure. You can't survive being placed in a deep freeze for two weeks.'

'Even that is debatable.'

'You certainly can't survive having your brain hacked out of your head with the eyes intact.'

'That is definitely true.'

'Are you Burke or Hare?'

'I'd prefer to be Hare. Burke was hanged.'

'But Hare turned Queen's evidence against his partners. Is that what you would do?'

'Nobody has caught us yet.'

'We must hope that it remains that way.'
'I'm not sure that I trust you.'
'I definitely don't trust you.'
'Shall we go for a drink?'
'When we've finished this one.'
'OK.'

*

- The News at Two on Independent World Service. Darcy Macaroon will fight for more recovery of powers from the EU. Manchester United to play the first zombie footballer in the premiership. But firstly...Mrs. Mary Atwell, renowned as the witch who beat the devil, has died. Julian has been at the funeral and is outside the crematorium.
- Thank you Crispin. Yes. The witch is dead and for a moment we thought that the devil had come to claim her. Something went wrong with the organ and a strange sound, much like a supercilious laugh, emanated from its depth just at the time of the committal. A member of the packed congregation had a cardiac arrest and if it had not been for the quick thinking and actions of Lady Sienna Scott and her husband Lord James Scott, there would have been a double funeral.
- Two for the price of one, Julian.
- Thank you Crispin, but at the time it was very scary. Back to you.
- OK. Manchester United have been having a few troubled seasons and today signed their first zombie player.......

Chapter 19

Skaaa - shkeeee, skaaa - shkeeee, skaaa - shkeeee.
Arrgh. Another silent scream as the knife plunged in.
Bzzz, bzzz.
The anaesthetist was staring at me in a knowing way and the surgeon was continuing with his sharply pointed examination of my back.
'How much of this can you take before you crack completely, Chambers?' asked the gas man in a conspiratorial whisper. 'I don't think your mind will ever recover.'
I continued to scream silently.
'That's if I let you come round at all,' hissed the mad doctor who was supposed to be ensuring that I suffered no pain but was purposely doing the opposite.
My scream was heard all round the inside of my head.
Outside just for a moment there was silence then ..... Skaaa - shkeeee, skaaa - shkeeee, skaaa - shkeeee.

*

I looked around me. I was lying on the rotting corpse of the octopus, our protector. The coils had gone limp around me.
'Now you can have some tapas,' laughed the blind man as he climbed onto my back once more and put his long fingers round my neck.
Fiona opened her eyes and looked around.
'What happened?' she asked.
'The octopus appears to have died,' replied the blind man before I could speak.
'Then perhaps we are safe for a time, dearie, and we do not need his protection,' suggested Susan.

She had staggered to her feet on pin-like legs, anomalous compared with her bloated body. They looked incapable of taking the weight but were presently achieving it.

'Our time has come and judgement is on us,' cried Maud, blissfully unaware of the changing scene around her. 'Thou shalt not bear false witness against thy neighbour. Honour thy father and thy mother that thy days shall be long in the land that the Lord thy God has given thee. Love your neighbour as yourself.'

'I'd like to love all my neighbours, dearie. Yes I would,' murmured Susan. 'Just as soon as I have had a hearty brunch. Eggs, bacon, sausage, beans, black pudding.'

When I heard the words black pudding I could not prevent a shudder from running down my spine. Warm blood congealing in a bowl. That had been my latest nightmare. Before this one, of course. But when would I wake up? Was I being sedated in some ghastly mental hospital and knocked out by the chemical cosh?

What are these nightmares all about?

'You've forgotten about the letter of introduction, haven't you?' demanded the blind man clinging to my back. 'It is vital that we find it.'

'Why?' I asked. 'How can it be important?'

'If we knew that we probably wouldn't have to find it,' replied Winter.

'I think we should move away from here before more people start looking for us,' urged Fiona.

The roles were reversed. I had been the one advocating that we kept moving and now it was Fiona whilst I no longer knew what to do.

'By the way,' she said looking me in the eyes. 'Thank you for saving me from the wave. If it were not for you I would have been drowned near the church.'

'Unless you'd managed to climb the tower,' I replied. 'But thank you for being grateful.'

She was actually looking more attractive as time went on.

'Go on,' suggested Winter in my ear. 'Strip her naked.'

'Get thee behind me,' I replied. 'Don't tempt me, devil.'

'Better the devil you know than the devil you don't know,' wheezed Winter, laughing with amusement at my discomfort.

'You can always strip me naked if you would like to, dearie,' Susan leered at me lecherously, her huge morbidly obese body quivering with desire.

I shuddered once again.

'Wrath, greed, sloth, pride, lust, envy and gluttony. These are the mortal sins,' Maud was still mouthing away.

'Yeh, yeh,' muttered Winter. 'Rant, rant, rant. As if any of it meant anything at all.'

Maud continued.

'A proud look. A lying tongue. Hands that shed innocent blood. A heart that devises wicked plots. Feet that are swift to run into mischief. A deceitful witness that uttereth lies. Him that soweth discord among brethren. These are seven abominations unto the Lord.'

*

- Dr. Diana Bones is with me today. Welcome back Dr. Bones. May I call you Diana?

- Certainly Julian, good afternoon.

- Our viewers are dying to hear more about your research with Professor Pugh Cruikshanks. How is it proceeding?

- On a general basis it is going very well.

- And specifically?

- Specifically we have hit a few problems. Some of our rat specimens have died and our interrogative mechanism failed.

- Interrogative mechanism?

- Yes, Julian. We implant liquid metal electrodes into areas of interest and link the results directly to one of the researchers.

- So the researcher's brain is somehow linked to the subject? Is that correct, Dr. Bones?
- That's right, Julian, via the electrodes.
- Is it possible for the subject of the experiment to keep a secret from the investigators?
- Possible but very difficult.
- So could this research be used as a lie detector?
- Rather an extreme way of detecting lies, don't you think Julian? After all it requires an isolated brain specimen.
- Sorry, I was forgetting. That is a bit of a drawback.
- And as yet we have not experimented on human brain tissue.
- But you plan to do so?
- That is the ultimate goal, Julian, but there are many hurdles to overcome before we start on any brains from Homo sapiens.
- Tell me some of the hurdles?
- Ethical committee approval, funding issues, compatibility problems, public acceptability.
- So no human brains as yet?
- Absolutely not.
- Then why do we keep hearing rumours that human brain is already being used?
- Where are these rumours coming from, Julian?
- It's all over the internet.
- You shouldn't believe everything you read on the internet, Julian. It can be very misleading.
- OK, let's move on. The interrogative mechanism failed. Does that mean that you could not tell what was happening in the experiment?
- Not at all, Julian. We have the usual methods at our disposal including Functional MRI, MRS, Pet scanning, Electrode array analysis, EEG.
- So what did go wrong?
- It was the interactive interrogative mechanism. A fully submersible module.

- *Submersible? Under water?*
- *No , not under water. The experimenter was able to enter the mindset of the rat brain and fully immerse herself in the experiences of the rat.*
- *The experimenter could tell exactly what the rat was experiencing?*
- *Better than tell what it was experiencing. The experimenter could actual experience the sensations themselves.*
- *That's very exciting.*
- *Yes, but it is temporarily unavailable.*

*

'Did you hear what happened to one of the research workers?'

I could hear the disembodied voices again. It was the female speaking.

'No. What?' replied the male.

'In a coma. They're calling it locked-in syndrome.'

'Count of Monte Christo Syndrome?'

'That's another name for it. They think that she is conscious but unable to communicate.'

'So not really a coma.'

'Not strictly speaking.'

'Ghastly! How did it happen?'

'Some kind of feedback, they think.'

'Was she linked up?'

'I expect so or how could there have been a feedback problem?'

'Was she working on the rats?'

'No. She was experimenting with the human brain tissue.'

'None of this will rebound on us, I hope!'

'Highly unlikely. The researchers don't even know our names.'

'The professor does.'

'We should make this the last one for a while.'

'Sound policy. I agree.'

*

'How can we possibly find the letter of introduction when there has been such a severe flood?' I was perturbed and puzzled. How indeed?

'If it is important its existence will persist,' replied the blind man.

'Why do you think that?' I asked.

'Information is never lost from the universe. It's a fundamental principle.'

'That's ridiculous,' I replied. 'If I have a unique book and I burn it whatever was in the book is lost.'

'Theoretically the positions of the atoms of ink and paper will influence the way the book burns, the ashes produced, etcetera. Thus the original scrawling lives on in the later smoke and debris,' replied the blind man. 'The information is still there.'

'But in reality nobody does know all the atomic configuration,' I replied. 'So the information is lost.'

'To us,' answered Winter. 'But not to the universe.'

'I'm not too concerned whether the letter of introduction is still available to the universe,' I argued. 'What is important is whether it is available to me.'

'Or us,' added Winter.

'Why are you so intimately concerned with what is happening to me?' I queried.

'That is for you to find out, I suspect,' replied the blind man.

'Why not for you to find out?'

'Because I don't care and I only do what I want to do,' countered Winter.

'You're no better than fat Susan,' I said quietly.

'Fat Susan?' questioned Winter. 'I'm not as greedy but you are right. I am no better than her but I am not as mad as Maud.'

The skinny harridan was still ranting on, showering us with verses from the Bible, quotes from theologians, speeches from religious demagogues, texts from Proverbs and commandments from Moses. I tried to blank my mind from her persistent gabble.

*

'Do we have any guests?' I asked Ivan.
'Yes sir,' replied the deformed servant. 'We have one. A young lady.'
'Has she arisen?'
'No sir.'
'But we are expecting her to do so?'
'Any time now, sir. In fact she is a little slow in rising.'
'Worrying?'
'Just a little.'

*

I was still picking up snatches of radio and television sandwiched between disembodied voices and juxtaposed with the anaesthetist's crossword clues.

- Astounding scenes at the United Nations building in New York and now equalling amazing events in the world of finance. The former Vice President of the United States, Adolphus, Fourth Baron de Ragestein arguably the world's richest man, has liquidated all of his assets and given the funds raised to charities for the poor. Pedro Lupino, rumoured to be one of the five richest men in the world, has given his money to the chronically sick and crippled and become a care assistant in a nursing home.

- Once again the world owes a large debt to Lord James Scott, known to everyone as Jimmy. He has told us that he could not have succeeded without the help of a large team including his family, Lady Aradel from Faerie and even the Queen.

*

We stumbled onwards along the road that led towards Bristol, away from the Somerset levels, away from Burnham. Time was not behaving properly. I was starving hungry but I did not know what to eat. We passed several inns but none of us had money.

'Where are we going?' asked Fiona Makepeace-Smythe.

'Away from Burnham,' I replied.

'That much I realised,' she retorted. 'But why, specifically, are we going towards the city?'

'I just feel obliged to do so,' I answered.

The road was changing and the season with it. We stumbled into a dense fog in which I could only just see my hand held out in front of me.

We had somehow bypassed Bristol and were now, impossibly, in the East End of London.

Fiona marched along beside me and behind us, leading the blind man, was Susan. She had slimmed down under the influence of the constant heckling from skinny mad Maud.

It was Victorian London near the end of the nineteenth century. The streets were lit with gaslights that flickered in the gloom casting an eerie appearance on the entire scene. A pall of smoke hung over the capital and it was raining, a misty, drizzling rain which became patchy smog. A clock chimed three and since it was very dark I could tell that it was the middle of the night rather than mid-afternoon. Some people were already up and going on their business.

'Look out,' came a cry and a horse cantered past us pulling a Hansom cab. Close behind came a man furiously peddling a bicycle whilst wearing a tall hat and garbed in a dress suit with tails. He had obviously been to a late revelry of some sort, presumably official, and was now making his way home.

Two women walked past us, deep in conversation. They were

hugely overdressed with bustles and gowns right down to the pavement. Why they were about at that ungodly hour I had no idea. A piece of paper fluttering in the road caught my notice so I stooped and picked it up. It was a poorly printed newspaper dated Thursday 30th August 1888.

'Where are we?' asked Susan.

'Definitely London,' I replied and then looked at a street sign. 'Buck's Row, Whitechapel.'

'Buck's Row?' queried Fiona. 'I lived in the East End. This road has not been called Buck's Row for many years. Its Durward Street now.'

'There's something special about Buck's Row,' I mused. 'I wish I could remember what it was.'

A blood curdling scream emanated from further down the ill-lit backstreet. We ran towards the sound. A lady and a man were standing staring at a body. It was that of a middle-aged woman. Her throat was severed by two cuts and the lower part of her body was partly ripped open. The woman was telling the man that she recognised the victim.

'That's Mary Ann Nicholls,' she told him, sobs punctuating her delivery. 'She works this patch.'

'I don't think we want to stay around here,' I pronounced quietly. 'This means trouble.'

'It's very interesting,' said the blind man. 'I'd like to watch what happens.'

'With someone else's eyes, I presume?' I looked hard at the blind man.

'That's right,' he answered with a smug smile.

'Well, we are not staying.'

So saying I picked him up and swung him onto my shoulders then marched away from the scene of terror.

'What is the urgency?' asked Fiona. 'Shouldn't we have stopped to help?'

'That was Jack the Ripper's first definite murder,' I answered. 'I finally remembered where I had heard the name of this street and the name of the victim was a clincher.'

'I thought that Jack the Ripper was fiction like Sweeney Todd, the demon barber of Fleet Street,' Fiona panted as she struggled to keep up with me.

'The murders were real,' I replied. 'A whole spate of them. Who did them nobody knows.'

'Turn right,' ordered the blind man after we had traversed several blocks. 'Then into the mews.'

I obeyed his command for want of anything better to do and I was followed by Fiona, Susan and Maud.

'Second on the right,' Winter pronounced. 'Key under the mat.'

I knelt down and lifted the heavy rush mat which was situated under a small porch. Sure enough the key was there. I picked it up and tried it in the door. The lock opened smoothly and we stepped inside.

'You are home,' stated the blind man, waving his hands expansively. 'Or at least you are at one of your homes.'

'I'm home?' I queried. 'If so why can't I recall it at all?'

'I can remember it,' replied Winter triumphantly. 'So what does it matter?'

Who is Winter? I wondered. Who is he really? *Why does he know so much about me?*

'Anyone care for a drink?' asked the blind man. 'I believe that there is a particularly nice claret in the cellar.'

*

'It would be expedient if I saw the guest,' I suggested to Ivan.

'Certainly your lordship, sir,' replied the hunchbacked servant. 'Follow me.'

'Do we have any detainees?'

'Only one sir. A lady.'

'And what was she doing?'

'She was snooping round the castle sir. I have her in suspended animation.'

'Good, good,' I replied. 'I would like to inspect her also. Is she in good condition?'

'Very good. Almost perfect.'

I followed the factotum along the corridor between the rows of portraits and to a door beyond the one which led to the cellar I had emerged from. Ivan pulled on the door and it creaked open. Taking a lamp from a table to one side of the door the man led the way down the cold stone steps into the gloom of the unlit chamber.

I followed, wrapping my black cloak around myself to keep out the chill, the deep blue silk-lined collar turned up.

When we reached the bottom of the steps Ivan turned to me.

'I will go ahead and light the lamps, your lordship. If you wait here for just a moment or two I will not be very long.'

He sidled off into the cavern leaving me in the darkness, something which I found surprisingly comfortable and comforting.

In minutes he had lit all the lamps and in the flickering light I walked over to the first coffin. Lying in the old wooden casket in a bed of pure white silk was a young woman. She had a faintly smug, condescending expression which at first glance was off-putting. She was just a little wide in the beam for true beauty of form but otherwise she looked very trim and her hair was a superb brunette colour. I recognised her at once for it was my fellow escapee from Burnham. I was looking at Fiona Makepeace-Smythe. Dripping onto her was a large sachet of red fluid with the words "Cross Matched Rhesus negative A" written in indelible felt tip on the polythene.

'No difficulties with supplies?'

'Not since you organised the blood-bank and transfusion centre, your lordship, sir,' replied the servant. 'And the local people are very grateful for the donation of a hospital.'

'Good, good. And the detainee?'

'Over here,' replied Ivan.

I looked in the general direction that he was pointing to and could discern a smaller, less grand coffin. I hurried over and peered inside. I did not recognise the occupant. She was a young woman in her thirties, she had a very prominent nose and smallish chin giving her the appearance of having a beak.

'You implied that she was not quite perfect. In some way less than complete?'

'Indeed, sir. Her little finger of the left hand is missing.'

'Something that we did?'

'No sir. The wound has long since healed but she has nine fingers rather than the full complement of ten.'

Now I knew who she was. I had found our octopus, or nonapus.

'We had better let her go, Ivan,' I ordered him. 'She is a mere researcher. An underling with no malice or evil intent towards us.'

'But she may have gained some knowledge about you, sir.'

'Indeed she probably has,' I replied. 'But does she understand it? I doubt it very much. Let her go. She will not be a problem.'

'Certainly sir. If that is your wish.'

The factotum walked over to the coffin and turned a small crank using a handle which was situated below the casket. The entire structure tipped up and the young woman's lifeless body slid out. I expected her to fall onto the floor but at the same time I knew I had seen this happen many times before. As she was about to hit the cold stone slabs her body faded into a myriad of small stars and disappeared without a trace.

*

- Hauber's Humble Pie protects you from Evil Spells. Eat one a day and you will not be troubled by flummoxed identity, misplaced magic

or even Lucifer's bane. Available at all the best stores at a cost of only.....

'Turn that thing off, can't you?' came the disembodied female voice. 'I'm trying to concentrate.'

'Any news about the researcher?' I could hear the male voice and I pictured him with a rather thin beard and slight ponytail.

'The one who was in a coma?'

'Yeah,'

'She's woken up. Luckily she is unharmed so no repercussions are likely.'

'Did she have anything to report?'

'A garbled story about being an octopus with nine tentacles and helping a hugely obese girl and a blind man.'

'Anything specific? Anything that will help or hinder the research?'

'You mean expose our identities?'

'OK. That's what I really meant.'

'Nothing to worry us. She did identify the two successful specimens.'

'That's good, I suppose. She was involved in their dream sequences?'

'Deeply, I understand.'

'Who told you all this?'

'The Professor.'

'Pugh Cruikshank?'

'Cruikshanks. With an S.'

'There are more than one of him?'

'You know what I mean.'

'How come he's telling you all this.'

'We have an understanding.'

'?!'

Chapter 20

I lay in a comfortable bed for the first time since I had apparently awakened from the dead. True it was still the wrong century but a comfortable, warm, feather mattress was not to be sneezed at. Unless you were allergic to feathers like my dear Mama. Actually I did not have a dear Mama. I must have done, of course, but not one that I knew. I was an orphan brought up in an orphanage and now I was also a chronological orphan. Displaced in time with a batch of weird companions, none weirder than the blind man lying on a mattress next to me. There were several other rooms but he insisted on sharing this one. I had the devil's own job preventing him from sharing the bed also and he had the lion's share of the blankets. Still, I was comfortable.

I remembered virtually nothing from my childhood...it was a blur. The first significant event I could recall was going to university to study physical education but doing extremely well at geography and history, which I studied as subsidiary subjects.

Would I get back to that former life? I had no idea. I had learnt to take one day at a time.

This house for example? The blind man had announced that it was my home. How could that be the case when I was born in 1978? It was absurd.

But he certainly appeared to know his way round the abode so I had decided to flow with entropy instead of constantly fighting it.

And Fiona? What was she? How come she had arrived here with me in the nineteenth century?

What did Maud and Susan represent? Were they here for a purpose?

I thought back over the previous day. I had found some money in a bureau and had ventured out to buy some victuals. The local shopkeepers had been very respectful but had seemed surprised to see me, almost as if they knew me but felt it was not my role, my place in society to be out and about buying food.

The paper had a report of the murder in Whitechapel. The newspaper story indicated that several other murders had occurred recently in the neighbourhood but no definite connection had been made between them.

I awoke from my reveries with a start. There was a severe and very loud knocking at the door.

I stood up from the bed in my borrowed nightclothes, found a dressing gown to wrap around myself and opened the front door. Two constables stood outside clad in their customary blue uniforms and the tall, rounded police helmets. The night air was still thick with fog and smog and the yellow smoke of a million coal fires.

'Please pardon us for intruding at such an early hour but we have been told that the night before last you were seen in Whitechapel.'

'You should come in,' I said with a slight shudder.

'Thank you, Count Luiskovo,' replied the leading policeman. 'Or should I call you Dr. Alexander Pedachenko?'

'Either will do,' I replied easily as the policemen entered the house.

My accent sounded foreign even to myself. Russian perhaps or Slavic?

'Which one is your actual name?' asked the other policeman.

'They are both my names,' I answered with a smile. 'In Russia we have multiple names and titles. Perhaps you have read Tolstoy's War and Peace?'

'I must confess that I haven't, your lordship,' replied the leading uniformed man.

'You should try it some day,' I suggested. 'But do come right in. Would you like a drink?'

'You seem very self-assured in the presence of a policeman,' said the leading officer, taking off his helmet.

'A Russian is self-assured simply because he knows nothing and does not want to know anything, since he does not believe in the possibility of knowing anything fully.'

'A bit deep for me, sir.'

'Tolstoy,' I replied. 'But why should I not be confident?'

'This is a murder enquiry, your lordship. You were seen and recognised with companions in Whitechapel in the early hours yesterday.'

'Entirely possible.'

'And one of your colleagues, an old fellow who was seen riding on your back, was also espied at the scene of the murder of Mary Ann Nicholls. Apparently he was wielding a knife and drinking the blood.'

'Have you met Mr. Winter yet?'

'No sir.'

'He is the person you are referring to,' I answered. 'And he has no eyes. He is therefore completely blind. How could he have done such a crime?'

'He couldn't if he is completely blind.'

'Exactly. Would you like to meet him?'

'We must indeed meet him.'

'But first have another drink.'

'No sir. One was enough.'

'Then follow me to see Mr. Winter. He is still asleep.'

I led the two policemen into the bedroom where Winter lay snoring on the floor. Even though he was asleep it was possible to tell that the blind man had no eyes. The sunken skin over the orbits was clearly obvious.

'We are sorry to have intruded,' stated the lead policeman,

'That is fine,' I replied with a polite smile. 'You were only doing your duty.'

*

We climbed up out of the cellar and walked back into the large room which housed the organ.

'I have written a poem for you,' said the general factotum.

'I didn't know that you wrote poetry, Ivan?'

'Yes your lordship. It fills the hours of light.'

'Quite, quite. Let's hear it then!'

'You would like me to read it to you?'

'Of course. Nothing better than to hear a poem from the mouth of the poet himself, or of course, herself.'

'Certainly sir. It is rather long.'

'I'm in no hurry.'

To emphasise the point I sat down on a chaise longue.

The servant stood and cleared his throat.

'What genre is it from?' I enquired before he started.

'Gothic Horror, your lordship.'

'Most appropriate.'

'It is entitled Count Dracula,' he said and paused for a reply.

'Naturally.'

'It is somewhat fanciful and loose with the facts.'

'Poetic license. I won't be offended. Go ahead.'

The misshapen servant took out a few sheets of paper, cleared his throat again and started to read.

'Count Dracula by Ivan the Terrible. I added the words the Terrible because they seemed to fit, sir.'

'Quite.'

'Here goes, sir:

Count Dracula

In Dracula's castle Dracula wept
Longing for daytime when Dracula slept
Bored with a diet consisting of blood
Dracula longed for a smidgen of love

He remembered a time before vampire's curse
Had altered his body for better or worse
A time when the ladies admired his style
A time when admirers thronged all the while
The hubbub of parties he recalled with a smile
And the beautiful lady he walked down the aisle

But now in his dungeon he sat in the dark
Nobody admired his beauty mark
Nobody wished to be near his reach
They knew he would drain them just like a leach

So how had he come to this existence surreal
With haemoglobin for each bloody meal?
He recalled it exactly, as he stroked his cravat,
The sharp pricking fangs of a vampire bat

Then awaking with horror and a life un-dead
Appearing in films after the watershed
Where they'd all try to stake him
Or chop off his head

The castle was draughty, the castle was wet
For he hadn't mended the heating yet
His servants had fled after the last raging mob
Had burnt down their quarters and exposed him to light
He was pretty certain it was an inside job
As he faded to dust, and a very long night

Then awakened once more by the dripping of blood
His body reformed but not his taste-buds
Doomed to eternity craving gore

Dracula cried and Dracula swore
If he couldn't find love
His un-life was a chore!

So one dark deepest night like a quiet cockroach
Dracula sat in the back of his coach
Four proud black horses pulled it along
And for just this once it didn't seem wrong

He was not out on the prowl looking for blood
This time the vampire was searching for love
But where would he find it, the love that he craved?
For any girl that was bitten was simply enslaved
(Or even worse, if he took too much of a tottle
Left cold, dead and lifeless like an empty milk bottle)

Many nights and days the coach would travel
Whilst Dracula's un-life began to unravel
In his coffin at daybreak deep in the coach
During the night he was happy, beyond self-reproach

Till finally reaching a place on the coast
In the light of the moon he saw a signpost
It was written in Greek but he could translate
It said "Go no further or meet a bad fate"

Reasoning that fate had already happened to him
Dracula mused that the chances were slim
Anything there could upset the un-dead
So he whipped up the horses despite their dire dread

Soon the horses refused, despite all his bidding

For in front was a cave, deep dark and forbidding
Changing into a bat, which he found quite easy,
Dracula flew, though he felt a mite queasy

Stone statues were toppled to left and to right
Most were of soldiers in terrible fright
Athenian and Spartan, Roman and Greek
In splendid armour, still bright and still chic.

The statues so lifelike he could not dismiss
And Dracula knew there was something amiss
These statues he realised were petrified men
Changed into stone in the depth of this den

Still looking for love, onwards he flew
And the deeper he went the hotter it grew.
Passion was pushing the vampire on,
Something was calling, how could he go wrong?

In the deepest extent of that dark musky cave
Something stirred, something depraved
Also craving for love (let's hear the loud organs)
In front of the bat was the last of the Gorgons!

With hair of terrible venomous snakes
The Gorgon turned with the merest of shakes
Looked at Dracula right in the eyes
And the bat fell like stone, to his utmost surprise

He changed back to a vampire and the Gorgon could see
That Dracula had recovered his "joie de un-vie"
"How did you do it" she asked with a groan
"All my other suitors have turned to cold stone"

Dracula smiled with a look debonair
And with a sweep of his hand reshaped his black hair
"Your gaze made me feel just a little bit heavy
But tell me, my Lady, are you one of a bevy
Of sisters I've heard of in ancient myth
Or are you a footloose and fancy-free miss?"

The Gorgon let out a bellowing wail
And with a laugh replied "My name's Euryale,
Cursed by Athena for my sister's sin
I've been here for centuries, the joke's wearing thin"

"Was your sister Medusa" was Dracula's query
" Yes, that's true" she replied with a voice that was weary
"She loved Poseidon in Athena's temple
But Athena returned and the heaven's trembled"

"She turned all three sisters into creatures like me
And all people are stone if they're people we see
So how can it be that has not happened to you?
And, by the way, how do you do?"

"Pleased to meet you" Dracula replied
"You cannot kill me for I've already died
For year after year my heart's been like stone
But, seeing you, I'm feeling re-grown"
"Apart from your attitude, which some would say's feisty,
And your hair, which is somewhat untidy
You're a good-looking dame of the classical school
Why don't we wed and merge our gene-pool?"

The Gorgon and Vampire were hastily wed
In a civil ceremony on the deepest seabed

> *Poseidon presided, it was the least he could do,*
> *For he was partly to blame, as the Gorgon well knew*
> *Now they are un-living happily ever after it's said*
> *In marital bliss, the unholy un-dead*

'Very good!' I applauded loudly. 'It is long as you said but not overlong. Well written.'

I could hear a smattering of applause coming from the other servants and, on looking up, I see that the spectral guests were also applauding in the gallery.

'Do you have another poem to read to me?'

'I have written more but they are not on me right now, sir,' replied Ivan.

'Never mind. That was excellent.'

I stood up quickly, the first lights of the day were beginning to filter through the dark, drawn curtains and through cracks in the old wooden shutters.

I felt immediately faint. The descent into the cellar, the organ playing, the poem, the light…all had sapped my strength.

'You should return to your bed, sir,' solicitously the factotum spoke. 'Let me help you.'

I shook my head.

'I'm sure there is work to be done.'

'Nothing that cannot wait. We wouldn't want a repetition of the Vladivostok affair, would we, sir?'

I recalled that I had been caught in daylight to my impermanent demise.

'I shall do as you suggest,' I agreed. 'It may be some time before I arise again.'

'I understand that sir.'

'If Fiona awakens before me tell her that I will not be too long.'

'Certainly sir.'

'Don't shock her too much.'

'No sir.'
'Has the heating been mended?'
'Not yet, sir.'
'You could try making that a priority before she awakens.'
'If she awakens.'
'Quite.'
Ivan led me down to the other cellar and helped me into the stone cold tomb.....

*

A week had gone by and the police were back at the Mews.
'Count Luiskovo,' stated the leading policeman. 'We would like you to account for your whereabouts yesterday morning at 5.30am.'
'Yesterday morning?' I replied. 'I imagine that I was in bed at that hour. No, wait a minute. We had a small fire in the Mews. The Metropolitan Fire Brigade were called and the constabulary.'
'What time would that have been, sir?'
'I looked at the long case clock, officer. The fire occurred at five in the morning, the alarm was raised and the brigade were here by five-fifteen.'
'They were very prompt, then sir.'
'The police took a little longer and I remember remonstrating with the sergeant about it.'
'Which sergeant would that be sir?'
'Sergeant Eric Lacey-Brown, if I recall correctly.'
'I believe you do, sir,' replied the constable with a perceptible depression of his manner and downward slope of his shoulders. 'He is the sergeant in charge of the night watch.'
'I looked at the clock again and told him that it was not good enough taking ten minutes longer than the fire brigade.'
'So they arrived at 5.25?'

'Correct,' I agreed. 'I took the trouble of telling the officer, Lacey-Brown, about my experiences in Russia where the militia arrive almost before you call them.'

'To be fair, sir, our society is very different. Maybe the militia are already busy watching you in Russia?'

'No, officer, that would be the Tsar's secret police .'

'And how long did you spend talking to Sergeant Lacey-Brown?'

'Not less than fifteen minutes whilst the brigade put out the fire.'

The policeman looked ever more crestfallen.

'Anyway, what is this all about?' I asked more firmly.

'Another woman has been killed in Whitechapel, your lordship. By the name of Annie Chapman.'

'Why have you come to me?'

'Your name was mentioned by a witness. He said he saw a dark-haired man of shabby-genteel appearance and the man reminded him of yourself.'

'Is my appearance shabby?' I demanded to know the answer .... this was an insult! An outrage!

'No sir, not at all. You are very smartly dressed. What of your other companions?'

'Winter is often shabby but never genteel.'

'Winter?'

'The blind man. The rest of my companions are women and they live in the other part of this house.'

'Quite sir. They are presumably the servants?'

'In a manner of speaking, yes.'

'I'll trouble you no more, your honour.'

'Good. By the way, you may be interested to know that the brigade believe that the fire was arson. Somebody started it deliberately.'

'Really sir, did you inform the night Sergeant about this?'

'He did not stay until the fire officer told me his conclusion.

After our little discourse he left.'

'Did the fire officer say how it had been started?'

'Rags and some oil and a candle that had burnt down to the level of the inflammable material.'

The constable rapidly scribbled in his notebook then questioned me again.

'Couldn't it have been an accident?'

'The fire officer did not think so. He believed that somebody was trying to burn me in my sleep.'

'Have you any idea who would do that?'

'Russian dissidents, I expect.'

The scribbling continued then the constable spoke once more.

'I shall have to speak to the Night Sergeant about this but if he corroborates your alibi you are in the clear, sir.'

I arched my eyebrows at this and the policemen left with no further comment. The second policeman had said not a word.

Chapter 21

- Breaking news…Lord James Scott is missing. The pound has reached a new high against the Dollar. Elton to sing at the double Royal wedding.

'This James Scott,'
'Yeah?'
'Gets himself into all sorts of trouble.'
These were different voices. They were both female and less educated. I could not tell whether we were in the same room as before but I thought probably not. The morgue or funeral parlour, or whatever, was more echoey. This was muted.
'What is he? Magic or something?'
'Dunno. 'Spose 'e must be. What d'you think of all this magic?'
'Frightening innit?'
'Yeah. Definitely that. The devil at stonehenge and now that money god at the UN. Scares the willies out of me.'
'Were they ever in you?'
'Nah!'

*

Diary: Susan has put much of her weight back on. She had slimmed down to about twelve stone but is now over twenty again. She has spent much of the time over the last month or so drinking in the local gin palaces. There were two more grotesque murders in Whitechapel, both in the early morning on Sunday 30th September and the newspapers are calling the perpetrator Jack the Ripper, as I knew they would. For those murders I was fast asleep in my bed in the small mews house. Apart from that I had no alibi but the police did not come to the Mews, for which I was most grateful.

The day before yesterday I heard a kerfuffle in the street outside the Mews. I ran out to see a small crowd of ruffians, young fellows, chasing after Susan and calling her names. I rushed over and confronted them, keeping them at bay with my stick until one tried to attack me. He had not realised that the stick I carried was in fact a sword cane. I drew the blade and pierced his arm as he swung at me. He hopped around in pain then ran off and the rest of the hooligans dispersed. Yesterday there was another disturbance around Winter, the blind man. A similar, or maybe even the same, crowd of young ruffians had gathered and were throwing stones at him. Fiona heard the noise first and went out to confront the mob. When I realised what was happening I had to hurry out and dispel the crowd as she was also under attack. This time I took my sword cane and a trusty revolver that I had discovered in the roll top desk and the mob responded to a little gentle persuasion from the two weapons.

But worst of all, earlier this morning Winter, the blind man who tells me that he can see with other people's eyes, returned covered in blood. He claimed he had been attacked but he had no wound upon his own body.

So what has he been doing?

Fiona and I spent some time cleaning him up, berated all the time by Maud who is still exhorting us to confess our crimes and repent. I have decided that we must move out very soon and continue our quest elsewhere....there are too many strange happenings around these parts. I have therefore started making plans.

One thing positive that has happened is that I have discovered the whereabouts of the locket. I saw it for sale in a jewellery shop. How it came to be there I have no idea but I am certain that it is the same object as the one I saw in the bugler's house. This surely must contain the information the priest was searching for. I have arranged an appointment with the jeweller for 10.00am and we must leave immediately to meet that commitment.

*

'The two specimens are doin' well.'
'Yeah. But only the two.'
'Do you think they can hear us?'
'Don't s'pose so. They haven't got any ears, just holes.'
'They've got eyes though, haven't they?'
'That's a point. Maybe they can see us. What do you think they intend doin' with them in the end?'
'Putting them into another head, or making androids?'
'With human brains they would be cyborgs like robocop.'
'Maybe that's what they are goin' to do.'
'What, make robocops?'
'Yeah..'

*

I lay down in the stone cold tomb, pulled my cape around my body and the collar up around my neck. Whatever anybody imagined it was never nice to surrender oneself to the un-death of the vampire's coffin. It was cold and soulless and I never knew how long I would have to spend in that peculiar limbo. This was particularly true in the present circumstances. Something was blocking my regeneration and that of the girl called Fiona. She was a new guest, not a detainee and this was her only hope. Somehow we were both being thwarted.....prevented from getting that which we needed. I sighed, a long sad sigh. It was my last breath as I closed my eyes and sank back into the oblivion. My last breath for a long time and I listened to it ebbing away....

*

We all walked over to the jewellery store in Hatton Garden in the district of Holborn. The jeweller met us most civilly and I purchased the locket for a reasonable price. I instantly opened it when we were outside the store but could only discern squiggles written on the inside back wall of the small ornamental case. These will require further examination later.

We strolled back to the Mews. Winter was in a state of high excitement, gibbering and capering around, more than once he fell of the pavement and had to be rescued to avoid being run over by a passing Hansom cab.

Back at the old Mews cottage I saw police in a cordon round the house. I was all for turning tail and moving out but Fiona marched straight up to the officers and demanded to see whoever was in charge. Winter skipped along behind her and bumped into a small signpost, knocking himself senseless to the amusement of the constabulary.

I held back but when Fiona was detained I felt obliged to also speak to the police. They promptly arrested me. Susan, Winter and Maud were ignored by the officers and I heard a sergeant tell his constable that two was enough, the local village idiots would have to wait their turn.

'There has been another murder, your lordship,' remarked the sergeant. 'But then you would know all about that wouldn't you, Count Luiskovo.'

'Would I?' I enquired politely.

'What is your first name, Count?'

'I am known as Dr. Alexander Pedachenko and as Count Andrey Luiskovo.'

'Am, I right in thinking that your coat of arms incorporates a double headed eagle of Russia and a dragon, or possible wyvern on a background of the alternate blue and white stripes of the Lords of Lusignan?'

'You are very well informed, officer.'

'So I am correct?'

'Indeed you are. I am most impressed by your erudite knowledge of my heraldic conceits.'

'Don't be too amazed, your lordship, but rather consider your position.'

'My position?'

'We have evidence that links you to this latest homicide.'

'That is impossible since I have not been involved in any murders.'

'I have in my possession a warrant for your arrest, your lordship. Anything you say may be taken down and used in evidence against you.'

'Or made up, for that matter.'

'I shall write that down, sir.'

'I shall require the Russian consul to be informed of this and I imagine that I will need a solicitor.'

'We can arrange that for you, sir,' said the policeman, saluting. Are you armed?'

'I have a Russian army issue revolver. Yes, I am armed. You had better take the gun.'

I reached into my pocket and handed the weapon to the sergeant.

'I would like to thank you for being so civil,' stated the policeman.

'I have no quarrel with you or anyone,' I replied. 'I expect whatever evidence you have was planted by some dissident.'

'Where would they obtain one of your crested handkerchiefs, your lordship?'

'From my laundry, I expect.'

I had no idea whether or not I had sent out my handkerchief with the laundry. In fact I was not aware of the fact that I had crested napkins.

'What of Fiona, my companion?'

'She has been arrested as an accomplice.'

'May I ask where the offending item was found?'

'Clutched in the dead woman's hand and soaked in her blood,' replied the sergeant.

Then I am in trouble, I thought grimly. *Evidence of that nature was considered as absolute proof in the nineteenth century. After all it was not long since they hanged people for stealing a loaf of bread.*

'And we have found identical crested handkerchiefs in your bedside cabinet,' added the sergeant.

I held onto my cane sword very firmly. It was well disguised and had fooled many an expert. It was good to have something up my sleeve.

In fact I also literally had a dagger there, hidden, up my sleeve.

*

'So what have they done with the other specimens, eh?'

I could hear the disembodied voices again...no, wait a minute! I could just about see two shadowy figures through the fog-like gloom. Yes, two cleaner ladies.

'Chucked them in the garbage I expect.'

'Nah! They wouldn't do that.'

'Yeah they would. It's illegal, this experiment.'

'Is it?'

'Course it is. That's why they pay us so much. Why the 'eck do you think they pay us four times as much as we got on our last job?'

'Don't know, Myrtle. You arranged the job, not me.'

'They need cleaners even if they're illegal. That's why the Professor asked me.'

'Yeah. Be a right mess in 'ere if we didn't always clean up after 'em. Right messy bunch.'

'Yeah. 'Ow's your Bert?'

'Our Bert? Still the same, no progress. What about your Annie,

George and Pete?'

'Our Pete's doin' great. Annie's got another bun cooking and our George is still in the slammer.'

'Oh. What d'you really think will 'appen with this experiment?'

'When these two fail?'

'Yeah.'

'Knowin' this lot they'll start takin' them out of living people rather than dead ones.'

'Nooo?'

'Yeah. I heard them say that the main problem was dealing with already dead brains.'

'Go on!'

'Yeah. What they want is a couple of fresh brains to work on.'

'Human brains?'

'Course.'

''Ow come these two are doin' so well?'

'Don't know. I think it's the magic they're usin'.'

'Thought it was only to observe their thoughts.'

'Nah! More to it than that. They've got some poisonous little dwarf in here every other day and they've recruited the help of that Tinkerbell.'

'Is she beautiful?'

'Beautiful? Not when she's resting. Gorgeous when she's working her spells but looks like a cross between a wasp and a mosquito when no-one is looking.'

'Go on!'

'Yeah! Looks like a beautiful film actress with wings when people are watching but when they turn away she's this great big ugly insect.'

'Gawd almighty! Myrtle, that's a fright. 'Ow come she didn't keep up the illusion when you was watchin'?'

'Hilda! We're cleaner ladies. Nobody notices the cleaners, not even the fairies.'

'The big nobs are comin'.'

'Yeah. We better move out. They don't like it if we are under their feet.'

I watched with blurry sight as the cleaners scurried out of the room taking their buckets and mops with them. Two people entered. A man and a woman, relatively young and both in white lab coats.

'The Prof will be here any minute so we must look busy,' said the woman.

'He's very pleased with this experiment,' said the man, who I could now see was younger than the woman. 'But he would like to take it one stage further.'

'That's all very well but we still don't know why these two have done so well compared with the other specimens. He didn't tell me he wanted to move on.'

'True, but I heard the Prof tell our financial backers that the earlier we get the specimens the better.'

'These were extremely fresh. Only just into the mortuary.'

'The previous cases were possibly even fresher and they did not do as well as these.'

'Exactly. So we have no idea why these are better.'

'Their fantasy world is more complete.'

'If it is fantasy.'

'What do you mean?'

'Maureen said that her time as an octopus was completely convincing.'

'But listen Di, she never actually left the laboratory.'

'Try telling her that. Don't forget we have used the fifth force and that can move people through time and space.'

'I know. But surely there would be some sign that the person had moved?'

'Maureen did not initially return when the electrodes were disconnected.'

'Food for thought.'

'Earlier specimens than these will be difficult to source, Rees.'

'They would have to be taken pre-mortem.'

'That involves a lot more people. It's one thing robbing a grave but quite another robbing a cradle.'

Good slogan, I thought. *That woman has an ear for a catchphrase.*

'Transplant surgeons do it all the time.'

Not so good. The lad's slogan won't make it big time.

'They do,' agreed the woman. 'That's where we will have to get our material but the ethical committee will be difficult.'

'I don't think he was going via the committee. They don't even know that we are utilising human specimens.'

'Officially speaking we are not doing so. These are classified as "mammalian brain tissue of more than one origin".'

'That's a clever one. Not exactly a lie but not the whole truth and nothing but the truth.'

He's getting better. But is that what I am? Mammalian tissue of more than one origin?

'We've got the DNA analysis back on the larger brain,' remarked the woman whose name was probably Diana.

'The man's?'

The guy speaking. Is his name Rees? It might be important to know these things.

'That's right. It may give us a clue to why his was the first truly successful isolated preparation.'

'You've not looked at it yet?'

'Only cursorily. That's more up your street.'

'Well come on then. Get it up on the computer. I'd like to have something to report to the boss other than just "more of the same".'

'Here it is,' said the woman.

I could see the two of them squinting at a large plasma screen.

'That's an unusual sequence.'

'Where?'

'There, amongst the telomeres.'

'What do you think it is?'

'It looks as if a whole virus has been incorporated into the DNA. Maybe even two viruses.'

'Is that unusual?'

'In that site on the DNA? Very unusual. We'll have to compare this section with known pathogens.'

I cannot and will not believe that I am an isolated brain experiment. I am Peter Chambers and this is another nightmare which has been brought on by the General Anaesthetic. I will blank out this nonsense....

*

'Would you object if I collected a few things from my room and changed my clothes?' I asked in a very reasonable tone. I was banking on the constabulary deferring to the gentry.

'Certainly sir, that would be fine. We've searched your room and discovered no hidden weapons apart from the handkerchiefs,' replied the sergeant, chuckling at what he obviously considered to be a witticism.

As soon as I was in my room I closed the door and bolted it. A constable was outside the door and indeed another was outside the adjoining bedroom where Fiona resided. I had seen her go to her room, also ostensibly to collect personal items.

I gently knocked on the dividing wall and a knock came back in reply. Much of the previous month had been taken up in creating an escape route from the Mews cottage. I had papered over the communicating door between the two rooms on both sides but this was easily reversed with a sharp knife. I could hear Fiona doing the same on her side of the wall. In a moment I was through and opening the hatch into the stable. This I had also concealed with the aid of a very moveable wardrobe. We both jumped through and down onto a pair of waiting horses. Now we had to pick up the village idiots and make haste to Chesham House in Belgravia, the home of the Imperial Russian Embassy.

We could hear the police trying to break down the doors into our bedrooms. They were taking some time due to another of my innovations.... sheet steel reinforcement bolted to the doors, painted over to look like wood.

I knew where the idiots would be. Susan would have led the capering blind man and the castigating woman to her favourite haunt, a gin palace by the name of the Black Swan but known to all as the Dirty Duck.

The horses responded well to our directions and very soon we were at the door of the inn.

It took some persuasion and coercion to induce the three to leave the public house but eventually they came with us. I had commandeered a hansom cab. Susan and Maud travelled in that out of the rain that had started to drizzle on us. The capering blind man climbed up behind me and put his thin bony hands round my waist.

In a matter of moments we were at Chesham House. The doorman led us round the back of the Imperial embassy. I paid off the cab driver and gave him an extra sum to go to the other side of London and wait for a non-existent passenger.

The horses were stabled and I met the ambassador. I had been in frequent communication with him and he was expecting something of this nature to occur. A large black carriage was brought to the front of the embassy and we all climbed into it along with an attaché from the house. Four superb black horses pulled the coach and we set off in a southward direction. We were making for Dover where we would take a small boat out to a waiting Imperial Russian battleship.

The boat was small and unpleasant, rowed by four large Slavic seamen. The battleship, however, was large and impressive, a steam-propelled ironclad that was clearly very new.

The five of us boarded the ship and, after the captain had toasted us with vodka and we had returned the compliment, we were shown to our cabins. The three ladies were in one cabin whilst I and Winter were quartered in the other. Late at night I noticed that Winter had disappeared. A tentative knock came at the door. I opened it and Fiona stood there.

'May I come in?'

I raised my eyebrows in mock surprise but ushered her in.

'Winter is in my cabin bunked up with Susan,' she explained.

'And this offended you?'

'Not really. It was Maud's tirade at them for their sins that was really getting me down. I couldn't sleep.'

'There's a spare bed in here now that Winter is in your cabin.'

'I'm rather cold and wondered whether shared bodily warmth might help me.'

'I'm sure it would,' I smiled and welcomed her into my bed.

I looked out through the small, round porthole and could see that the ship was steaming into a fog bank. Within seconds the view of the sea was completely obscured by the thick, enveloping mist.

Chapter 22

'This is my colleague, Dr. Diana Bones, and with her is her assistant, Peter Rees Chin, known as Rees, originally from the Republic of China but who has been over in the UK for some considerable time. Diana and Rees let me introduce Mr. Stiltskin and Lady Tinkerbell.'

I could hear the Professor's voice but I could not see him. I had only ever seen his back... I had never been correctly positioned to see his face.

Diana Bones was clearly the name of the female researcher and Chin the male but more interesting were the visitors. Stiltskin was a poisoned dwarf with large ears, long unruly beard and long nose. Tinkerbell was a fairy. I could not tell whether she was actually an insect as she was consistently staying in her fairy form. She looked like a beautiful teenage girl with gossamer thin wings and she hovered a few inches off the ground. No... for a moment I saw the illusion slip and there was a monstrous insect just as described by the cleaner, a cross between a mosquito and a hornet, then she was a soft focus movie starlet with wings.

'The experiments have been highly successful in large part due to your fifth force component,' said the professor.

I recognised his voice. I had only heard snippets from him before but I definitely knew this person. I could still not see his face.

'You mean magic,' growled the dwarf, Stiltskin.

'If you like,' agreed Cruikshanks. 'But I find that most scientists prefer the term "fifth force". It sounds more scientific.'

'I don't think it matters, really, Rumple,' trilled the fairy stroking the dwarf's hair.

'I suppose not,' Stiltskin grumpily acquiesced. 'But I like to call a pickaxe a pickaxe.'

'You mean call a spade a spade,' interposed the professor.

'I know what a pickaxe is and what a spade is,' growled the squat man. 'All dwarves know the difference between the two. I knew fourteen different names for spade and ten for pickaxe by the time I was three years old.'

'Errr, yes,' the professor coughed. 'I invited you here today to see a new phase in the experiment. We will disconnect one animal specimen from another and then reconnect the intra-brain divisions.'

'The intra-brain divisions?' queried Stiltskin.

'We have divided the corpus callosum on several specimens and made incisions in the frontal lobe white matter and elsewhere. Reconnection will be performed using liquid metal.'

The dwarf and the fairy looked on with blank expressions. My vision, already dim, became ever more blurred.

*

Sometime in the night I felt Fiona rise and then return. I turned over and went back to sleep. Hands groped my body and I woke with the dawn and turned to look at Fiona. Horror upon horror! She was gone and the blind man Winter was in the bed with me! Long thin fingers were clawing at my neck. I brushed them aside and clambered off the bunk. He immediately swung up behind me and hung onto my back.

Despairing of removing the blind man I ran out of the room with him still clinging to me. I knocked on the next cabin where Fiona and the other two had their sleeping quarters. Receiving no reply I tried the door and it opened to a turn of the brass knob. The cabin was empty. There was no sign of Fiona, Susan or Maud and no evidence that they had ever been there. Was I, Count Luiskovo, going mad?

No. There was just one thing. Lying on the bunk that Fiona had briefly occupied was a strange glass orb. Perhaps four inches in diameter it was green and had an indentation at one side which created a ring for a rope to be attached. I had seen the object at the Mews but had ignored it.

The blind man could tell that I was staring at the orb.

'It's a float,' he remarked.

'Afloat?' I queried.

'It would be if you put it in the water.'

'Why is it on the bed?'

'I brought it with me,' replied Winter, the cause of much of my discontent as he clung to my back.

'You did?'

'Yes,' he answered. 'I secreted it in my pocket. Heh, heh, heh.'

'Why did you do that?'

'I wanted it and now it is yours.'

'Why should I want it?' I enquired.

'I don't know,' he answered. 'But one thing I do know.'

'What is that?'

'It's time that you got this poor old man some breakfast.'

I groaned. Before breakfast I would need a little rest. Then I would have to tackle the captain of the ship. Perhaps he knew where the girls were. If he didn't then nobody did.

*

My vision was clearing but I could still not see the professor's face. The poisoned dwarf, Rumple Stiltskin, and the fairy, Tinkerbell, were watching attentively as the mad professor and his two assistants leant over a computer screen.

'All the connections are computer controlled using robotics,' remarked the professor.

'So what are the tube-like machines that the specimens are moved in and out of?' trilled Tinkerbell.

'Magnetic Resonance Imaging units or MRI,' replied Cruikshanks. 'Small in size but large enough to take the neurological experiments.'

'And what do they do?' growled the dwarf.

'They provide imaging information from the brains and more,' explained the scientist. 'They are very high field strength machines at eight Tesla. We obtain exquisite images, functional data, spectroscopic info. The lot.'

He said this with pride.

'Is that any use?' asked the dwarf.

'We couldn't conduct the experiments without it,' stated Cruishanks.

'And that narrower unit?' the dwarf pointed at a ring-like machine.

'PET-CT,' replied the professor. 'Positron Emission Tomography coupled with Computed Tomography.'

'I don't understand any of this terminology,' trilled Tinkerbell.

'MRI uses magnets, PET uses radioactive isotopes and CT uses X-rays,' explained Pugh Cruikshanks.

'I don't understand either but I don't care,' growled Stiltskin, the dwarf, proud of his ignorance.

'We've got more,' bustled the professor, just a little hassled by the dwarf's angry countenance. 'Quantum interference devices, magnetic stimulation machine, artificial wombs, EEG. We've got the lot.'

He waved his hand around the large laboratory in an expansive gesture.

'Neuroscience is the must-have subject at the moment,' he added. 'The sexy forefront of medical research.'

'Sounds good,' squeaked Tinkerbell excitedly.

'What I want to know is how you use the equipment and when

will you deliver?' grunted the squat figure of the dwarf.

'OK,' replied the professor sighing, clearly a bit exasperated. The meeting was not going quite as planned. 'It is all computer and robotic controlled. The important factor is keeping the brain tissue viable both biologically and mentally.'

The two visitors were listening intently so Cruikshanks continued.

'We store various memories in the computers so that we can kick-start a sequence by dual hippocampal stimulus and computer generated imagery.'

'Where do the sequences come from?' queried the female visitor.

I was by now convinced that the cleaner was right. The fairy was not entirely humanoid.

'They originate in the subject's own brain but with the assistance of the fifth force we can store whole memories on a hard disk.'

'Am I right in thinking that the two human brains are the only functioning units out of many?' asked Tinkerbell.

'We have two human brains presently functioning and just under twenty animal brains,' answered the professor.

'But only two out of how many human experiments?' asked Tinkerbell, her questions more pertinent than would have been expected given her fairy starlet looks.

'Sixty,' answered Cruikshanks.

'And how many animal brains have you used and which sort?' asked the dwarf, interested again now that the high tech machinery was not being discussed.

'About thirty animals have been used in toto and the species include rat, feral cat and chimpanzee.'

'Just three animal types and all mammals,' mused the dwarf.

'Correct,' agreed Cruikshanks.

'And a twenty times better yield,' muttered the poisonous midget.

'True.'

'Why is that?' trilled Tinkerbell.

'All of the animal experiments have been successful since we started using living brains rather than harvesting them from recently deceased animals,' explained the professor.

'Were the two functioning human brains harvested from live humans?' asked the dwarf.

'Not exactly but they were very recently deceased,' answered Cruikshanks, shuffling slightly.

'But so also were many of the rest of the sixty human brains, surely?' queried the dwarf, with a penetrating look at Cruikshanks. 'You wouldn't have used old tissue.'

'True.'

'So what is the difference with these two?'

'We are not sure yet but we are getting there,' replied Cruikshanks.

'And if you don't get there,' grunted the dwarf. 'Are you going to use live human brains?'

'If needs be, yes,' agreed the professor. 'The research must go on.'

'Ha, ha!' laughed the dwarf, a nasty chuckle full of evil. 'Always the excuse. The pursuit of knowledge. Can't give it up now. The end justifies the means.'

'That is quite right!' exclaimed the professor. 'Medical science is a very difficult subject.'

'It's not rocket science,' snorted the dwarf.

'True,' the professor nodded violently. 'Medicine is not rocket science. It is far more complicated than mere rocket science.'

The dwarf leant over and pressed several switches randomly before the mad professor could stop him.

I blanked out.

*

I felt a wrench running through my guts, my soul turned inside out and my mind did a flip. The weight on my back disappeared and I felt more whole in myself but strangely ruthless, a razor sharp brain with a predator's outlook. I surveyed the scene looking for my prey.

A small rat ran past me and I pounced.

'Come to me little ratty,' I laughed, smiling at the rodent as I enticed it to run between my paws..

'Don't play with your food,' came a familiar voice.

The skinny Maud was standing looking at me with an angry face.

'Be a good kitty or you will end up in bad kittyland where all bad kitties go.'

She was Maud but she was also more frightening than previously. Her fingers ended in talons and her face was grotesquely contorted.

I purred at her and she stroked me on my head. I could not resist the desire to scratch her hand. So I did it.

*

I was back in the laboratory looking at the mad professor whose face was still turned away from me as he fiddled with the computer controls.

'You shouldn't have done that,' he shouted at the dwarf. 'You mixed up the animal and human brain circuitry. I've only just about succeeded in putting it straight again.'

'Isn't that the final aim of the experimentation?' asked Stiltskin.

'Not entirely,' sniffed Cruikshanks. 'Any more behaviour like that and I'll ban you from the lab.'

The dwarf laughed, unimpressed by the threat.

'You are going to provide me with a troop of sentient, trainable, semi-human animals that I can use as an army of miners. They will be able to work in the deepest of mines, endure hardship and not complain.'

'Whilst I get a docile and obedient lover,' trilled Tinkerbell. 'That was the deal.'

The professor squirmed. This was all too public in front of his two researchers who had stayed so quiet.

'True, true,' he acquiesced. 'You will both get your wishes but we will have moved medical science forward. We will be able to save the lives of people with intact brains and diseased bodies.'

'If the brains can be re-implanted,' said the dwarf. 'Otherwise this will all be a waste of time from your point of view.'

'Not at all,' replied Cruikshanks, happy to rebut that argument. 'We know a lot more about how the brain functions than we did before.'

'Such as?' asked Tinkerbell, always keen to learn more about the men she wished to dominate for the sake of love.

'We have been able to make careful incisions in the brain and then create artificial switches,' explained Cruikshanks. 'Thus we have separated the hemispheres by cutting the corpus callosum, isolated the frontal lobes, motor and sensory cortices, hippocampus and limbic systems. All can be connected back together at a push of a button or united with the system of another animal.'

'So where has our magic helped all of this?' asked Stiltskin.

'Helping the brains remain functioning such that they believe they are living a full life and by enabling us to participate in those imagined lives,' replied the mad professor.

'The lives they live are experienced and may not necessarily be imagined,' countered Tinkerbell. 'The spells used are remarkably robust.'

'You can have a look at whatever the male brain is perceiving if you wish,' answered the professor.

'Oh do let's,' squealed Tinkerbell. 'That would be oodles of fun, fun, fun.'

'We will have to connect ourselves to these helmets,' replied

Cruikshanks. 'Our researchers use full immersion but this time we will only be partially on line but it should be sufficient.'

'What is he up to at the moment?' asked the dwarf. 'And why can't we be connected to the female brain as well?'

'We've taken the female offline,' replied Cruikshanks. 'We are having some trouble keeping her functioning since we detached her from the cross-link with the male brain.'

'And what is the dear, darling boy doing?' trilled Tinkerbell.

'Let's have a look, shall we?' replied the professor, picking up one of the helmets. 'When we put these on we will put ourselves into his environment. He will believe that we are people who should be there so keep in character.'

The professor turned to his two researchers.

'You are in charge Diana, whilst we are in the sequence. Immediately we are ready provide a small electric shock to the specimen A, then stimulate the hippocampus.'

*

For a moment I could not understand where I was then I analysed my surroundings. I was back on board ship. No rat, no cat, no Maud and no Winter.

I believe that I should speak to the captain, I thought. *He may shed some light onto the whereabouts of Fiona, Susan and Maud.... and where has Winter gone?*

I walked down the corridor trying to shake off the feeling that I was being observed by myriads of unseen eyes. Winter appeared from a cabin and skipped along beside me without saying a word, his sightless orbits surveying the scene in the disconcerting way that he did.

I reached the ladder to the next level and spoke to a rating.

'The captain is on the bridge,' replied the seaman to my question. 'You most probably will be allowed to see him.'

He then pointed out the exact route to take. I obeyed the instructions, hastened up the rungs followed by the sightless man and thence to the steps that took me towards the bridge. When I got there I would demand to know what the captain had done with my companions.

Within moments I was standing in the bridge. The captain had his back to me and was looking out to sea. Staring intently at me were a young lady who appeared to be hovering above the floor of the bridge, next to her was a dwarf.

Seeing my perplexed gaze the lady lowered herself until her feet touched the floor. I shook myself trying to make sense from that which I had seen. People do not hover above the floor so it must have been a trick of the light.

The captain eventually turned and looked at me. I had not met him since I had been aboard ship but I was sure that I had seen him before.

Yes, I had it. The captain was the spitting image of the Reverend Theodore Dean, the vicar who had persecuted me and pursued me in Burnham!

The surprise made me feel faint and I sat down quickly on one of the leather bound chairs.

*

'Welcome back, your lordship,' lisped Ivan the Terrible.

'Status report,' I demanded.

'You are eighty percent whole with sixty-five percent incorporation,' replied the general factotum.

'Almost sufficient but not quite,' I answered. 'Do you know what is blocking full regeneration?'

'No sir but the details may be hidden in your mind. If you will let me use hypnotic regression we may be able to recover the information?'

I stared at the misshapen servant trying to determine whether this was a ploy to gain an upper hand over his master. If it was I would have to kill him immediately. If not it would be safe to allow the analysis. Which was it to be?

His mind was relatively simple and there were no telltale signs of deception. I surmised that he wished to assist me and that it would be safe to submit to hypnosis.

'Guests, detainees, enemies at the door, mobs at the gate, creditors, debtors?' I asked peremptorily.

'Several short term debtors otherwise the answer is no to all of the questions, sir,' whispered Ivan.

'Then I will submit to hypnosis.'

'Very good, sir.'

'So not even a guest?'

'No sir.'

'Fiona has gone?'

'Disappeared.'

'Unusual.'

'Unheard of, sir.'

'Disappointing.'

'I thought you would think that.'

'Hypnosis then, Ivan.'

'Very good, sir.'

*

I woke up to see the young lady from the bridge fanning me with a towel. I was in my cabin and the lady seemed most attentive to my needs.

'What you really need is a massage,' she said to me in a husky voice. 'That will tone up your blood pressure no end.'

'What happened to me?' I asked. 'And who are you?'

'I'm Miss Bell,' replied the young woman. 'But you can call me

Tinker.'

'But why am I now in my cabin?'

'You fainted on the bridge and the captain thought that it would be a good idea if I looked after you. I agreed,' smiled the girl.

The captain! I suddenly remembered .... He was Theodore Dean, the mean clergyman who had done so much to persecute me! how could this be the case?

'Do you know the captain well?' I asked.

'Not very well,' replied Miss Bell.

'How long has he been captain of this ship?' I enquired, trying to speak in an innocent voice.

Something was undoubtedly going on that I could not understand and could only partially remember.

'He's the Professor, really,' she trilled and then put a hand over her mouth. 'I shouldn't have said that.'

I sat up on the bed.

'I need to speak to the captain again,' I stated.

'Do lie down,' soothed Miss Bell. 'I can help you to recover.'

'No,' I protested. 'I must speak to the man in charge.'

'Lie down,' she shouted and waved her hands.

I lay back down instantly. I could not disobey, something about Miss Bell forced me to comply.

'That's better,' she trilled, smiling widely. 'I really think that this is going to work just as I want it to.'

Chapter 23

I was convinced that she was no human girl. I gradually relaxed as the insect fairy, for surely that was what she was, gently massaged my legs. It was actually very pleasant. I would have felt completely at ease if I had not suspected that lurking beneath that beautiful exterior was a giant insect with disturbingly ugly features.

As I daydreamed I heard disembodied voices again. They undoubtedly emanated from the researchers in the laboratory.

'Diana, your main field is neurosciences and your doctorate was on the use of high Tesla magnetic resonance spectroscopy. Is that right?'

'You know that Rees. I've told you before.'

'How come you didn't study DNA?'

'I did but I'm not the expert on it that you are.'

'Makes sense. I'm not so au fait with the spectroscopy. What exactly does it do?'

'Magnetic resonance spectroscopy or MRS uses magnets and radio waves to study the range of molecules in the sample,' explained Dr. Diana Bones in a bored voice. 'I'm sure you know that.

'Not the details. I'm much better with nucleic acids.'

'I've been watching the sleepers and the specimens for the last hour, Rees. I want to know how you have got on with analysing the unusual bit on the DNA?'

'I was going to tell you, Diana. Don't be impatient.'

'Go on then, tell me.'

'It's at least two viruses.'

'Do you know what they are, Rees?'

'I know what they resemble.'

'What's that?'

'The larger virus is very like rabies and the smaller is a bacteriophage.'

'Rabies! So the male brain specimen carries rabies!'

'It's not exactly rabies, Di. It is just very similar. In fact I suspect the subject would be immune to actual rabies.'

'Any idea what it does?'

'None as yet but it is sure to be significant.'

'Could it explain why this specimen has survived the best?'

'Not entirely. There are also other changes in the subject's gene code.'

'Such as?'

'A blood dyscrasia.'

'Explain.'

'There are gene changes similar to haemophilia although this is not sex-linked.'

'So a genetic disorder that causes bleeding?'

'Something to do with haemoglobin production and the clotting mechanism, certainly. Maybe aplastic anaemia.'

'Fascinating. Would it mean that the person had specific requirements? Would they have needed transfusions or injections of clotting factors?'

'Maybe. I've never before seen exactly these changes.'

'And the female brain?'

'Interesting also. Just the bacteriophage.'

'Nothing else abnormal?'

'Not that I can find. What were your views on the morphology of the two successful human brain specimens?'

'Basically normal although the male brain is larger than the female and both contain more haematite than normal.'

'Significantly?'

'At the very upper limits of normal. Maybe the male brain is much as seven percent heavier than normal. But less frontal cortex, proportionately.'

'Really?'

'Yes... and the male specimen responded better after we blocked off part of the frontal lobes.'

'With incisions?'

'That's right. The part I am referring to might be referred to as the conscience but that is a really loose term.'

'The superego?'

'Again a vague term invented by Freud.'

'But the part of the brain that does a good part of the cognitive undertaking? The thinking person?'

'Without the frontal lobes a person is very disinhibited. We have found that the specimens last better if we disconnect the two sides of the brain by cutting the corpus callosum and make them disinhibited by creating incisions in the white matter of the frontal lobes. We can reconnect them using the liquid metal switches.'

'That's in addition to temporary disconnection and reconnection by the use of electro-magnetic pulses?'

'That's right, Rees, but why are you asking me all of this? I thought you knew this already.'

'I'm writing up my PhD thesis and I want to get it right. You've got yours already so it won't do you any harm if I include some of this stuff in my dissertation.'

'You'll have to acknowledge the rest of us.'

'Of course I will. Prof is my supervisor so he will insist that I acknowledge the source.'

'You'll get your name on all the papers anyway.'

'I'm more worried about my thesis at the moment. Do you think the work is good enough for a PhD?'

'Good enough? It's brilliant. This is Nobel Prize territory once we overcome the ethical committee problem.'

'Do you really believe that Professor Cruikshanks wants to use live human brains?'

'He hasn't mentioned it before. I think he only said it to please the ugly gnome.'

'I think he's a dwarf rather than gnome. I understand that gnomes are much smaller.'

'How big?'

'Just a few inches tall.'

'Golly, that is small.'

'Diana, just look at him lying there with the helmet on. He certainly is ugly. You're right about that.'

'Huge ears, shaggy beard, great big hooked nose. He's a right sight.'

'And that enormous battle-axe he carries. Frightening.'

'Miss Bell hardly looks human. More like a monstrous insect.'

'She looked OK when she was awake.'

'You men are all the same. It's an illusion. She's a fairy.'

'You don't think that she is the original Tinkerbell, do you?'

'And that he is the original Rumpelstiltskin? The stories are very old so it doesn't seem possible.'

'I've heard that they live for a very long time and that in the Faerie Realm time passes at a different rate.'

'They're taking their time in this poor man's fantasy world aren't they?'

Diana Bones examined the computer console.

'The professor will signal to me when he wants to come out. At the moment the Prof is having long discussions with Mr. Stiltskin on the bridge and Miss Bell is massaging the man's legs.'

'What is the name of the male brain specimen?'

'No idea. We weren't told his name. I call him Brainiac.'

'OK, so the fairy is massaging Brainiac's legs. I thought she was a bit too eager to enter his fantasy. What do you call the female brain?'

'I call her the Grey Lady.'

'Why has Professor Cruikshanks taken the Grey Lady off-line?'

'The specimen is deteriorating and he thought that it might last longer if we don't overuse it.'

'Is it working better now?'

'Worse. It was better when it was linked to Brainiac.'

'When the Prof comes out ask him if we can reconnect the Grey Lady.'

'Good idea...oh..there's the signal to pull them out.'

*

Suddenly the massaging of my legs stopped and Miss Tinker Bell disappeared.

My full awareness was now through the murky fluid of my specimen jar in the laboratory. Miss Tinker Bell was furious with Professor Cruikshanks.

'I was just developing a good rapport with the male brain specimen when you ripped me away from him,' she screamed. 'He's bound to suspect something is amiss if his masseuse just disappears mid-massage.'

'Sorry my dear,' replied Cruikshanks in an avuncular tone. 'Mr. Stiltskin and I had finished our discussion and I thought you would probably be getting bored.'

The ugly dwarf laughed in a disgustingly lewd manner and muttered something that I could not hear. Tinker Bell responded by slapping Stiltskin on the face.

The team all disappeared from the laboratory and I heard the words "tea and crumpets" being bandied around.

I was left in the semi-gloom of emergency lighting, staring out through the large Kilner jar at a world that I now knew I no longer inhabited. I was certain that all that remained of one Peter Chambers was a specimen in a glass bottle. For some reason this specimen was still thinking but I was under no illusions. I was dead. But then I had been dead before, of that I was sure.

Dead?

I do not want to be dead. I think therefore I am. Je pense, donc je suis. Cogito ergo sum.

I do not want to be dead!

*

'Just concentrate your vision on the pocket watch, your lordship, sir,' ordered Ivan, politely.

I stared at the handsome gold watch as it swung backwards and forwards like a pendulum at the end of the long golden chain.

'You are feeling sleepy, so sleepy, you will relax, relax, relax,' chanted Ivan. 'Your eyelids feel heavy, so heavy.'

The misshapen factotum's voice droned on and I did, indeed, feel sleepy and my eyelids drooped.

'By the count of five you will become fast asleep and you will then answer my questions,' the manservant's voice intoned. 'One, two, three, four...'

I did not hear number five.

'Who are you and what is your name?'

'I am the Prince of Wallachia or Count Dracula, posthumously known as Vlad the Impaler,' I replied like an automaton. 'Also known by many other names throughout history in my many resurrections as the living dead'

'What are you?'

'I am a vampire. The original vampire.'

'Name a few of your names through history.'

'John Appleshanks, Dr. Alexander Pedachenko, Count Andrey Luiskovo, Joseph Stalin, Peter Chambers.'

'What was your last reincarnation?'

'As Peter Chambers.'

'Where is he now.'

'Imprisoned in a bottle.'

'In a bottle?'

'More correctly speaking the brain of Peter Chambers is in a large glass jar in a laboratory.'

'Why have you not regenerated?'

'I am being kept partially alive in an unauthorised medical experiment.'

'And this is preventing your regeneration?'

'That would appear to be the case.'

'As Peter Chambers were you aware of your previous lives?'

'No. I decided to hide that history from my latest incarnation.'

'But you left information about your nature in some form?'

'That is correct. I left clues so that I could regenerate.'

'Tell me more about the clues.'

'A locket with written instructions and an inbuilt desire to be buried with a sachet of my own blood.'

'But somehow these have not yet worked?'

'My instructions to my executor have not been followed.'

'Who disobeyed your instructions?'

'My fiancée had definite instructions regarding type of coffin, sachet of blood etcetera.'

'But she sold your body for medical science?'

'Highly unlikely. I am certain that she has no idea that my brain is being used in an experiment. No. For some reason unknown to me she agreed that my body should be cremated and, with the best of intentions, has ignored my instructions.'

'Tell me more about the medical experimentation.'

I squirmed a little as I sat staring at the watch swinging back and forth, back and forth.

'It is most uncomfortable to talk about my own brain.'

'You must tell me about the medical experiments.'

'I am in a bottle and can see through the fluid and glass.'

'And what are the scientists doing?'

'Cutting into my brain, severing my nerve pathways and then

stimulating the neurons.'

'If they are keeping the brain alive they must be feeding it with oxygen and glucose, and removing waste products. Why has the blood not initiated your revival?'

'They are not using blood! They are not using blood!'

'On the count of three you will awake from your trance and remember everything we have talked about. One, two, three...'

I awoke with a start.

'I don't think that I'm in the best strategic position, Ivan.'

'That is an understatement, your lordship.'

'I do litotes better than hyperbole, Ivan. The outlook is grave.'

'Was that humour, sir?'

'My time here is limited before they drag me back using the brute force of electrical shocks and magnetic pulses.'

'Yes sir. We must make plans.'

'Indeed we must...and quickly.'

'We need to continue the hypnosis, 1,2,3,4,5.'

Chapter 24

'Long live the revolution!'
'The Tsar must die.'
'Kill the Royal Family.'
'Anastasia must go. Kill the bitch!'
'Bolsheviks for ever.'
Iosif Vissarionovich Dzhugashvili hints too much at my origin. Stalin sounds like a good name... it is the one I shall use.
I smiled with the insincere grin that many learnt who had been educated in the seminary. The harsh vision of the Russian Orthodox Church had entered my soul like barbs of steel. I no longer believed in a personal God .... except myself of course. I knew that I was different. I was a direct descendant from Vlad the Impaler, the original Count Dracula. Perhaps descendant is not the right word to use ... I was the reincarnated evil vampire and I intended to use the power vested in me via the revolution to rule with a rod of iron.
But first Lenin and Trotsky must die.
Within five years from now I shall be general secretary of the Communist Party and I shall rule it for decades. Then when I die I shall return and rule the world.
First I need to remove the real revolutionaries Vladimir Lenin and Leon Trotsky. That will take some time but I shall succeed.
'Long live the revolution.'
'The people must rule!'
'Workers Unite. We'll keep the red flag flying here.'
'Death to the Tsar.'
'Long live the workers' paradise.'
The fools. Little do they know..........

*

I expelled Trotsky from the party in 1927 but he kept writing and acting as a thorn in my side. He never understood why Communism is a disappointment. People are weak, they do not possess the right outlook, the right nature for pure communism to work. They are too selfish, too concerned about themselves, what they own, what they earn. But I have made the State work. Leon Trotsky is an idealist. My assassin will blunt his ideals.......

*

Many of my own people have to die to fight Adolf Hitler. He was in a pact with me but he never meant to keep to the agreement. That does not worry me .... I never intended honouring it either.

Hitler should have read about Napoleon. Lev Nikolaevich Tolstoi described Napoleon's failed invasion of Russia in his epic book War and Peace. As it was for Napoleon so shall be for Hitler. We shall destroy the Austrian. The Motherland will suffer but survive. I have become the Father of the USSR, the Union of Soviet Socialist Republics, and the suffering of the people is my suffering.

*

I am dying and few will mourn my passing. Tolstoy asked whether events create people or people create events. Was Napoleon inevitable? If the Corsican had not taken the lead would someone else have been pushed into the position he took and done the same things? If Hitler had not led his party would Rudolf Hess or Hermann Wilhelm Goering taken his place to the same inevitable war and defeat? If I had not taken control of the USSR would someone else have held the State together?

Many people think that I am a monster but I did what I had to do. I have done monstrous things but perhaps not as monstrous as my nature would incline me to.

I am tired of being feared but unloved. Thirty-one years leading the Party, Premier of the Soviet Union for twenty-nine of those years.

In my next reincarnation I shall try to be a normal person, loved and wooed, not feared and hated.

*

'So you tried to control your Id, your subconscious?'
'Yes Ivan. I hid my true nature from myself and that has led to this impasse.'
'Were you loved? Was it a success?'
'I believe that it was but not with my fiancée. I found true love by chance whilst I was a specimen in a jar.'
'How?'
'I met a young lady named Fiona and came to realise that she and I made a great team.'
'Where is she now?'
'In another jar, I suspect.'
'Then our plans should include her, your lordship!'
'If they can, Ivan, if they can.'
'If you are able to regenerate surely you will be able to assist her to do so too?'
'Maybe she will not want to live the lonely life of a vampire?'
'But then, sir, maybe she will, rather than die and be discarded as a piece of rotting tissue.'
'Put like that it doesn't sound such a bad option.'
'No sir.'
'So plans must be made.'
'I'm already busy doing that sir with the help of the other servants.'

'Well done Ivan.'

'Thank you sir.'

'I cannot remember anything that happens here in limbo when I am stimulated to undergo a dream sequence. Something about the experimentation wipes my memory.'

'No sir. That is the problem. I am hoping that a post-hypnotic command will assist. I have utilised a fairly commonly used word in your present environment. It will stimulate you to seek your hidden message.'

'I have to find that since I must reverse my own hypnotic command. It is imperative that I do that. Your own command cannot reverse mine.'

'That is correct, sir.'

'I have to go now.'

'Yes sir. Good luck.'

'The luck of the undead!'

*

'On this the XVII day of January 1606 it has pleased the Lord to take unto himself His servant John Appleshanks of Burnham'

Oh god, not again!

I was back in the coffin in Burnham. I looked at my body.... spindly and skinny. I had the old Appleshanks body back. I knew that. I also knew that I had forgotten some very important facts. I stared at the notice. I could remember being here before at least twice, if not more. There would be a woman asleep outside the door. I would have to avoid her. Then I would be in trouble with the militia and the local clergy.

I may or may not meet a young woman who would be accompanied by a skinny harridan and a greedy fat girl .

I would definitely meet an old blind man, the Winter of my

discontent.

There would be a huge tidal surge or Tsunami and I had to be away before it hit this part of the coast.

The clergyman was the clue. I was sure of that but exactly why I did not know.

Plan: avoid the sleeping woman, find the clergyman, kidnap him and determine why he has been persecuting me.

I crept out of the room and tiptoed round the sleeping woman. I was going to make for St. Andrews Church … if I wanted to find the local clergyman that was the place to look!

Out of the front door, down the rough path and into the church with the leaning tower, into the vestry and put on a black cassock over my funereal garb.

Then wait.

I sat on a hard three-legged stool in the vestry and examined my arms and legs again. They now looked like the appendages of Peter Chambers. As the blind man had once said I was gaining control of my morphic projection.

'The eleven o'clock service on Sunday will be attended by all the local families.'

It was the voice of the vicar talking to his curate as they walked towards the vestry where I was hiding. The vicar continued.

'I shall be going up to London to meet some colleagues. I shall leave you in charge of the experimentation.'

Experimentation?

That was a non sequitur. The word experimentation did not make sense in the early seventeenth century. Something was not quite right in the things the vicar was saying. Theodore Dean, I remembered his name. The Reverend Theodore Dean... that was it…. and he was very keen that I should give him a letter of introduction. I had no such thing to give him. What was he after?

'So you run along now and I will see you and Bones later.'

'OK, Professor,' replied the curate.

Professor? Professor!

This was a command. I had to find the hidden message. It was in the locket and the key was the green glass float but they were both in another century on board ship or perhaps in the USSR.

No. My thinking was flawed. The hidden message was initially here in Burnham so presumably would still be here. If this was all unreal and I was the subject of experimentation then the locket and float could be anywhere. They were probably in the upstairs room in the little cottage.

Do I need the clergyman?

Every other time I had let the man chase me. This time I would change things. Overpower him, take him back to the house and retrieve the message then find out what he had been doing to me and why.

No. It was too risky.

I now knew what I had to do. I had to retrieve the locket and the glass float. It was therefore imperative that I was not found.

The door swung open and the clergyman walked in preceded by the capering blind man Winter. I was hidden behind the door.

'You are behind the door, Peter Chambers. I know you are there so there is no point in hiding,' shouted the professor.

The professor walked into the vestry. He was wearing his white lab coat over the top of his clerical garb. Winter pointed out where I was hiding and laughed with his wheezing evil chuckle. Cruikshanks looked me up and down.

'The female specimen is failing, Chambers, but you continue to function. I need to know why,' said the clergyman/professor. 'We are running out of time and I need to be more direct. I have decided that it is pointless avoiding shocking your psyche since you are determined to do that to yourself.'

I stared at the man. I could now remember that this was Professor Cruikshanks and I had the distinct feeling that there was much more I should know.

'Why are your memories covering centuries, Chambers?' asked the professor. 'And why does your brain specimen continue to live despite all the insults we give it.'

I said not a word.

'Answer me or I will arrange for Rees and Bones to shock you into submission,' screamed the fake clergyman.

I still stared at the man speechless.

'Let me explain the situation,' said the professor. 'You are a specimen in a bottle kept alive by artificial blood and electrical stimulation.'

I knew this much already and continued to stare at the evil scientist.

'All this,' the man waved his hands expansively. 'All of it is in your imagination, fleshed out by the use of computers and some use of the fifth force, that which you would call magic.'

'So why did my mind decide to persecute me with tidal waves and chasing militia?' I broke my silence.

'At last you speak,' replied Professor Cruikshanks. 'And I cannot answer your question.'

'You can try!' I retorted.

'OK. Two experiments have done well. Yourself and Fiona Makepeace-Smythe. Other brain specimens have worked for only a day or two.'

'How does that relate to my peculiar worlds of the 17th, 19th, 20th and 21st centuries?' I demanded to know.

'That's just it. It doesn't,' answered the professor. 'Makepeace-Smythe and all the other brain specimens simply re-ran memories of their lifetimes. You seem to have a deep fantasy world that has supplanted your actual memory.'

The professor twisted something in his hands and I felt an excruciating shock run down from my head to the base of my spine.

'But enough of this chit chat. I believe that you know why you are different and I want you to tell me. Do so or the shocks will increase.'

The man is a monster!

I realised this with a profound feeling of shock. I was in the complete control of a psychopathic madman.

*

I had been lying down on the sofa in the kitchen-diner of my Clifton flat. I awoke with a start. The dreams had been really bad, true nightmares from which I had been unable to wake myself. Horror piled upon gothic horror but at last I had woken up. Residual thoughts of operations, coffins and vampires filled my mind.

I looked at my watch. Gawd, I was running late! It was almost six in the afternoon and the lads from the rugby club would be arriving at eight. I had to clean up the flat, get the curry cooking, peel some veggies and then tidy myself up. The fiancée hoped to arrive around eight but would not be able to help before then as she was working all day. She was a doctor, a paediatric surgical trainee registrar at the local children's hospital, and had been drafted in for an extra shift due to the absence of a colleague. Arrival at eight could, in fact, be optimistic since it depended on a number of extraneous factors... the paediatrician who was returning to relieve her would be arriving in Temple Meads by train and we all knew how unreliable the rail service could be!

I set to work, pushing my two bitches, Gemma and Lizzie, off the bed. First things first. The labradoodle and the greyhound had been in all afternoon whilst I was sleeping my restless dream-plagued sleep and as soon as I had the curry on the go I would have to take them out for a very quick walk on the Downs.

Chapter 25

I walked the dogs down the short flight of stairs that wound down past the back of the surgery. The night was drawing in already and the sky was heavily overcast. In the back garden my canine companions growled and sniffed at imaginary foes. As I passed the lone tree in the garden the dogs pulled away from the shadows which gave me a start. They were usually so prepared to tackle anything. For a fleeting moment the horrors of my nightmares returned unbidden to my mind but it must have been a flight of fancy affecting the animals. I opened the little gate at the end of the garden and this let me out onto a narrow alleyway. As I closed this portal I fancied I heard a scream from the dental surgery where a light was still burning away and the drill was still whining. The scream was not repeated and I decided it was my overwrought imagination.

The alleyway led out onto the Whiteladies Road and I turned up away from the small Sainsbury's where I had purchased most of the provisions for the party. I was still feeling dissociated from my surroundings and the passing cars sounded too loud, the lights of the shops were excessively garish and the pedestrians were giving me strange looks. I glanced down at my clothes. They all looked normal. I had not gone out without my pants or wearing odd shoes...no particular fashion faux pas. I pulled my jacket around my body and shivered just a little. There was something peculiar in the air, surely that woman had stared at me most oddly and that cat had the most strange markings?

The big issue man smiled at me as I passed but he was not the usual person that I bought the magazine from and the gap toothed smile of the new fellow was not encouraging. I hurried on with the dogs straining at the lead.

A new clothes shop on my left had a display of mannequins in the window and I stopped for a moment to look at a jacket on one of them. To my horror the dummy moved and opened the jacket. My heart had stopped for a moment but I then realised that this was animatronics like Disneyland.... just a man-shaped robot for displaying the clothes. Unfortunately it was far enough into planet weird to be off-putting and in my present state of residual anxiety this was not what I wanted to see. I hurried away from the display and as I went I could not help but have the distinct impression that all of the dummies turned to watch me, although I knew that this had to be nonsense.

I passed several charity shops, an estate agents and and an excellent stationers then reached the Downs. I let the dogs go loose and stood on one leg wondering whether to have a cigarette. I had a packet in my pocket but had given up smoking a week before. So far I had managed to resist the urge but perversely keeping a packet handy made me feel that I could smoke if I wished to and this had been a comfort. Alternatively I could use an e-cigarette although I was not convinced that this was the answer since the addiction to nicotine would still be there and the products had not been proven to be safe. The dogs scurried into the undergrowth and I had almost decided I would indeed have a cigarette when they returned yelping in fear with their tails between their legs. This was unprecedented as I usually had to shout to get them to come back to me. Despite my best efforts I could not persuade the dogs to continue walking in the greenery and I had to put them back on the leads. Truth to tell, I was just a little spooked by their performance and thought that it was better if I got away from the dark trees and tangled undergrowth. They then dragged me back down the hill towards the dental surgery and my little flat above it..

The dogs yelped again as we passed the shop with the android display but I ignored the movement... if they wanted to use such frightening models I would not buy their jacket...simple as that!

Back into the garden and a lone light flickered like a flame in the dental surgery but now no noise emanated. The dogs whined cravenly as we passed the shadows behind the tree but I continued walking and we climbed the stairs.

Mysteriously the internal door to the flat was open. I was convinced that I had left the door locked but perhaps my fiancée had arrived back early. With that thought in my mind I walked boldly into the main room.

Three of my rugby pals were already there sitting round the table, drinking my beer.

'We let ourselves in, Pete, old boy,' remarked a particularly large guy named Dave.

I did not know Dave too well. He had only joined the club at the beginning of the season and I thought he was just a little too cocky but he was one of the crowd so I had invited him.

'Arrived early then?' I enquired.

'Not really,' replied Dave, looking at his watch. 'It's already half past eight.'

I looked at my watch. He was right.. it read 20:31.

Where had the time gone? I was convinced that I had only been out for ten or fifteen minutes.

'The curry?'

'We took it all off the gas,' answered Wankers, the guy whose real name was Wayne but who had received the nickname after telling us that his new yacht had a mooring on two anchors. 'Would you like me to serve up?'

I nodded acceptance of the idea. Kat, my fiancée, had not arrived home and I felt unusually weary.

George, the third of my rugby compatriots, looked at me with some anxiety but I ignored his glance and took off my coat. Throwing the garment onto the sofa I sat down at the table where the others were already seated. Wankers came back with four steaming bowls of rice and curry, George opened a bottle of wine and we started to eat.

'This is a great place,' remarked Dave.

'It's OK,' I replied noncommittally.

'Flat in Clifton, all the mod cons, fabulous view,' added the latest recruit to our team. 'Hard to beat.'

'He hasn't just got one flat,' interjected Wankers. 'He owns the whole building including the flat above and the surgery below.'

'Really?' questioned Dave. 'Must be worth a bob or two?'

I gave no response, simply wishing that Wankers had kept his mouth shut.

'Not just this building but several others,' continued Wankers. 'Told me that he was putting money into property rather than boats. That's right, isn't it Pete?'

I nodded. It was public knowledge so it was not worth denying it.

'How do you do it, mate?' asked Dave interrogatively.

'Do what?' I was somewhat irritated.

'Success,' replied Dave with a sweep of his hand taking in the surroundings. 'There must be a secret to your success. After all, you are only a school teacher and they don't earn much.'

'The pay's not too bad and the income is constant,' I answered.

'Not so good that you could buy several properties,' countered the self-confessed property expert.

'There's no secret,' I answered. 'Just hard work and an eye for a bargain.'

'There's more to it than that,' remarked Dave. 'What is the secret of your success?'

'Leave it,' interposed Wankers. 'I should not have said anything about Pete's property. It was out of order.'

'I still want to know his secret,' repeated Dave sullenly but Wankers stare forced him to shut up.

We finished our bowlfuls and the wine in silence. I opened

some bottles of lager.

'There's a bit more curry in the pan,' stated Wankers. 'I'll give everyone some seconds.'

'I hope you left some for Kat?' I remarked as he dolloped the food on our plates. 'She'll be hungry when she gets off her shift.'

'Forgot to tell you, mate,' stated Dave, his sullen look vanishing. 'She can't make it.'

'What?' I cried. 'Not at all?'

'Seems that the bloke who was supposed to relieve her is stuck in Reading,' he added.

'How do you know this?' I asked.

'Picked up your phone when it rang,' mumbled Dave, stuffing great fork-loads of curry and rice into his already full mouth.

'So she's not off until tomorrow?' I queried.

'That's about it,' agreed Dave. Then he grinned. 'Unless what really happened is that she gone off with her consultant on a tryst.'

I stared daggers at the rugby prop.

'No need to look at me like that,' Dave tried to look all innocent. 'I'm only relaying what I heard on the grapevine.'

'People have told you that my fiancée is having an affair with her boss?' I was incredulous. How could he have heard such a thing?

'Yeah,' he swallowed a lump of meat noisily. 'That's right. Duncan told me.'

It suddenly became believable. Duncan was another rugby player and another trainee registrar. He moved in the same circles as my Kat and he would indeed know what was going on. All my previous fears about surgery, death and the undead suddenly became so much mundane moonshine. This was real. This was shattering. I felt a hollow sensation of pain in my belly.

'Thought you probably knew,' added Dave. 'Sorry to be the bearer of bad news.'

I stared at him again. He did not look the slightest bit sorry...in fact he seemed to be relishing my discomfort.

'You're not really her type,' he continued.

'How would you know?' I blurted out.

'Kat?' he replied. 'How would I know Kat? We all know Kat, she's been around a bit.'

I stood up. Adrenaline was surging through my body and I wanted to hit the man but as I stood a weariness struck my body as if all the blood was draining to my feet. I sat down again, aware of the fact that if I did not do so I would probably faint.

'You don't look at all well,' stated Wankers, leaning over the table to look at me more closely.

'I'm OK,' I denied what he had said, brushing him away from me.

'No you are not,' he insisted. 'You should lie down. You look as if you are about to faint.'

He came round the table and took my arm.

'Come on old buddy,' he demanded. 'We'll get you onto the sofa. You've had a bit of a shock.'

I still tried to push him off me but found myself guided over to the settee....a long, modern, grey leather affair on which I often lounged or even lay out flat to watch my large flatscreen TV.

I lay down now, still protesting that I was fine.

'We need to get your feet up a bit,' Wankers was the only one of the three who appeared to be practical at all.

He obtained a cushion from the adjacent armchair and lifted my legs. In doing so my trouser leg rode up a little.

'Hello!' exclaimed Wankers in surprise. 'What have we got here?'

'I don't know,' I replied thickly. 'I can't feel anything. Maybe just a very slight itch.'

'There's a tick on your left calf,' stated Wankers. 'It's a mighty big one.'

A tick? A parasitic arachnid? I had never been troubled by one before.

I struggled up into a sitting position and stared at the creature. Its body was over two centimetres in diameter and appeared to be swelling as I looked. It had little legs that were waving energetically and its head was burrowed deeply into my skin.

'This little critter will be making you feel faint,' announced Wankers.

'I'll pull it out,' I replied.

'No. Don't do that. It might regurgitate straight into your blood vessel and then you will have a really nasty reaction,' countered Wankers.

'What should I do then?' I wailed. 'I can't go round with that thing hanging off me.'

'Listen to the big boy crying!' laughed Dave. 'A little tick and he's wailing away.'

'Shut up!' ordered Wankers. 'These things are no laughing matter.'

Dave clammed up but Wankers comment made me feel just a little scared. What could a tiny spider-like bloodsucker do to me that Wankers was wary about?

'I think I have a tick-removal device on my penknife,' said George hesitantly. 'I've never used it.'

'I've used the devices before,' said Wankers. 'If you get the penknife I'll have a go at Pete's leg.'

'Whoa there!' I exclaimed. 'Shouldn't we go down to casualty and get them to remove this bloodsucker?'

'Theoretically correct but practically only one out of ten,' replied Wankers, looking carefully at the Swiss Army knife that George had retrieved from his pocket. 'We would have to wait for four hours before anybody sees you and how are you going to get there. We're all pissed!'

'We could call an ambulance,' I suggested.

'Do you think they would come if we told them that you had been bitten by a tick?' Wankers ridiculed the idea.

'You better have a go with the penknife,' I reluctantly agreed.

Wankers approached my leg and slid out a wire loop that looked surprisingly like the needle threader that Kat occasionally used when forced to do some sewing of her favourite clothes.

At least it is not a sharp blade, I thought as the loop slipped over the swelling bulbous body of the bloodsucker.

'This bit won't hurt,' said Wankers as he tightened the loop.

He was wrong. I screamed with agony as Wankers tightened and twisted. With a foul sucking sound the tick relinquished its hold on my skin and came out intact. By this time the body had swollen to gargantuan proportions, easily the width of my calf. The monster was still waving its little legs and I stared at the face of the arachnid.

Bizarrely I recognised the features. It was the blind man Winter from my worst nightmares.

I looked again at my rugby pals. Dave was undoubtedly Professor Cruikshanks, George had changed sex and was now Dr. Diana Bones and Wankers was the Chinese researcher, Peter Rees Chin. As my consciousness faded I perversely thought that Dave's truculent and sullen indignation was explained…the professor did not like taking instructions from his most junior researcher!

*

The scenario shifted.

Drip-splat, drip-splat. Skaaa - shkeeee, skaaa - shkeeee, skaaa - shkeeee.

I was in the operating theatre and I was on my own with the anaesthetist. But when I looked closely at the gasman I realised that he was the professor.

'I'm convinced that you know why you are different. I can tell it in your eyes, Chambers.'

'How did you change my reality?' I gasped, fighting to speak against the movement of the breathing machine. 'And how come I can speak? I couldn't move every time this happened before.'

'I signalled my researchers,' replied the anaesthetist-professor. 'And this is only part of your memory....look around you.'

I did so. There was a bare room. No operating gear, no surgeon, no doors and no windows. Not quite bare for in the corner of the room, almost out of sight, huddled Winter, whimpering slightly. He was constrained by iron bands on his wrists and ankles, binding him in an unnatural position. He had clearly thought that he would be rewarded for leading the professor to me but his reward was not to his liking.

'This is where the fifth force, magic, comes in handy,' chuckled the villainous doctor. 'Now will you tell me the answer or must I bring in the surgeon and start the operation all over again?'

I stared at him imploringly but he simply continued.

'You should have seen your face when we were in your flat. You really thought that you had woken up from your nightmares!'

'But I hadn't?'

'Of course not. You should have realised by now that there is no real awakening from your evil dreams. You're in a bottle, Chambers.'

'So what makes you think that you can hurt me any more?' I asked. 'If I am already in a bottle that's the worst of it.'

'No, no. That's not so,' cried the monstrous anaesthetist, the evil professor. 'You know the surgery hurts and it will start again. In fact you know it will be excruciating pain because that is how you died. So tell me why you are different. Answer me!'

He pushed a small lever and another electric shock ran through my body.

'OK, OK,' I gasped. 'I believe I do know the answer but it is not simple. Take me back to the Church.'

In a blink of an eye we were back in the vestry. The professor was still clad in his white lab coat over the clerical black costume.

Winter was now in the corner of the vestry but still bound in iron manacles and chains.

'So what is the answer,' Cruikshanks demanded.

'We need to return to the cottage and search for a locket,' I replied.

'No need to do that,' said the professor. 'We can find the memory on the computer and stimulate it in your mind.'

'How will that help?' I queried.

'The locket will simply appear in your hand,' answered Cruikshanks.

'I need something else as well,' I added. 'There was a green glass float.'

'Yes,' agreed the professor. 'I believe we have that catalogued also.'

He appeared to be staring into middle distance but was presumably looking at a computer screen.

'There it is... green glass orb.'

He wriggled his fingers around and immediately in one hand I was holding the locket and in the other the orb.

'If you are attempting to trick me I will make you suffer,' muttered the mad scientist.

'There is no point killing me when I'm already dead,' I replied. 'And I am your best experiment so far.'

'That is true but you have "died" several times over and simply continued so I will have no compunction over using maximum force,' grunted the scientist.

'Let me see if this does provide the answer before you attack me further,' I countered as calmly as possible.

I took the locket and opened it. I could remember looking inside the thing before but this time I intended placing the glass orb over the locket.

The light was dim in the vestry and I could see very little. The professor realised this and, muttering a few words, he waved his hands around. A small electric spotlight appeared hovering over the locket.

'There are some words,' cried the professor, grabbing the locket from me. 'Let me read them first.'

Staring at the small ornamental case the scientist was puzzled.

'They are written in capitals in a circle and I shall read them out, starting from the raised star. EVIL WON A LU CARD.'

He thrust the locket back into my hands.

'That is meaningless,' he shouted and started to adjust his communication device.

Chapter 26

'Wait,' I cried in reply. 'You read it clockwise. If you read it anti-clockwise it obviously reads Dracula Now Live.'

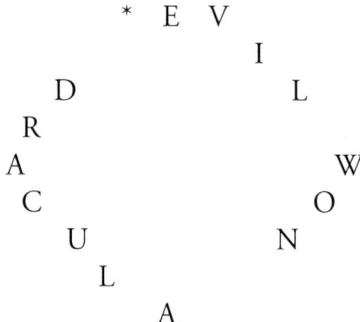

'That explains nothing,' screamed the professor but I was not really listening. Cosmic changes had occurred in my awareness. Winter had disappeared, the vestry room was insubstantial and I could see Ivan the Terrible hovering over my body whilst I was simultaneously lying in a coffin, standing in the vestry and staring out from the glass bottle in the laboratory.

'Capture this one, Ivan,' I commanded.

'Certainly sir,' replied the general factotum.

In a further coffin I could now see the professor lying stretched out cold and lifeless. His thin ghost-like body also stood in the vestry.

'What have you done?' screamed the ghost. 'Why do I feel dead?'

'I have captured you in the same manner as the unfortunate

researcher was detained,' I replied coldly. 'I believe her name was Maureen?'

The professor head nodded in reply, both in the coffin and in the vestry.

'But now it is my turn to be the mad psychopath and your turn to answer questions,' I continued. 'I need to know exactly why you are conducting these experiments. What the dwarf and fairy really want. Where you obtained all the specimens and, perhaps most important to myself, how you can help Fiona Makepeace-Smythe and myself escape from the trap you have put us in.'

Again the professor nodded. There was little else he could do for now I saw that the chains and manacles he had used on Winter were comprehensively binding him and he was tightly gagged.

'Ivan,' I said calmly. 'We need to let the professor speak.'

'Sorry, your Lordship,' replied the faithful servant.

The gags fell off the professor who slumped to the floor in the vestry but remained still in the coffin.

'So I have many questions and you will have to provide many answers.'

'I will, I will,' cried the mad scientist.

'So first questions first. What is the purpose of these experiments?'

'To build an army for Rumpelstiltskin,' cried the professor.

'An army for mining or for fighting?' I asked.

'Fighting. Taking over the world.'

'And Tinkerbell... what is her role and her involvement in this?'

'She has provided invaluable control of the fifth force, magic,' replied the mad scientist.

'And why is she helping you?'

'She just wants a man she can control,' replied Cruikshanks.

'You have been very helpful,' I said. 'But now tell me where you obtained the specimens.'

'Most of them came from the hospital straight after the flood,' replied the scientist. 'You were one of the unfortunates whose operation was halted due to the tsunami.'

'And were they all dead?'

'None of them were actually dead but they all looked dead due to the zombie drug tetrodotoxin.'

'So it was murder?'

'Technically. But all of the specimens were nearly dead. Or might have been.'

'It was murder.'

'Look, I didn't ask questions. Please let me go. I don't want to have locked-in syndrome.'

'Nobody would,' I replied. 'And nobody would like their living brain confined to a glass jar with somebody giving it electric shocks.'

'I did it for medical science.'

'You did it for money and power,' I growled. 'Was Fiona Makepeace-Smythe a victim of the floods when her brain was harvested?'

'I don't know,' replied the murderous experimenter. 'She came via a different route.'

'Ah ha!,' I cried. 'And what would that have been?'

'She was brought to us in coma by the dwarf,' replied Cruishanks. 'Now will you let me go?'

'It is not as simple as that,' I replied. 'I need further information and then I will give you some instructions.'

'I'll help you but let me go!' pleaded the professor.

'Who are Winter, Susan and Maud?' I asked.

'You haven't discovered that?' sneered the professor.

'Careful how you answer,' I replied and the scientist saw the anger in my face.

'Winter is your Id and Susan is Fiona's Id,' replied the professor, clearly wishing that he had not had to impart the information.

'That mad blind man is my subconscious, my urge, the seat of my desires?'

'Yes,' he answered. 'Amusing isn't it?'

I ignored this and continued the questioning.

'And Maud?'

'Maud is Fiona's superego,' replied the scientist. 'Although strictly speaking these terms are not exact.'

'So you split our brains into pieces and from the pieces cobbled together different aspects of our personalities.'

'Yes,' agreed the mad scientist. 'You could put it like that.'

'And what about my superego?' I asked. 'Do I not have a conscience?'

'You appear to function better without one,' answered Cruikshanks.

'So I did have one?'

'Yes... and you metaphysically buried her in the Forest of Dean.'

'The Maud I met in the old man Winter's cottage. But she was already dead!'

'Your conscience was already feeble and we excised it,' replied the scientist.

I stood for a while looking at the bound wraith of the professor, overlaid, as it was by the image of his body lying in a tomb deep in my castle. I considered the loss of my superego and decided I could do without it until I had fully regenerated. Winter had presumably been reabsorbed into my psyche when I had read the instructions in the locket. I could certainly access his memories as well as my own and I intended sitting down and studying this with the help of my hypnotist, the loyal Ivan.

'I need to know more about your researchers,' I finally said, after a long pause. 'There are two I can see busy in the laboratory, unaware as yet of your plight.'

'Yes. Dr. Diana Bones and Peter Rees Chin.'

'Tell me their exact roles, please.'

'Dr Diana Bones is my post doctoral researcher and Rees Chin is a PhD student. They cannot help you in any way.'

'Really,' I replied. 'Very interesting. I did not ask whether they could help.'

'They cannot,' screamed the wrathful wraith of the professor. 'Only I can help and I can only do that if you let me free.'

'I do not believe you,' I countered. 'You see I have been observing the activity in the laboratory for some time and the pair seem quite capable of running the entire show.'

'Not true,' answered the mad scientist. 'I am indispensable.'

'You'll be telling me next that you are also invincible,' I smiled wryly. 'They can help me and you will tell them to do so. Firstly I need to speak to Fiona.'

'She is offline.'

'Put her back online!' I demanded.

The professor did not reply.

'Ivan!' I cried. 'The professor should be taken entirely into limbo.'

'No, stop!' cried the mad scientist. 'I'm sure that they can help.'

'Go ahead,' I said quietly. 'But I need to know exactly what you are telling the researchers.'

The professor nodded.

'I will. But I need my hands to be free.'

I signalled for Ivan to free the professor's hands. He immediately started to push buttons on his communication device. The researchers looked worried and responded by tapping commands into the computer. They became more alarmed and pressed a few more buttons. They then tried to take the helmet off the professor's head and the electrodes away from his body but every time they did so alarm bells rang from the bio-monitors.

'Stop, stop!' cried the professor into his communicator. 'That is not working.'

'You tried to double-cross me, I presume?' I lifted my eyebrows in a questioning manner. 'If you do that again it will harm you irrevocably.'

'I'll do what you say,' cried the professor. 'But let me back into the real world.'

'Welcome to my world,' I smiled. 'This is as real as it gets, right now. But you will help me.'

'I will, I will,' cried the evil creature.

I knew that I had to persuade the man that helping me was in his best interests.

'Time is running out for all of us,' I declared. 'So get Fiona back online straight away and it will help you too.'

The man thumbed some buttons and Chin's voice came over the device.

'The female specimen is offline as you ordered, professor.'

'Patch into her memory sequence immediately,' replied the scientist.

'OK. I will do as you say. Any particular sequence?'

'Some recent ones after the two experiments were separated,' suggested Cruikshanks.

'Wilco!' replied Chin and I could see through the cloudy perception provided via the eyes in the jar that the Chinese man was pushing buttons furiously. Abruptly the professor and myself were standing in a school gymnasium. The dwarf, the evil Mister Rumple Stiltskin, was acting as the gym master. Fiona was aged about fifteen and was running around with all the other girls. When she caught my eye she obviously recognised me and gave me a big welcoming smile. The dwarf turned round and saw us standing by the door and immediately waved us away in considerable annoyance.

We instantly returned to the vestry of the church in Burnham.

'What was the dwarf doing there?' I asked the professor.

'He is obviously the gym master,' replied the mad scientist.

'But he can't have been Fiona's teacher,' I answered. 'It's impossible.'

'No, but he can take part in the re-creation of the event just as the other researchers have done with you,' answered Cruikshanks.

'But why is he here at all?' I queried. 'I thought that he had only been to the laboratory for the first time earlier today.'

'You saw that, did you?' asked the professor.

'Indeed.'

'It was for the benefit of Miss Bell,' continued the scientist. 'She had not been in the laboratory when the specimens were active and experimentation was underway. Stiltskin has been here often.'

'I bet he has,' I replied grimly.

'He has taken particular interest in Fiona's development throughout the project,' answered the professor, speaking with an intermittent sniff as if my suspicions were completely beneath him and had generated some kind of strange and nasty smell.

'I wish to go back and speak to Fiona in one of her later sequences,' I demanded. 'I need to do that right now.'

'A sequence after you two were parted?' leered the scientist.

'Yes, that's right,' I agreed. 'Something more recent.'

The professor talked into his communication device and we were instantly in a small hovel, not dissimilar to Winter's cottage in the Forest of Dean.

Fiona was sat on a hard round-topped wooden stool stoking a poor wood fire. She was dressed in ragged clothes and was considerably thinner than when I had seen her last but she looked beautiful, truly stunning. She also looked just a little ill.

'Hello Buttons,' she said as I entered the room. 'Who is that with you? Is it Madam Twankey?'

I turned and looked at Cruikshanks. He was dressed in pantomime dame clothes..... billowing brightly-coloured dress, a blonde wig and a wild hat with sticks of rhubarb poking out of it, blue stockings and huge clumpy shoes.

'Yes. He's Madam Twankey,' I replied.

The professor made a noise of annoyance and in the limbo I could hear laughter from Ivan the Terrible... presumably he had some input on the professor's clothing.

'I'm pleased to see you, Buttons, but I do feel down,' said Cinderella, for that was clearly the role that Fiona had taken.

'What has upset you Cinders?' I asked.

I was not surprised by the answer.

'The Palace is having a ball,' replied Cinders. 'And all the ladies in the realm have been invited.'

'Then you should be pleased and go to the party,' I answered, fitting in with the sequence.

'I can't because I have no clothes to wear, only these rags,' cried Cinders with a sob. 'And my step-sisters won't let me go.'

'Of course you can't go,' uttered a hoarse voice. I could not initially work out where it was coming from.

'She's behind you,' said Madam Twankey.

I spun round and saw Maud climbing down the rough wooden staircase. She was thinner than ever and was dressed in a very tightly fitting tubular dress which accentuated the fact that she had no breast development. It was not becoming.

'You cannot go to the ball because you are a sinner,' continued Maud in a haughty manner. 'You are lazy, work-shy and no use to anyone.'

'But I try so hard,' cried my Fiona, the Cinderella.

'Trying is no use, you have to succeed,' sniffed Maud.

'And you're ugly,' came a laughing voice. 'Don't want to spoil the party by having ugly girls around the place.'

Susan came down the stairs like a barrel on legs, rolling from side to side. She was larger than ever, fat hanging down from all parts of her obese body and limbs. She had several hairy chins and her clothing was grotesque, a bright pink sheet wrapped round her body and a green turban on her head.

'Please let me go to the ball!' pleaded Cinders.

'No!' cried the ugly sisters, speaking in unison. They ignored Cruikshanks and myself and swung out of the room and off into a waiting Hansom cab.

I hurried over to Cinderella.

'You are not really Cinderella,' I said urgently. 'You are Fiona Makepeace-Smythe.'

'I know that is what I am called,' replied the ragged female urchin. 'And I know that you are Peter Chambers..... and yet I am Cinderella and cannot be anything else and you are Buttons.'

'We are not really here in a hovel of a cottage,' I added. 'None of this is real.'

'No,' replied Fiona in a depressed voice. 'We are not here but it is all that is left to me.'

'You realise that we have been used in experimentation?' I asked.

'Yes I know that Buttons but do you know when the Fairy Godmother will arrive.'

'There is no Fairy Godmother, Fiona, and you must concentrate,' I implored her.

'It's no good Peter,' she replied. 'I'm finished. I'm not even in the jar any more.'

'So you know that we had our brains put into jars and operated upon.'

'Of course, Peter. That much became obvious. But I am not in the jar.'

'You must be, Fiona, or you could not be speaking to me.'

'No Buttons. I cannot go to the ball,' said the girl. 'This is just one of my memories, reconstructed on the computer. I watched as they poured the liquid away and threw out both the specimen and the jar. Now I just have these repeating sequences left to me stored on the computer.'

'What if I found you?' I asked. 'Would you be prepared to accept a life as one of the undead?'

'Would you take me to the ball?' asked Cinderella.

'I will try,' I answered.

'Oh Buttons,' cried the computer generated sequence. 'I do

love you Buttons but I have nothing to wear only these rags.'

Cinderella turned back to stoking the fire. When I stirred slightly she swivelled round and saw us standing by the door.

'Hello Buttons,' she said. 'Who is that with you? Is it Madam Twankey?'

Chapter 27

We were back in the vestry.

'What the bloody hell have you done to her?' I asked.

'The specimen started to deteriorate,' said the professor. 'It is a miracle that it lasted as long as it did.'

'But what have you done with the specimen?'

'We have thrown it out.'

'Why?' I asked, very angry indeed.

If there was no specimen I could not offer Fiona the option I was considering. It now seemed likely that I could force the professor to provide that which I required for my own reincarnation but without Fiona's physical remains I could not do the same for her.

'As I said,' replied the professor. 'It had begun to deteriorate. It was beginning to smell.'

She smells a bit but she has got a heart of gold came unbidden as a half-remembered phrase to my undead mind.

'Then I will have to find her,' I replied.

'The bottle will have been thrown out for recycling or dumped in a tip,' snapped back the professor. 'You'll never find it in a month of Sundays!'

'And the contents?'

'We don't wash out the jars. They go to our clinical waste disposal agent intact.'

'Don't they object when they see bits of brain in a jar?'

'They're used to it. Anyway the jar was dirty and obscured so the mushy contents were no longer all that visible.'

I stretched my arms and cracked my joints. I was now very angry indeed. To have found true love of all places in a bottle and then to have it ripped away from me was cruelty

I, Count Dracula, Drakula, Dragwlya, Vlad Ţepeș, Vlad the Impaler, the evil 15th-century Prince of Wallachia had lived in an undead state through nearly six centuries, longing to find love.... and I had found it only to have it snatched away from me! I let out a wail of anguish.

'Can I help, sir?' asked Ivan the Terrible, hearing my wail from his place within my limbo castle.

I explained the situation.

'May I suggest that you reincorporate as soon as possible and chase the bottle, sir,' replied the factotum.

'Yes,' I answered. 'It is the only thing to be done but rest assured the perpetrators of this crime will have to suffer.'

'Yes sir,' replied Ivan. 'We shall see to that, won't we, sir?'

I turned to the wraith of the professor who had a cold smile on his psychopathic face. He wiped the smile from his visage when he saw me looking but a cruel glint persisted in his eyes.

'Is there something amusing you?' I asked.

'There is,' replied the scientist.

'And what is it?' I asked pedantically.

'Prince Charming usually looks for Cinderella with a glass slipper which he wants to fill with her foot.'

'Yes?'

'And you will be going on foot looking for her in a glass jar which has slipped into a landfill.'

The professor let out a long maniacal laugh.

'I don't find that even vaguely amusing,' I replied. 'Now when you took my body there will have been several packets of my cross-matched blood with it?'

'That is true. We did not know why you needed them,' answered the professor, sobering up a little.

'They were not, in fact, just cross-matched. They were my own blood, kept for the contingency of my body ceasing to function.'

'Your death?'

'Yes, my death. The instruction was that they should then be left in the coffin on top of my body. The envelope of the packets would then bio-degrade and the contents would spread over me, leading to my reincorporation.'

'That is completely impossible!' exclaimed the scientist. 'There is no way that a packet of blood could reinvigorate a lifeless corpse!'

'You have not been reading the vampire legends,' I countered. 'That is what always happens. It is how I return. It is why I am the immortal undead.'

'I still say it cannot happen,' sneered the professor. 'It is a delusion on your part.'

'So your captivity here and in limbo is all a delusion?'

'It is part of your memory re-inaction... it is your imagination fleshing out impossible deeds with the help of a computer and a little bit of the fifth force.'

'Oh dear,' I replied. 'Where have your scientific principles gone?'

'What do you mean?' demanded the wraith of Cruikshanks. 'I adhere firmly to scientific philosophy. What you have described is simply mumbo-jumbo nonsense. No scientific theory would permit such an idea.'

'You should only stick to your theories until such time as they are proven to be wrong,' I parried. 'Once a theory is proven to be wrong it should be altered or discarded.'

'You have proven nothing I believe in to be wrong!' retorted the scientist.

'I have no further time for your refutations and contradictions,' I answered. 'Your argument only leads me to believe that you have kept the blood. Presumably you thought it was of interest?'

'It is true that I have kept one sachet,' murmured the scientist. 'But how could it possibly work?'

'My DNA is unusual. Your researcher Chin discovered that but you did not stop to listen to him.'

The scientist nodded and I continued.

'It includes a rabies-like virus and a bacteriophage, some haematitie for magic manipulation and...'

'So what?' interrupted Criuikshanks.

'.....And genes for some very powerful stem cells,' I continued, ignoring the interruption. 'The blood is packed full with stem cells that regenerate my body and mind when they come into contact with my remains.'

'That's preposterous,' opposed the professor. 'Stem cells couldn't retain your memories, your phenotype, your whole being.'

'They don't have to,' I replied. 'That is provided by the version of myself that is stored in limbo. That is where the manipulation of magic comes into the game.'

'So even if you did have the remains of Cinderella, your Fiona, you would not be able to regenerate her as you do not have her stem cells and her image in limbo!' exclaimed the professor triumphantly. 'So I will have triumphed in the end.'

'Only if your aim was to defeat me, which it certainly wasn't initially,' I replied.

'Well it is now,' answered the psychopathic scientist.

'You are still wrong, professor,' I countered. 'If I find her remains my stem cells can configure themselves to her brain cells, reconstruct her body and her mind.'

'But not her completely!' laughed the professor. 'You'd have a mindless hulk.'

'She is presently somewhere in limbo,' I replied. 'And given that she has lasted this long I suspect that she is near my castle.'

'You'll never find her!' exclaimed the spiteful madman.

I looked into the limbo world and could see Ivan the Terrible carrying a body down to the basement towards a waiting coffin.

'It looks as if Ivan has already done just that,' I replied. 'So I need to proceed with my own regeneration.'

'How do you intend doing that?' asked the professor. 'Given

that your brain is presently in a bottle.'

'This is where you can help me,' I replied. 'You shall tell your researchers to retrieve the sachet of my blood from the freezer and empty exactly half of it into the bottle containing my brain.'

'Why should I agree to that?' queried the professor. 'What would I get out of the transaction?'

'I will release you from limbo with your mind almost intact.'

'Almost? Almost!'

'Well now professor, you have been a naughty boy,' I replied. 'Killing people and putting them into bottles is a serious crime. You are a psychopathic mass murderer.'

'It was in the interest of medical science.'

'All in a good cause, all for the betterment of humankind? I've been there before. Heard all of the arguments.'

'You can talk, you bloody hypocrite!' screamed the professor. 'If you are to be believed you are the reincarnation of Vlad the Impaler. The Impaler!'

'True,' I nodded. 'That is the case.'

'Well, Mister Dracula, in case you didn't realise it you are the biggest, most sadistic psychopath of the lot.'

'You are forgetting that I was also Stalin, Count Luiskovo and the bugler.'

'They were all probably monsters. Stalin certainly was.'

'No doubt about it. Even the bugler enjoyed his time as a soldier and unbeknownst to his relatives terrorised the neighbourhood at night flying around as a blood-sucking vampire bat.'

'There you are then. Calling me a psychopath is the pot calling the kettle black.'

'But we are in a new age, professor, and the pot on the induction hob is as shiny and clean as the kettle.'

'So what?'

'I am pointing out that it is possible to change. My time as Stalin tired me. The killing, the horror.'

'How can a psychopath change? That is one of the hallmarks of psychopathy...the inability to learn from mistakes.'

'The psychology of psychopathy is poorly understood but even psychopaths show some rudimentary grasp of morality,' I replied coldly. The professor disgusted me and arguing with him was taking longer that I wanted it to do. He simply laughed at my reply.

'They cannot learn,' he repeated.

'That is obviously untrue,' I contradicted him. 'There are many talented psychopaths who are CEOs of large companies. They've learnt how to blend in with the business mentality and, just like yourself, have risen to the top of their chosen career.'

'But you are worse than all of those,' hissed the scientist. 'So I will not help you.'

'I was worse,' I agreed. 'But I conducted an experiment. I hid the knowledge of my past from my latest incarnation and led a blame-free life...well, almost blameless.'

'You bit rugby players.'

'Only if they bit me first.'

'You required blood regularly in order to survive.'

'In my latest incorporation I utilised a blood bank. It was far simpler than wandering the streets looking for an innocent victim.'

'So you broke into a blood bank!'

'No, I endowed a blood bank and received regular blood as treatment for my blood dyscrasia. As far as the blood bank is concerned I have aplastic anaemia and I am their founder and patron.'

'But you were not a happy soul. Your memories are the most troubled we encountered.'

'That is where you have assisted me,' I replied with a thin smile.

'How?' asked the bemused scientist, aware of the fact that he had not intended helping me in any way.

'You removed my conscience, my superego,' I answered.

'How did that help you?'

'Only when my own Maud was removed did I realise that I did not need it. My evil deeds were not directed entirely by my Id but also by my perverted superego.'

'In what way?' the professor was now fascinated. I could tell that I had gripped him with this twist to the usual story.

'It was my superego that forced me to kill so many of the invaders of my country in such a foul way, both as Count Dracula, the Prince of Wallachia, and as Stalin the ruler of the USSR.'

'How can your conscience make you kill people?'

'I believed that it was right and necessary to defend my country in whatever way I could. I now know that this may or may not be morally correct and that the balance of probability is that it is incorrect.'

The professor did not reply but I could tell that he did not agree. I expanded my argument.

'Look at the statistics. Twenty million people, soldiers and civilians, died in the USSR fighting against the Germans...about a fifth or sixth of the population. France, which did not fight as hard as the Russians and did not suffer so greatly, lost a tiny proportion in comparison, perhaps one and a half percent of the population as opposed to twenty percent.'

'But France was occupied and the USSR won its war. The USSR was victorious,' countered the professor.

'At far too great a cost in human lives,' I replied. 'The superego pushed nationalism into me, duty to the fatherland and all of that nonsense. Without it I was able to see that the victory was a pyrrhic one.'

'You can't argue that people are better off without a conscience. It's an obscene argument.'

'I am Dracula. I am an obscene character and I can argue that no conscience is better than a perverted one. I will also aver that most people had perverted superegos in the past.... kept that way by religion, nationalism and politics.'

'You are suggesting that for the greater part of history people would have been better off with no conscience? That must be rubbish…people would have just given in to the most basic desires. The primitive id would have ruled.'

'Look how well Susan and Maud got on together,' I answered. 'Fiona, or Cinderella, had her conscience and her subconscious travelling with her and they teamed up together just fine.'

'That was simply in the experiment,' replied the psychopathic professor, the mad scientist of legend. 'That's not real life.'

'And yet you argued that you had obtained invaluable information about the way that the brain works. I think that your exact words were "We know a lot more about how the brain functions than we did before."'

'You heard all of that conversation?'

'And many more.'

'But I still disagree with you about the superego,' replied the professor. 'I, for example, am motivated by the very best of intentions. The furtherance of science, the increase in medical knowledge….these are my motivations.'

'Straight out of your superego,' I pointed out. 'And fitting in just fine with your innate desire for power, position and gratification. In other words your superego and your id have you stitched up. You have not used your conscious intelligence at all in deciding on your course of action.'

'Gratification?' the professor sounded insulted. 'What form is this gratification suppose to have taken.'

'Don't try and kid me that you have not been having affairs with the mortuary staff and with your researchers.'

'Well…'

'Probably including the dwarf, the fairy and the Chinese researcher, Chin.'

'Not the dwarf and Chin,' replied the scientist.

'But all the others?'

'Maybe.'

'Hence I rest my case. We are ruled by our prejudices, in the form of our superego, and our desires, via our subconscious or id. You freed me of both and I realised that I could live without them.'

'But you have integrated them back into your undead self now,' argued the professor. 'So what you have learnt was wasted.'

'When I have not lived my life in vain I have lived it in vein,' I murmured.

'That doesn't make sense,' replied the scientist.

'It was a feeble pun on the word vein, a blood vessel taking blood back to the heart,' I answered, baring my sharp canines.

'Oh, I see.'

'Yes, but you don't find it funny because of your overarching Superego. So before I let you go I will remove some of that Superego and a section of your Id. This will be done using psychology and magic rather than surgery,' I explained.

'I'm not going to help you so you can disabuse yourself of the belief in that possibility,' hissed the wraith and his body writhed in sympathy within the limbo coffin.

'Then begone to limbo and I shall work through another plan,' so saying I dismissed the wraith and saw it shrink down into the corpse within the limbo coffin.

'I'll keep good watch on him, your lordship,' said the ever attentive Ivan.

'Good work, Ivan,' I remarked. 'And there may be two more to capture very soon.'

'Very good sir. We have not run out of coffins.'

'I don't suppose that we have,' I replied with a sardonic grin.

Chapter 28

I sat for a long time in the vestry of the church deciding what should be done in order to achieve my objectives. When the wraith shrank away the communication device that the professor had used had fallen to the floor. I picked it up and spent some time studying it. After a while I decided that iteration and reiteration would be the best ploy..... guesswork. I pressed a random button and found myself back in the Victorian London memory.

'There he is,' came a cry and a red-faced policeman came running in my direction.

I pushed another button and I was instantly standing in the operating theatre.

On the third pressing I was back in my flat, the table covered with used crockery and the room smelling of curry, beer and sweaty rugby players.

'You're back in the flat, is that right, professor?' asked Dr. Bones, over the communicator.

'Yes,' I answered, trying hard to sound like the scientist.

'Do you want us to join you like before?' she asked.

'Certainly,' I agreed.

'Righto!' she replied cheerfully. 'Rees is having a short break and I will tell him when he returns. Can you wait a few moments?'

'Definitely.'

'Will I be seeing you later?'

'If you wish.'

She chuckled.

'It's usually if you wish, prof. Your place or mine?'

'Yours.'

'OK. Right, Rees is just coming back. We will be with you right away.'

I sat at the table with my back to the door. I had put on my rugby shirt since Dave was wearing one when he had been in the flat and they would be expecting the professor to look that way. I did not want them winking back out again the moment they arrived. This was a trap and I needed to spring it exactly correctly.

Rees was the first to appear.

'Take this one Ivan,' I commanded.

From the limbo I could just hear my servant reply in the affirmative.

'What going on, prof?' the Chinese researcher started to ask then he felt his soul being sucked into the void and down to the coffin in my basement. His wraith was left sitting still in a chair opposite me, immobile.

Doctor Diana Bones appeared in the middle of the room rather than coming through the door.

'And this one,' I cried.

She looked first at me and then at Rees. She tried frantically to press the automatic release on her communicator. Too late! The trap was sprung. Down to a coffin next to Rees went her soul.

I sat looking at the two wraiths, Peter Rees Chin sat opposite me and Dr. Bones standing motionless in the middle of the room.

'Now I have you as you had me,' I remarked coolly, removing their communicator devices.

I looked at them with the frozen smile of the hunter, the cat playing with the mouse.

'When you chose to amuse yourselves with my brain you made a mistake,' I stated coldly. 'Let me make this clear,' I said. 'I am not the prey. I am the predator. You are the meat, I am the carnivore.'

They stood and sat transfixed, held by Ivan's spell.

'What the odds were that you should have randomly picked on me I do not know,' I said, studying my fingernails. 'But perhaps I can hazard a guess. You have experimented on sixty human brains, is that right? Dr. Bones you can answer.'

Ivan was listening and relinquished some of the grip on the post-doctoral scientist. Her wraith relaxed slightly.

'Yes, that's about right,' she answered the question then looked around her. 'What's happening? How have you done this to me?'

I waved my hands and Ivan controlled her again.

'All shall be revealed,' I smiled coldly. 'So sixty brains out of six billion. That makes the odds of choosing my brain roughly one in a hundred million. Far too unlikely to have been due to chance. I suspect the dwarf was involved in my case as well as in that of the Cinderella. Is that so?'

Again Ivan released the researcher.

'Yes, yes, of course,' replied Dr. Bones impatiently. 'But where is the professor and why do I keep feeling that I'm in an icy coffin?'

'Because you are, dear girl,' I continued to smile, the game beginning to amuse me. 'And I put you there with the help of my dear friend Ivan.'

I could see my servant beaming with delight at this description of him.

'I still don't understand what you have done,' complained the researcher. 'How can I be in a coffin, in this flat and in the laboratory?'

'It's the coffin that is confusing you, isn't it?' I asked as benevolently as a dog worrying a bone.

'Of course. The other two are obvious but where is the coffin?' she looked around bemused.

'The coffin is in my castle in limbo,' I answered but this still did not appear to satisfy her so I continued. 'You see it is like this. I have captured your souls and placed them in limbo.'

'There is no such thing as limbo,' the researcher contradicted me. 'The pope has decreed that limbo does not exist.'

'Well now,' I almost laughed. 'It's a pity he did not bother to tell me that!'

'Who are you really?' asked the scientist. 'You can't just be a simple PE teacher.'

'Well there now,' I said condescendingly. 'It has taken you some time to come to that conclusion. You have been playing through my memories for weeks, maybe months and you have not guessed who I am?'

'Years actually,' stated Dr. Bones. 'We have kept your specimen going for over two years.'

'That figures,' I prompted. 'Go on, have you guessed my identity?'

'Are you Rasputin?'

I laughed.

'Somewhat worse, I'm afraid. I am Count Dracula, the Prince of Wallachia.'

'Ridiculous!' she exclaimed. 'He died centuries ago.'

'And I have been resurrected multiple times and led many lives since then. Nevertheless I am he.'

For a moment I felt slightly pompous and silly as if the girl's scepticism might actually break my own self belief but the moment passed. After all, it was no lie. I was Count Dracula, the vampire.

She looked on in amazement.

'No wonder your specimen was successful,' she concluded. 'And that you had abnormal DNA.'

'Chin was right,' I stated. 'My DNA has incorporated a virus or two. The rabies-like virus was caught from a vampire bat and the bacteriophage prevents my tissues from being eaten by bacteria whenever I happen to die.'

'Is that why Cinderella, the Fiona girl, kept working?' asked the researcher. 'She had the bacteriophage too.'

'Correct,' I agreed with the supposition.

'But that still doesn't explain all this limbo stuff,' protested Dr. Bones.

'That's where the supernatural comes into it,' I smiled as I said it. 'My mother was a witch. Simple really.'

'So why should I help you?' asked the post-doctoral researcher.

'Why not?' I replied. 'You are already compromised. If this laboratory is investigated by the police you would be finished anyway and I am certainly no worse a person than your psychopathic boss.'

'If you really are the vampire you are a monster!'

'Maybe I was in the past but over the centuries I have learnt to at least simulate goodness.'

'What value is there in that?'

'It is what most human beings do,' I replied. 'They learn to be good or at least pretend that they are. I just happened to take longer coming to that realisation.'

'And if I do help you what will happen to the three of us?'

'The professor, yourself and Chin?'

'Yes.'

'I cannot permit you to pass the knowledge you have gained on to other people so I will wipe your brains of the memories. I will expunge the experiments from your long term recall.'

'Can you do that?'

'Certainly. With the help of my colleague, Ivan.'

'Then you will let us go?'

'I will.'

'How do I know that I can trust you?'

'The question should be the other way round,' I retorted. 'How do I know I can trust you?'

'Why do you say that?'

'Because I will have to release you and you will be almost free to ignore my requests.'

'Almost free?'

'It would be foolish of me to let you go completely. I will keep Chin and Cruikshanks in limbo as safe keeping and a small part of your soul.'

'A small part of my soul?'

'Perhaps fifteen percent.'

'What will it mean to me?'

'You will move around the laboratory in a slight daze, obeying my instructions and then you will return here. I will expunge the memories and you will wake up with the other two in the altered laboratory.'

'Will any of our work be left intact?'

'The laboratory will be there but none of the specimens and you will all have a burning desire to research into botanical specimens rather than zoological.'

'But I'm a medical researcher not a botanist! I'm a doctor not a plant gatherer!'

'You are an unethical criminal. That is the best offer I can make. Perhaps you can put your remaining knowledge to the development of new herbal remedies?'

'I won't do it. I flatly refuse.'

'Off!' I cried and the shade of Dr. Bones slid down into the coffin in my castle.

Peter Rees Chin, the PhD student, woke up.

'I assume you heard that discussion?' I enquired.

'Yes sir,' replied the Chinese scientist.

'And what is your response?'

'I will do whatever you say,' said the man. 'I did not know that the brains were harvested from the living.'

'Yet you came from China where you were working on the transplant teams taking parts from executed criminals,' I answered.

'But not directly...'

'You are not blameless Chin, but I am willing to spare all three of you as offered.'

'I will do it!' exclaimed the researcher.

'Good,' I replied then detailed exactly what I wanted doing with the blood and that I wished to find out where Fiona, or Cinderella, had been sent .

'And there is something more,' added the post-graduate researcher.

'What may that be?' I asked.

'Cinderella,'

'Yes,' I encouraged Chin to continue.

'The specimen was not put out for recycling. Tinkerbell took it.'

'In the jar?'

'Yes. In the jar. She took some apparatus as well.'

'So Fiona Makepeace-Smythe was not sent off for recycling?'

'The professor lied to you. I think from what you have told us he thought that it was funny.'

'He thought that he was amusing?'

'Perhaps he did.'

Once again I felt very angry but pushed the sensation down. I had given in to my id and my superego on too many occasions. Now was a time for careful reasoning.

'Tell me everything you know about Miss Tinker Bell and the dwarf,' I suggested.

'Very little, although their addresses are in my research book,' answered Chin.

'That could be most valuable,' I nodded. 'So you are happy to continue with my plan, fifteen percent of your soul will remain in limbo. After pouring half of the blood into my jar you return here and I will wipe these memories from your brain and also from the other two. Then I shall release your soul.'

'Yes sir,' it was his turn to nod. 'I believe you are being very fair to us considering what has been done to you.'

'I have spent many lives being less than pragmatic,' I replied. 'This time I will be as practical as possible.'

'Thank you sir,' he answered. 'We may yet become friends.'

'Maybe, Chin, maybe,' I answered. 'Just don't make any mistakes.'

I nodded to Ivan the Terrible, the wraith fleshed out considerably and Chin pressed his communicator, disappearing back into the laboratory.

Chapter 29

'Cruikshanks!' the name came unbidden to my lips.

I could see the man temporarily stopped at the border of my territory. The psychopathic professor looked around him wildly and then focussed on one spot where he could see me standing quietly waiting to gain his attention.

Almost simultaneously Ivan appeared in my consciousness.

'I'm sorry to interrupt you, your lordship but......'

'Professor Cruikshanks has risen from his coffin and broken free from the castle?'

'Yes sir. I have just discovered that myself. I presume that he must have set off one of your alarms and that is how you know? Shall I send out the spectral hunting dogs?'

'Not this time, Ivan. I shall spend some moments talking with the professor and then we will decide.'

'Very good sir.'

'Incidentally, how did he gain the strength to escape?'

'He drained the life essence from Dr. Bones, your lordship.'

'What of Chin?'

'Spared. Perhaps his coffin was too far away from the professor.'

'The professor's mind force is greater than I expected. I imagine that Dr. Bones has completely expired?'

'Yes sir.'

'Then there is nothing we can do for her. That's all for now.'

'Call me if you need me, sir.'

'Rest assured that I shall, Ivan.'

'Thank you , sir.'

Ivan's image disappeared and I concentrated on the professor whose image I could see at one of the borders of my land.

'So your slave has just notified you that I have escaped,' sneered the professor. 'It took him some time. I've been out of the castle for several months already.'

'Time is not universal,' I replied. 'What seems like months to you may only be minutes to Ivan and myself.'

'Rubbish. I don't believe you,' contradicted Cruikshanks. 'That cannot be the case.'

'Of course it can,' I answered. 'Think of Einstein and the travelling twins.'

'What are you babbling about, vampire?'

'Put simply if I accelerate away from you and reach near to the speed of light whilst you remain stationary then when I return you will have aged considerably whilst I have changed little.'

'I have not moved that quickly, nor have you!' replied the professor.

'That is just one example of the relative nature of time. In this case the terrain you have been crossing is not part of the normal space-time continuum.'

'I survived it well enough.'

'Maybe, but if you think that you can escape from my land safely you are mistaken,' I stated the bald facts.

'You would say that when I'm right at your border,' answered the professor. 'You can't stop me, that's why you say it.'

'You are wrong,' I answered. 'I have saved many people from making a terrible mistake by the use of the alarms. You are definitely better off in my dungeon than in the bordering territories.'

'Rubbish. You are trying to prevent me from going by arguing with me.'

'I'm sorry to have to tell you that it is not rubbish,' I answered. 'The enemy lives over the border you are standing next to. Through that gate waits the enemy.'

'I can see another gate not far away. I can go there.'

'......And if you move to the next border crossing you will be going to something almost as bad.'

'What is something almost as bad as your enemy?' asked the professor.

'The Devourer of Souls,' I replied.

'So this way leads to your enemy?'

'Correct.'

'Well the enemy of my enemy is my friend,' espoused the mad scientist.

'That philosophy is frequently untrue and has led to many unhappy conclusions,' I countered.

'Why is it untrue?' asked the evil doctor.

'We may both have a common enemy and still be enemies ourselves,' I replied. 'Because A is the opposite to B and C is the opposite to A it does not mean that B and C are necessarily the same.'

'Yes it does!' answered the professor. 'You can't have more than one opposite.'

'Black is opposite to white,' I replied. 'But white is colourless so a colour, for example red, is also opposite to white. Red is not the same as black.'

'Life isn't just black and white!' screamed the professor. 'You are just trying to keep me talking while your men creep up on me.'

'Untrue,' I countered. 'They would have been on you in minutes if I had commanded it to be so. I am trying to save your soul.'

'My enemy, you Count Dracula, are trying to save my immortal soul?' laughed the professor derisively. 'Spare me the fiction. I would rather meet your enemy any day.'

'The enemy,' I answered.

'Whatever,' replied Cruikshanks. 'I'm passing over.'

'Let me tell you again that the enemy of your enemy is not necessarily your friend.'

'Your black and white analogy was not convincing.'

'OK, you consider yourself to be my enemy, yes?'

'Correct.'

'But we have common enemies, anthrax, polio, smallpox. Choose any of them. For example smallpox is my enemy but it is not your friend.'

'It could be if I used it as a biological weapon and I had been vaccinated against it.'

The professor moved closer to the gate.

'I'm definitely going over, away from you and your coffins and your specious arguments.'

'So be it,' I answered, releasing the locks. 'Once you have passed through you will not be able to pass back.'

The professor smiled condescendingly and walked quickly over the threshold, the gate into eternity.

*

The blood was having the desired effect. Chin opened the glass jar and I could see him standing amazed at the apparition that rose before him. I stepped out as a fully grown six footer, wearing evening dress and a black cape, the collar turned up. My dark hair, almost blue-black, peaked over my forehead and my long fingers flexed in anticipation.

Chin stepped back, worried as to what I would do next. I smiled but this did nothing to alleviate his anxiety..... it simply revealed my fangs.

I flicked my fingers and my appearance more closely resembled that of Peter Chambers, my immediately previous embodiment. Chin relaxed perceptively.

'Well done Chin,' I remarked. 'You shall be rewarded.'

'Thank you sir,' replied the Chinese researcher.

'Collect some of the immersion devices and the computer. We are moving out.'

'What about the laboratory?'

'Ivan will cross over and deal with it. He will dispose of the bodies.'

'I thought that you were going to revive them. You promised.....'

'That was before Professor Cruikshanks killed Dr. Bones and escaped from my clutches,' I answered. 'Now there is nothing that I can do for them.'

'But there will be an enquiry, the police will be involved, we shall all be ruined,' the researcher sat down and cried.

'Chin up Chin,' I said gaily. 'Not all is lost. We shall set you up in this laboratory and you shall be the professor.'

'But I don't even have my doctorate yet!'

'Easily arranged with a little persuasion. Everybody knows that the professor was having an affair with Bones so we shall tell the world that they have run off together. There will be sightings of them in exotic places and they will never come back.'

'But, but....'

'No buts, there is insufficient time. We must chase after Miss Tinker Bell and retrieve the remains of Cinderella, the erstwhile Fiona Makepeace-Smythe.'

*

We walked out into the car park and retrieved Chin's car. I looked at his vehicle with some apprehension. It was a very old and battered VW Polo. Chin saw my apprehensive glance.

'It works well, boss,' he assured me. 'I keep it serviced myself. It's very reliable.'

I jumped into the front passenger seat and off we went. I recognised the location almost immediately. The laboratory was situated near the junction of the M4 and the M5 on the outskirts of Bristol in a new industrial estate. I had lived in Bristol for many years as Peter Chambers so I was happy to direct Chin to Tinkerbell's address which was a small house in the south of Bristol.

As we drove we listened to the radio. In addition Chin filled me in on all the news I had missed whilst I had been in the bottle. Some of it I had already heard as disembodied voices but much of the news made me gasp..... no mean feat given my unshockable nature as a centuries old vampire!

So Parsifal X was behind the Tsunami! The irascible elemental from Faerie had contrived the merging of realities. I was conceited enough to believe that the clashing of worlds at that precise second was undertaken because X somehow knew that I was incapacitated. As Peter Chambers I packed no punch but in my full, knowledgable form as the vampire Count Dracula I was equal in power to most of the creatures from Faerie. I knew of X, of course I did. I had not considered him as a threat. After all, his world was decaying, the power of magic was declining. I had not expected X to go into partnership with the enemy and to try to merge the realities was an undertaking far greater than I ever expected X to attempt.

Having caught me unawares whilst being operated upon the dwarf must have harvested my living brain and taken it to Professor Cruikshanks.

But Parsifal X had been defeated so who was the dwarf working for now? The news on the radio right that minute was quite fascinating.

- Unlikely reports emanating from Downing Street. A police spokesman has denied that the prime minister was assaulted by clay monsters. "Golems, either mechanical or magical, do not suddenly appear and attack the Prime Minister of the United Kingdom," was the statement read out by the police at New Scotland Yard. However an inside informer tells me that solid baked statues of men in a variety of poses have been found inside number ten. These are being linked with Sir Robert Goodfellow who was temporarily arrested in connection with the matter and then released without charge.....

Robert or Robin Goodfellow. Puck! Now there was a name to conjure with. I immediately suspected that the dwarf was working for Puck and that the earlier brain specimens had been used to control the golems. A cyborg army was what the dwarf wanted and it sounded as if it was Puck who demanded it.

I knocked at Miss Bell's front door but received no reply. A wave of my hands and a few muttered words of magic later and we were inside. The place had been cleared out. There were no signs of Miss Bell, no personal possessions and no glass jar containing the last mortal remains of Fiona Makepeace-Smythe.

On to the dwarf's address next. This was a penthouse flat in a new block of apartments down in the Bristol Harbourside.

The area had been completely restructured several years before and this was a very expensive and popular residential development. I had decided that we would not knock at this door. I would use my open sesame spell on the communal door and then repeat it when the elevator dumped us outside the door of the actual apartment.

In the event the first spell was unnecessary as someone leaving the apartment block held the door open as we arrived.

'More equipment for Mr. Stiltskin?' he enquired politely.

I nodded agreement.

'He's the little fellow who lives in the penthouse,' continued the man. 'He's a strange guy but he's no trouble. Take the express lift, the service lift is out of use at the moment.'

We both thanked him profusely.

'No trouble!' he exclaimed. 'That's what neighbours are for.'

Sure, I thought. *They're there to remove even the little bit of security that he might otherwise have had.*

I pressed the button for the top floor and the lift rapidly ascended and then opened right inside the apartment.

Again no spell needed!

I looked around warily and then heard strange sounds coming from a room off the hallway. We poked our heads round the door. The dwarf was lying on the floor with a full immersion set on, connected to a computer and to the specimen jar. In the glass container was the pulpy mass of brain that represented Fiona Makepeace-Smythe, known to the world as Cinderella.

I stared at the object which represented my love interest. I knew that she could be reconstructed but she did not presently look too inviting. I studied the entire set-up as dispassionately as possible.

The dwarf had obviously used this room as an extension of the laboratory. There were several empty discarded specimen jars and in addition a plethora of equipment. I had not been able to examine the lab apparatus in much detail as my own reincorporation had destroyed the experiment. But here the entire lab was reproduced. Attached to the specimen jar containing Fiona's brain were numerous wires and tubes. The wires connected directly to sites on her brain and out to junction boxes and thence to devices connected to the aforementioned computer. There were several slave computers in the system and these were running various other pieces of hardware including pumps, infusion devices and a drip mechanism that was constantly bathing the brain with turbid fluid. The main pumps serviced the tubes entering the arteries and veins of the brain. Here the fluid was almost blood red in colour although it was not exactly the right tone and again was presumably artificial rather than truly sanguineous.

The dripping fluid on the surface of the brain! I stared at it.

Rather than being totally immersed in fluid as I had originally believed I could now see that the yellow turbid fluid was being dripped onto the brain continuously. This was keeping it moist but not inundated. It was also the explanation for the constant dripping that I had assumed was Chinese torture. Partly I had heard the sound of the drip but also the distortion of the meninges could have been detected by my few remaining senses. Poor Fiona, or Cinderella, was still suffering from the torture and I could see from the expression on the face of the dwarf that he was relishing the situation.

Chapter 30

Cinderella...I knew that the story went back to the Seventeenth Century and could have originated even further back than that. The wicked stepmother, the ugly sisters, the glass slipper and various magical transformations. I was aware of all the stories.

But Mr. Rumple Stiltskin was a different matter. I could also recall his story. The imp, Rumpelstilzchen is the name I knew him by, and he was able to spin straw into gold and create great chasms by stamping his feet. His temper was legendary but he desired to remove the firstborn child of the king and although having extracted a foolish promise from the queen, the miller's daughter, he was eventually thwarted from his goal. He did not appear in the Cinderella legends so why he was after the girl now I could only imagine. He was, however, a distant cousin of Puck so it was highly likely that they were working together.

Quickly we set up our own equipment and, leaving Chin to watch the apparatus, I immersed myself into the world of Cinderella, the girl I had first met as Fiona Makepeace-Smythe.

I hid in the shadows of her memories watching the proceedings until I was completely au fait with the situation. At first we were in the hovel where Cinderella sat by the fire and the sisters prepared for the ball. I hung upside down from a rafter in the shape of a vampire bat.

Then the scene shifted and we were in the games room of a large school. Girls were running around in gym slips chanting Fiona's name. She was trapped in a large cage still dressed in her Cinderella outfit. The dwarf was laughing and joking with the ecstatic schoolgirls as they ran round shouting.

Next we were at the ball and Cinders had been drafted in to

wait on everybody. Not a single glance did she receive from the Royal Family...she might as well have not been present. I was there as a courtier. The dwarf was sitting at the top table eating prawn cocktails and melon with the ugly sisters, Susan and Maud, sat either side of him.

'We have another one to trap,' I said quietly to Ivan whom I could see in limbo waiting patiently for my instruction.

'Ready,' came the reply.

'Oh no you don't!' exclaimed Mr. Stiltskin.

He had obviously heard my comment to the factotum and instantly grabbed a sharp knife from the table and held it to the neck of the fat Susan.

'Cinderella is almost dead now,' stated the dwarfish imp. 'But she will certainly be dead if I sacrifice her Id.'

'I lived without my Id perfectly happily,' I replied without blinking, fixing the dwarf with a constant stare.

'It was still alive but simply separated from you,' replied the dwarf. 'Cinders can't live without her ugly sisters. She's too weak.'

With the hand behind my back I was signalling to Ivan and to Chin. The Chinese researcher appeared behind the dwarf and crept towards him. As he did so he hit against a gold plated chair and the dwarf swung round towards him. In his moment of distraction I flew through the air in my form as a bat. I sunk my teeth into his neck and paralysed the creature and as he fell to the floor of the ballroom Ivan caught his soul.

I released the dwarf's spectre and turned back into my human shape, veering towards the Peter Chambers form but perhaps slightly taller and more saturnine. I was dressed as a very smart courtier, an adviser to the king and queen.

Cinderella had been watching all this bemused and highly anxious. When I reappeared she ran up to me.

'Buttons,' she cried. 'They let you in here!'

'Indeed Cinders,' I replied. 'Or should I call you Fiona?'

She looked at me confusedly then nodded.

'You're right,' she agreed. 'I also knew you as Peter Chambers when I was Fiona, didn't I?'

I nodded.

'Cinderella or Fiona I have to ask you a serious question.'

'Go ahead,' she replied.

'If I offered you the life of the undead....that of a vampire. Would you take it?'

'Hey,' she answered. 'I thought for a moment that you were going to ask for my hand in marriage and I was all poised to say yes. I'm entirely fed up with this prince charming lark. Look at the boy!'

I turned and looked. Prince Charming was a mindless beauty, a handsome hulk of legend partially created by the computer and animated by magic. He smiled at everybody and clearly had no personality.

'I'm programmed to desire marriage to the legendary Charming but I've always been in love with you, Buttons,' continued Cinderella. 'You are the only person who ever treated me with kindness.'

'Apart from your Mum and Dad when they were alive and, of course, the fairy godmother.'

'Where is the fairy godmother?' asked Cinderella. 'isn't she supposed to have turned up long ago.'

'She's dead,' snarled the dwarf from his position on the floor. 'As you all will be when my boss gets here.'

'Your boss being Puck?' I enquired.

'That's right.... and he is on his way down to Bristol. He should be here any moment.'

'Did you call him down to deal with us?' I asked.

The wraith writhed slightly.

'Not exactly,' he finally replied. 'But he told me that he was coming down with his golems.'

'Why is he coming to Bristol?'

'Why should I tell you that?' asked the dwarf truculently.

'Because I have you completely in my power,' I replied.

'Not for long,' he countered. 'But it won't do any harm to tell you. You can't do anything about it.'

I waited.

'He's coming down to capture Lord James Scott and his family,' continued the dwarf after a pause.

'The Bristolian who fought Parsifal X and the Devil?' I queried.

'Yeah, one and the same.'

'Am I right in thinking that Scott is an archangel?' I asked, remembering that Chin had spoken about him during the car journey. 'What makes Puck think he can overpower Scott?'

'They say Scott is Saint Michael,' replied the dwarf, garrulous now that the damn had broken. 'But I don't accept it. Puck has caught the guy with a pair of clever spells and will now deliver the coup de grâce.'

'So he thinks that he is going to kill an archangel,' I murmured, stroking my chin. 'Angels are notoriously difficult to kill. Even I wouldn't try.'

'Even you, ha ha ha,' laughed the dwarf. 'Talking as if you are some sort of powerful force. An aged vampire that decided to be a schoolteacher. Ha ha ha!'

I found the dwarf's laughter offensive but decided not to rise to the bait. People could laugh at my journey of self discovery as much as they liked and it would not deter me. The dwarf was meat, I was the carnivore. My mind was clear on that issue.... the predator may play with the prey but it has no need to laugh at it or let it goad him.

'You have told me all that I need to know so you can sleep for now,' I signalled to Ivan and the dwarf slipped into a coma.

'OK,' I said. 'Cinders, you wait here and we will do something about saving you.'

Chin and I exited from the Cinderella memory and I immediately poured the remaining half sachet of my stem cells into the jar and over the brain. Within minutes the mix of potent cells and powerful magic had its effect and a solid, albeit weak, form of Cinderella was standing beside me. Not quite Cinders, in fact. This was a combination of Cinderella, Fiona, the sisters and something else. A vibrant, intelligent, exciting woman was standing next to me... her obvious beauty was secondary to these other attributes.

'Well done Vlad,' she said with a chuckle. 'You've saved me at last. What took you so long?'

I looked at her, somewhat puzzled. She was talking as if I had known her for an eon rather than a relatively short time.

The dwarf lay senseless at my feet. I stooped and picked him up effortlessly and threw him over my shoulder. My own strength was coming back by leaps and bounds but Fiona worried me. I was delighted that I had saved her but she was deathly pale. We needed blood and we needed it soon!

'I've brought the tea,' came a female voice.

We froze. We had assumed that we were in the apartment on our own apart from the dwarf but through the door came Mis Tinker Bell, the fairy. When she saw us she dropped the tea tray with a startling crash and waved her magic wand.

I was too slow in reply and she had me gripped, body and soul. The only thing I could do was move my head. I looked at Chin and Cinders, my beloved Fiona. They were also held by the powerful fairy's spell.

'So what have you done to my little dwarfy?' asked Tinkerbell. 'Tell me or you'll end up as a squashed frog.'

'Squashed frog?' queried Chin. 'Why as a frog?'

'I'll turn you into one, you yellow peril,' shouted the fairy.

'Careful there,' I cautioned the fairy. 'That was tantamount to racial harassment. You can't go calling my friend Chin the yellow peril.'

'I'll call him what I like, vampire,' spat the fairy.

I was trying to signal to Ivan to come to our assistance but he was having a job controlling the soul of the dwarf which was rising up out of the limbo coffin in the basement dungeon of my castle.

'And you will tell me what you have done to the dwarf!' she exploded with rage and threw another spell at me.

This pushed me to my knees in agony, my body was burning up and red hot needles were poking into my skin all over my torso. I writhed in pain, rolling over on the floor.

'Tell me,' she screamed.

'OK, OK,' I muttered. 'Just release the spell on me.'

The fairy removed the second spell leaving me bound from the neck down.

'Speak,' she ordered.

'The dwarf's soul is in limbo,' I replied.

'Then take it out of limbo,' she batted back her reply.

I was watching Cinderella from the corner of my eye, trying to keep the fairy's attention whilst Cinders underwent a transformation. Not this time into a princess clothed in a beautiful ball gown nor even into the upper class Fiona Makepeace-Smythe. Her face remained the same but all over her head snakes had started to appear, coiling out from amongst her hair then replacing it completely. Writhing, hissing snakes , their mouths opening and closing and bifid tongues darting in and out from the red raw orifices.

'Close your eyes, Chin,' ordered Cinderella. 'And turn your head away.'

'What about Vlad?' asked Chin, worried about my safety.

'He's immune to this,' laughed the Gorgon, Euryale.

Tinkerbell turned her attention on the Gorgon and the Gorgon, Euryale, the monster with the serpentine hypertrichosis, in turn fixed the fairy with her gaze.

The fairy froze and turned to stone. Euryale smiled, the snakes receded and the beautiful and clever woman I had known, both as Cinderella and Fiona, returned. I found that the fairy's spell had dissipated so I stepped over and held Cinders' hand.

'I had forgotten that Ivan's poem was true,' I explained. 'I'm truly sorry.'

'They messed with our minds,' replied Cinders. 'I also had forgotten who I was and what I could do.'

'A Cinderella story is always one about a person who has unexpected attributes ,' I could not suppress a slight chuckle. 'You've certainly got those a plenty.'

'Can I look now?' asked Chin.

'Of course,' answered Cinders.

Chin opened his eyes and looked towards us. The fairy was frozen in a position of attack and her insectoid origin was apparent.... she appeared to be readying a huge sting, like a scorpion's tail, presumably hoping to plunge it into my immovable body.

'Have you killed her?' asked Chin, worriedly. 'Seems a bit drastic if you have killed Tinkerbell.'

'Don't be alarmed,' replied Cinders. 'The effect is only temporary but we will have to get her and the dwarf back to Faerie to face trial for their crimes.'

'Shouldn't they be put on trial here in England?' asked Chin.

'Maybe,' agreed Cinders. 'But they kidnapped me from Faerie and it is more difficult to control magical creatures here in the normal world. You are just not used to it in the way that we are.'

'The dwarf told us that Puck is coming to Bristol. We had better look out for him,' I reminded the company.

'Don't worry sir,' came Ivan's voice. 'My son has been at the top of your tower keeping watch over Bristol.'

'Your castle is in Bristol?' questioned Chin.

'It's in limbo,' I replied. 'And limbo is a state of mind so it can be anywhere that you wish it to be.'

Chapter 31

It was a moonlit night and the limbo tower of my castle had been placed corresponding to the Cabot Tower on Brandon Hill commanding an excellent view over the city of Bristol.

I stood on the parapet looking down at a broad sweep of the town. All seemed quiet and then I observed a small twist of smoke rising in the Redland area. I narrowed my vision and with my vampire senses brought the scene into focus.

A hugely enlarged and contorted Puck was fighting with an equal sized angel. Presumably the latter was Saint Michael. As I looked my enhanced senses saw a small bat-like demon appear behind the archangel. I recognised that demon from the time when I was Stalin. It was the evil soul of Hitler, leader of Germany in the Nazi era.

The demon bat would sway the balance in favour of Puck, of that I was certain.

I turned to my companions.

'I have one more task before this day is done,' I cried, turning myself into a very powerful haematophagous flying mammal. 'I need to rid this world of a demon.'

I flew with immense speed to the site of conflict in the leafy suburb and latched myself with no more ado onto the neck of the Hitler demon. The creature's shriek was drowned by the noise of the fighting and the archangel was unaware of my presence.

'This one for limbo,' I said to the ever-watchful Ivan.

'Certainly sir,' replied the factotum and the bat-like demon of the German Führer faded into the aether and appeared in a suitable shrunken form in one of my spare coffins.

My strength was fading and I knew that Cinderella's own

longevity would not be great if I did not soon find some blood for both of us. Although by nature of sanguivorous habits we did not wish to inflict ourselves on the poor unsuspecting cattle that the people represented. I had done that many times before but now knew that it was unnecessary. The blood bank beckoned and then I could return to the fray if necessary. It was a much more civilised way of obtaining the blood I needed and I was sure that Fiona/Cinderella/Euryale would approve.

'I have to decide what to call you,' I said to the girl.

'I like Cinders,' she answered. 'I've grown used to the name. Do you mind being called Buttons?'

'Not in the least,' I answered. 'It's an improvement on Count Dracula or even Vlad. It's much more friendly.'

'Buttons the friendly Bloodsucker,' laughed Cinders.

'What do we do now, boss?' asked Chin, breaking in on our heart to heart chat.

'I shall not tamper with your memories. I shall release your soul and mind unharmed so that you can do as you wish,' I answered. 'I can set you up as a professor or you can join my entourage both here and in limbo.'

'I'll join your entourage,' Chin nodded furiously. 'Definitely the more exciting option of the two.'

*

The dwarf and Tinkerbell had been consigned to a magic nulling prison in Faerie. Chin was busy finding out all of the details of what had been going on in Redland. Apparently the devil incarnate had also arrived and a combination of Saint Michael and the Dragon King had defeated him.

Cinders and I sat outside my castle in the sunlight. The castle was now coinciding with Eilean Donan in the West of Scotland and had taken on the shape of that picturesque building.

'Regrettably I still do not remember our previous wedding

ceremony,' I said to Cinders, holding her hand. 'So will you marry me again?'

'Why not?' agreed Cinderella. 'The contract is probably null and void after all this time.'

'Would this be a suitable place?' I asked.

'Certainly,' she answered. 'If you weren't marrying me, you could be the organist.'

'Ivan the Terrible could do that for us,' I replied. 'He's not at all bad.'

'Let's go and speak to him,' said my newly affianced.

Like young lovers we went hand in hand to my factotum.

'I'll do that for you, of course ma'am and your lordship,' agreed Ivan. 'In fact I have a song that I would like you to hear.'

Ivan led us over to the harpsichord where a small piece of paper fluttered on a music stand.

'I thought this might amuse you sir....

Vampire's teeth are shining
Shining bright in the pale moonlight
Vampires looking for love
But finding only blood

Take care if you're out late
Vampires may be your date
Vampires looking for love
But finding only blood

Never let them put their probe in
Or they'll feast on haemoglobin
Careful of the night's miasma
Vampires love to feast on plasma

Vampires looking for love
But finding only blood
Vampires looking for love
But finding only blood.'

'Droll,' I replied. 'Most droll.'

'Don't you like it, sir?' asked Ivan.

'It fits your name,' I answered. 'It's terrible, Ivan, but it is so bad that it is good. I adore it.'

'So do I,' concurred Cinders. 'Let's have it at the wedding ceremony.'

'And Ivan can read out his long poem,' I suggested.

'His son can be our page boy,' added Cinderella.

Ivan beamed with delight and we went back outside to sit in the sun. Chin arrived and joined us and he congratulated us when we told him the tidings.

'Great news about the wedding,' he replied to us both. 'There are, however, a few things that puzzle me.'

'Fire away,' I replied.

'Number one...how come you are not susceptible to sunlight? Vampires traditionally die in the daylight.'

'Factor 60 sunblock,' I replied. 'Next question?'

'You told me what happened in Victorian England but who killed the girls in London? Who was Jack the Ripper?'

I looked at Chin for a while as I gathered my thoughts.

'You will find this hard to believe,' I answered. 'And you may find it easier to accept as a fiction.'

'As a fiction?'

'As if I made it up.'

'OK,' replied Chin. 'I'm happy with that.'

'My memories have almost completely returned and I am able to give you a definitive answer. You may have heard about the DNA evidence?'

'I've heard something about a shawl.'

'That's right. DNA from both the victim and one of the original suspects in the case, Aaron Kosminski, was found on a shawl left at the scene of the crime. The investigating policeman took the shawl and gave it to his wife who put it away. It was untouched for over a century.'

'So we know it was Kosminski who killed that victim?'

'No we don't. All we know is that it is likely that he was in intimate contact with the shawl and so was the victim. He could have been a client of the murdered woman.'

'So we still don't know who killed the women?'

'On the contrary if you are prepared to suspend your disbelief I will tell you who did it.'

'You've told me about your id, sir,' replied Chin politely. 'Was it the blind desire of Winter that killed the girls?'

'Did I, as Count Luiskovo, kill the girls due to innate mad desire? Is that what you are implying?' I chuckled. 'No. But I was a witness and I do know the name of the killer.'

'Who was it? Please don't hold me in suspense anymore. Who was Jack the Ripper?'

'The Ripper was none other than Prince Albert.'

'Queen Victoria's consort? That's ridiculous. He died in 1861 of typhoid fever. I've read a lot about him.'

'That was the story put out to the public. In fact he had developed a particularly vicious case of haematophagy and his sanguivorous habits disturbed the peace of the Royal Family.'

'Sorry sir,' answered Chin. 'Are you saying that Prince Albert had become a vampire?'

'Yes, he had a hereditary blood dyscrasia similar to my own. He passed it on to his children.'

'I thought that Queen Victoria was the one who passed on haemophilia?'

'Again that is the usual story.'

'So how did you know all this?'

'The reason that I was in Britain at the time was because I was a recognised expert on vampirism in all its forms.'

'Because you were the original vampire, Count Dracula?'

'Indeed. Of course they did not know that…I was an eminent

doctor who specialised in blood disorders.'

'By the name of Dr. Alexander Pedachenko?'

'Exactly. I arrived in England secretly having been invited over to discuss a matter of importance to the Queen and I travelled immediately to Buckingham Palace. I was taken by the palace chamberlain to Albert's room where he was kept under lock and key.'

'The Prince Consort was kept under lock and key?'

'Indeed. Initially his tendencies emerged as a simple desire to suck blood from his victims. They were not harmed apart from a couple of puncture wounds in the neck and a period of retrograde amnesia.

'They didn't remember what had happened?'

'Correct. But early in 1861 he killed a woman, perhaps unintentionally. He repeated this later in 1861 and it came to the notice of the Queen. A story was concocted that Albert was suffering from abdominal pain and diarrhoea. The convenient death of a servant about the age and height of Albert provided a body. Albert was locked away and the country mourned his death at the funeral of the unknown servant.'

'Explaining the extended mourning period of the Queen.'

'Quite right. The whole thing was totally abhorrent to her and she mourned him as if he was dead whilst all the time being aware of his incarceration.'

'What happened in 1888?'

'They kept Albert quiet by feeding him with live animals, mostly rabbits, until 1888 when he made his first escape.'

'Didn't anybody suspect that he was still alive?'

'The servants all knew, of course. Every day they had to go to his suite, his rooms were all serviced with hot water daily, clean sheets, the lot. Albert was kept out of sight but they must have known he was there.'

'How did he get out?'

'We believe that he obtained a duplicate key. Anyway, he killed two women in Whitechapel before I arrived. I went to examine him.'

'What was he like?'

'He was in a pitiful state. He had sores over his body, he was wasting away and his mind had completely cracked. He was still dressed in his well-made clothes but they were very shabby and worn.'

'He escaped again?'

'Several times and at the final case I managed to track him down and witness the murder. There was nothing I could do for the Prince.'

'Why did the killings stop?'

'The decision was made that he would have to die. He was basically a mindless idiot by that stage. Some forms of vampirism do lead to dementia.'

'How did he die? Who killed Prince Albert?'

'Archie Brown, John Brown's younger brother, delivered the final blow and the poor Prince was then pierced through his heart with a wooden stake. His body was burnt and the ashes scattered at sea so that he would not reincorporate.'

'Why did John Brown not do the dirty deed?'

'Because he died in 1883. He was one of the few people who could control the insane Prince and it was after he died that Albert kept trying to escape.'

'How did the Queen view all of this?'

'Albert's death was a great relief to Victoria and she visibly lightened up in the remaining years of her long reign.'

'So who inherited this condition? Are there any other members of the royal family who are vampires?'

'Basically all of them to a greater or lesser extent. Luckily the genes have been diluted and they do not tend to develop the insanity. Earlier offspring were not so lucky.'

'Which ones developed the full syndrome?'

'Prince Leopold, Duke of Albany had the full monty. Princess Alice passed it on to at least three of her offspring. I could go on but the list is endless.'

'Including many of the royals of Europe?'

'To a lesser or greater extent to all of them.'

'So the royals are all blood-sucking vampires!'

'You could put it that way if you wish but they are probably better for the economy than a President would be.'

'Do they have any other odd traits?'

'A certain degree of lycanthropy is not uncommon amongst them.'

'So you are saying that they are also werewolves?'

'It is because of their inbreeding, marrying first cousins etcetera. The recessive genes will out if there is too much inbreeding.'

'My final question is about Professor Cruikshanks. What has actually happened to him?'

'He escaped from my castle by killing your colleague, Dr. Bones,' I replied. 'And then decided to cross over from my land into one of the next territories.'

'What territory would that be?'

'The area in question is out of my purview but it is commonly known as Hell.'

*

'Welcome to Hell, Professor Cruikshanks,' came a deep multitimbral voice that could be heard even in my own fiefdom. 'I've been expecting you. My name is Lucifer. I shall take you to the deepest part of my domain, there to suffer for an eternity.'

The End

The Witch, the Dragon and the Angel trilogy, precede *Tsunami. Change* and the *Witches' Brew Trilogy* follow it.